We
only
know
so
much

ALSO BY ELIZABETH CRANE

You Must Be This Happy to Enter

All This Heavenly Glory

When the Messenger Is Hot

we only know so much

ELIZABETH CRANE

A NOVEL

HARPER ● PERENNIAL

NEW YORK ● LONDON ● TORONTO ● SYDNEY ● NEW DELHI ● AUCKLAND

HARPER ● PERENNIAL

HarperCollins books may be purchased for educational, business, or sales promotional use. For information please write: Special Markets Department, HarperCollins Publishers, 10 East 53rd Street, New York, NY 10022.

FIRST EDITION

Designed by Michael Correy

Library of Congress Cataloging-in-Publication Data is available upon request.

ISBN 978-0-06-209947-1

12 13 14 15 16   OV/RRD   10 9 8 7 6 5 4 3

We
only
Know
so
much

one

At the moment, the Copeland family is a bit at odds.

First of all, Priscilla is a bitch. Or at least a brat. An extreme brat. Look, we're just reporting what we've heard. Maybe bitch is too harsh. Let's say it this way: her attitude is often poor. The reasons are currently unclear. For one thing, her parents might have done better to rethink that name. Right? It's not very contemporary. Something about it's just bitchy-sounding. Maybe she knew that when she was little. She's been this way since she was born and she's nineteen now and it's only gotten worse. What are you supposed to do when your daughter's like this? No one wants to believe their own kid isn't the nicest person, but think about it, girls like this aren't born in a void. Jean and her husband, Gordon, have punished her, of course, told her no, admonished her, this sort of thing, but nothing's worked. They've come to think it's just innate. That may or may not be true. Maybe she got it from her great-grandmother. Genetically or otherwise. Just a thought. And Priscilla's like this everywhere. At home, at work, at school, everywhere. Let's hope that if you're a waiter she never sits at your table. If she sits at your table she will be sending some shit back, and if you do that waiter thing where you introduce yourself, you will rue that choice because she will use your name so many times that by the time she leaves you will want to change it. Jean and Gordon almost never take her to restaurants anymore. Dinner at home is tough enough.

Somehow Priscilla has friends, she's actually a fairly social creature, but even her friends know she's got an attitude, and much is said about it behind her back. How Priscilla sees it is that she's just *honest*. Her mother has of course pointed out many times that being honest doesn't have to mean being rude. Priscilla is pretty, not the prettiest ever, but pretty, and she has good style, and hopes to be on television one day. Right now that's a little nebulous in the sense that she's not really sure in what capacity she'd like to appear on television. She's still living at home, but she's been working at Express for a year, since she graduated. A long year. She's sort of interested in acting, but not really; really, she's just more interested in being herself on television.

The boy, Otis, is a sweet nine-year-old who does all his math homework as soon as he gets his new textbook at the beginning of the year, just because he likes to. He's been doing this since first grade, he's in third now. Otis likes math, likes solving problems, figuring things out, kind of just can't help but do one more, and before he knows it he's done with the whole thing. This, of course, makes the rest of the year pretty boring, but his family has other things on their mind, so sometimes he builds crossword puzzles and other times he pulls the legs off insects, caterpillars in particular. Otis feels kind of bad about this habit, but when he gets in the mood to do it he just can't stop himself. For this reason, Priscilla has not called her brother anything but *Freak*, *Baby Freak*, or *Freak Baby* for the past four years. Otis was named after the elevator company. Well, maybe not after the elevator company exactly, Jean wasn't trying to commemorate them or anything, she just noticed it in an elevator once when she was pregnant with him and liked the sound of it. Gordon has never known about the origin of his son's name. Jean has learned not to start conversations.

Gordon's not a bad guy, but he's kind of a know-it-all. He likes to tell you things he knows. Often and at length. He doesn't mean to condescend, though his comments are sometimes taken that way. He's a good bit away from pompous, and he's always friendly and upbeat. He spent a summer traveling around Europe with his parents when he was ten, which provided him with an inexhaustible supply of information about anything European. He's attractive enough, in a small-market weatherman kind of way. His hair is combed. Gordon has a degree in hospitality and an extensive background managing restaurants, and claims to have worked for the FBI, to have been a private detective and also a hospital aide (this qualifying him to discuss aspects of medicine and hospital management, almost as though he has a medical degree). As need be, if it pertains to the conversation, he will call up other brief careers and fields of study that date either to high school or to interim periods between longer jobs. It's not that it's not possible that he's had all these jobs, though it certainly doesn't seem probable. It's more like the extent of his responsibilities has been exaggerated, that along the way he just took a lot of notes. For as long as he has been married, though, Gordon has been in middle management at a local chain of supermarkets, giving him a vast knowledge of any and all products sold in these supermarkets as well as many competing supermarkets, along with his knowledge of marketing, advertising, and customer service. What it all comes down to: we get it, Gordon, you know stuff.

Once, Jean had *a lot of potential*. Her school counselors said so; lots of people did. She was a straight-A student (though she worked hard for it), and she loved reading more than anything, but she didn't know what anyone could do with that, career-wise. She started college with a major in library science, but found the required coursework dull, so she switched to liberal arts, taking a position as an administrative assistant in the English department of their local college that she kept until Priscilla was born. She was an attractive enough girl, long brown hair with a middle part and a nice slender figure, but was one of those girls who sort of went unnoticed. Picture: 1970s-era tenth-grade photo on the side of a milk carton with red-letter caption MISSING. Except she isn't. She'd never had much of a sense of style, would observe the other girls at school with their corduroy bell-bottoms and coordinated polyester shirts, but when it came time to go shopping, the choices baffled her, and she tended to end up with whatever her mother picked out: straight-leg Lee jeans and blouses with Peter Pan collars or ties at the neck. Cotton. Plaid, often.

Jean married young. Gordon was, still is, a few years older, and Jean was thrilled that someone so worldly would pay her attention. When they first met, Jean had never been anywhere more exotic than Yellowstone, hadn't been out of the country at all, so his stories about secret passageways in Bavarian castles and polo matches in Sardinia sounded incredibly romantic to her. (He hadn't actually been to these places or events, he just told stories about them.)

Jean had just graduated college when she met Gordon through friends at a potluck dinner party. The hosts, her college roommate Margot and her live-in boyfriend, Paul, made number eight spaghetti with sauce from a jar and garlic bread, standard fare for such events; another friend brought a salad and a bottle of Wishbone Italian dressing, another brought a gallon of jug wine with a screw cap. Gordon had clenched his teeth when he saw the screw cap wine open and flowing; he'd brought two bottles with him, for dinner a *sangiovese chianti* (Gordon cannot pronounce anything foreign without earnest efforts at exact pronunciation—his friends tease him about it, but he's committed) and a Sambuca (with coffee beans) for dessert (*This should complement the different notes in the dessert nicely*), and a tiramisu he made himself, with white chocolate mousse curls dappling the edges, a dusting of cocoa (with a flower stencil), all served in a swirl of passionfruit coulis. *I had something similar at O'Neal's Baloon in New York once.* The dessert was such a sight that the entire dinner party was left mostly speechless but stifling giggles. Sticking out of the eight servings were tall, cylindrical, white chocolate–dipped wafers, each with a violet blossom tucked into the top. *The garnish was my own touch.* Jean, though, was thoroughly dazzled. The dinner wasn't meant to be a fixup, mostly just some young college grads on a budget, celebrating their new lives, but Margot arranged for Jean and Gordon to sit together, just in case. And Jean had been thrilled, thought Gordon was quite nice-looking, more so because of his exciting stories and seemingly vast knowledge on any number of topics. Gordon, a few years older than the rest of the group, after a number of years at *exciting but less-promising* careers, had just been promoted to a dream job as a junior office manager at a small supermarket chain. *Off the floor.* Gordon had actually liked being *on the floor* while he was there, as much for getting to know the products as for the interaction with the people. Gordon has always considered himself a people person, though there are any number of people who might disagree. But he'd always wanted to move up, which was why he'd originally taken the job.

That first night, Gordon had talked to Jean exclusively for an hour over dinner, told her about his new promotion and his interest in cuisine. He asked her only a few, basic questions (*What do you do?* he asked; she said she worked at the college, and she might have said more, but he was already off, talking at length about how much he loved to read, and about some of his favorite authors—they both admired Vonnegut). But he looked directly into her eyes the whole time, laughed at her one joke (*Virginia Woolf walks into a bar . . .*), and told her he thought she looked like Katharine Ross, *Prettier, even,* which made her blush, and which was Gordon's way of saying he was hot for her, and he smiled at her and told her he'd make dinner for her sometime, if she were *so inclined*. Jean gave Gordon her number and he called her that same night, said he just couldn't wait to hear her voice again, which sent her swooning. Afterward, Jean called Margot to ask what she thought. Margot had suspected there might be sparks between them, but she had reservations about Gordon's being a great match for anyone, thought he was a nice enough guy who hadn't gotten his heart broken yet, and she was right. But she told Jean she thought it was *Great!* because she secretly considered Jean kind of mousy, and thought that Gordon might be about as good as it got for her.

Jean had never been to a man's house for a first date before. She hadn't been at all sure it was a good idea, and she knew it was okay to say no, but also didn't want Gordon to feel spurned. She liked him. But the date went well, and although Gordon did not miss mention of a lone ingredient or step in the meal, over dinner he took more of an active interest in asking Jean about herself, learned more about her love of books, though it gradually emerged that they didn't have many favorites in common, and Gordon was surprised at how many of the classics Jean had not read. *You haven't read 'A Farewell to Arms'? 'Madame Bovary'? 'Emma'?* That she was a woman who loved to read but didn't love Austen floored him; his first guess was that she was either a romance fan or worse, but in fact she simply preferred more contemporary stories and language to village dances and polite conversations. She was a fan of Carver, Oates, and Paley, she told him, even Pynchon, though she admitted to finding him a challenge, and had always loved Salinger. Gordon had also read some of these, and appreciated that Jean was reading such a variety of complex works, but used all his might to hide his disappointment when she mentioned Salinger, whom he'd always thought was overrated. He was equally surprised, but impressed, that she had read and loved *Lolita*, had always assumed that most women would read it *only superficially*, but when he mentioned this to her he left off the *most women* part of the comment, knowing it wasn't the right thing to say. So Jean had felt pleased with herself in keeping up with the sophisticated likes of Gordon Copeland, and when he drove her home, he told her he'd had a wonderful evening, and she could see that he was sincere, and shyly whispered that she had as well, and she let him give her a passionate kiss at the door that aroused her almost instantly.

Ten days later they were sleeping together. Jean had been with only one man before this, her high school boyfriend. It had never been very good, something she mostly just tolerated and hadn't much looked forward to thereafter, and had decided she was willing to wait until she was more sure about someone. And with Gordon she was sure. She had heard people talk about soul mates, and though she'd previously found that term somewhat vague—it brought to mind an image of Siamese twins floating in space, a sort of literal but mystical connection—she was surer than she'd ever been that Gordon was hers. Her mind, body, and heart had never responded this way for anyone else, and she couldn't imagine it ever would again. Gordon was stable but worldly. He told her he loved her, which was true (although it was subsequently said only at random, oddly timed intervals, like in the pitch dark of their bedroom as she pulled her pajamas on, intervals that made sense only to Gordon), and she was sure she felt the same way, that parts of her trembled that hadn't trembled before. She imagined, listening to stories of his travels, that he would take her to these places, that they would make love on the grounds of Egyptian palaces, that they would stay in *pensiones* tucked away on cobblestone streets in small Italian cities and have pasta and wine in bed with the doors to the balcony open, sheer curtains blowing like she'd seen in the movies, that she would get a short haircut like Jean Seberg and he would chase her through the streets of Paris, take her against a wall in an alley at dusk on a wet, gray day.

BUT IN REALITY, THOUGH their lovemaking had been passionate and exciting in the beginning (Gordon had picked up a few tricks over the years and took a certain pride in being willing to please a woman before he got his, and Jean, not having been especially pleased with her first go-round, was, indeed, impressed), their travels had never taken them farther than Mexico City, where they went for their honeymoon. They had climbed the pyramids at Teotihuacan, but the steps were so narrow it was hard to get a good foothold, much less lie down and hope to make love without sliding all the way to the bottom. More than that, though, Gordon's discourse on the history of the Mexican pyramids didn't enhance the moment for her—she wanted to take in the breathtaking view, to feel the history, not talk about it. In the six months they courted, Jean had been to enough work parties to last her a lifetime; Gordon liked his coworkers and they seemed amused by him, but Jean had never been all that big on parties, which she tended to get through mostly by nodding and smiling. She preferred staying in with Gordon, where there was still a chance they'd have a two-way conversation. Within two years, she was pregnant with Priscilla.

For a moment, after Priscilla was born, there had been a renewed burst of excitement and joy. Jean had suffered a late-stage miscarriage before Priscilla, less than a year after her marriage, had been crushed, of course, and it had taken some trying for her to get pregnant again. So when their healthy, beautiful baby girl was born, Gordon and Jean were briefly closer than ever. Gordon had been in the delivery room and everything, was *astounded by the miracle of the human reproductive system*, handed the slimy, new Priscilla over to her mother in awe, and they felt as connected as they ever had, for about three whole speechless minutes before Priscilla started screaming. Weird, throaty, scratchy, animal sounds came from this tiny life in her mother's arms, and no breast, no gentle touch, no lullaby would calm this child until she had thoroughly exhausted herself and everyone in earshot, sometimes not even then. In the first year, Jean made many more than the required visits to the pediatrician; Priscilla was diagnosed with croup and colic and was treated accordingly, but the cries were seemingly interminable. When she was old enough to take solid foods she ate as little as possible, refusing it, spitting it out or throwing it up. Jean tried every possible food in every possible combination. Gordon threw his many two cents in, and though this sometimes tested her patience, she tried all his suggestions too (*swaddling has been in practice since biblical times*), to no avail. The colic and the croup finally waned after a year, but Priscilla remained fussy and prone to crying, pouting, and throwing things as soon as she had the muscle to lift them. Jean read every book she could find on child care, tried everything from a family bed to tough love, experimented with "calming" foods and educational toys designed to focus a child's attention away from negative stimulation. Gordon drew the line at child psychology; the doctors had been adamant that Priscilla was a perfectly healthy, normal child, that some were just fussier than others, that she'd grow out of it; this was what Gordon wanted to hear, and he stuck with it. Jean secretly took Priscilla to a child psychologist anyway, who suggested things to try at home but essentially agreed with the doctors. And, of course, though Priscilla did eventually stop crying, she remained crabby, and pretty much refused to do anything she was told to do—not without sulking, anyway. By the time she was three and a half she was picking out her own outfits, refusing to wear most of the frilly, pink girl things her mother thought she'd looked so precious in, opting for surprisingly subtle shades and simple designs, until Jean started buying such things exclusively, knowing that anything else just wouldn't get worn.

When the time came for Priscilla to enter preschool, then, it was a relief; grade school was the best thing ever. Jean felt awful about how much she enjoyed it when her child was out of the house; she loved her, of course, actually loved her beyond words, but those hours of the day when Priscilla was fussing in someone else's care were wonderful hours of getting lost in the books she adored, a favorite pastime she'd put aside from almost the moment her daughter had been born. For a period of time, Jean even delved into erotica, had an anthology of erotic short stories she'd read over and over; she found herself suddenly interested in masturbating, learned to please herself quite handily, as it were, a sweet release from the tension of the rest of her day. And this, too, inevitably contributed to her drawing away from her husband.

JEAN HAD BEEN CAREFUL to use birth control after Priscilla, convinced that a second child would be no different in temperament. So when she got pregnant, accidentally, with Otis, almost nine years later, she spent most of those nine months worrying about repeating Priscilla's early years. It was a needless concern. Whatever Priscilla was, Otis was the opposite. Gordon had been as thrilled about this pregnancy as he'd been the first time; he'd hoped for a boy, a perfect set, and he'd seemingly erased Priscilla's croupy years from his mind, no doubt because he was at work for forty croup hours a week. Again, Gordon was in the delivery room for the birth, had wanted to videotape it because he was so sorry he hadn't the first time (Jean said *No*, and when pressed by Gordon, said only *It's not up for discussion*), but again Jean and Gordon had a moment in the delivery room—more than a moment this time, actually. Otis took to Jean's breast easily and hungrily as Gordon watched, rapt, as though he were watching Mary herself, after which Otis fell into a deep sleep and Gordon lay next to his wife and son, content and proud of them both. He stroked her hair, still sticky with sweat, and heaped rambly, damp-eyed praise on Jean, told her he'd never been one for religion but felt so grateful for what seemed miraculous to him, grateful she'd been willing to bear him another child, a son to carry the Copeland name, and Jean felt his sincerity. But Gordon, never one for brevity, went on. Gordon imagined going through the birth canal, told Jean *I know it's not an easy thing for the mother, of course, but imagine what it's like for the child,* he said, *it's like you're struggling against this vast darkness and then finally, light, a victory!* That, unsurprisingly, was the moment when the moment was lost.

GORDON HASN'T CHANGED MUCH. Once a month or so he still prepares a gourmet meal for the family, but it always comes with the entry fee of listening to every last detail of how the meal was prepared, along with any relevant cultural history of the ingredients and/or the dish itself. Jean does most of the cooking now, but even when she does, the historical commentary is hard to avoid. These days, if you should sit down to breakfast at the Copelands' and compliment Jean on her delicious pancakes, there's only a small chance that she might finish saying *Thank you* before Gordon starts in with something like this: *Did you know that the pancake originated in prehistoric times? They would use dry seed flours, which are rich with carbohydrates, and cook them on heated stones or in earthenware pots. The etymology of the word* pancake *dates back to 1430! Of course, there are regional varieties of the pancake around the world. For example, in Germany, pancakes are often made from potatoes; in Wales, they are sometimes made with oatmeal. In some Asian countries, pancakes are made with fermented rice batter and served with pickles! Can you imagine? Pickles! Also, one should never confuse a crêpe with a traditional pancake; although they have similarities, those are very different things, very different. Though it is true that either pancakes or crêpes can be served with either sweet or savory accompaniments, not just with butter and maple syrup, as Americans traditionally eat them.*

Gordon's diction is very precise; he leaves no syllable or letter unpronounced, and uses the word "American" as though he isn't one himself. Jean might take his comments about American cuisine as the mild insults they are, but refrains from pointing out that that's the way she and the kids like it. Instead she screws her mouth up into a tight little circle that she thinks no one will notice, although Otis actually does. In the earliest throes of her love for Gordon, Jean hadn't been bothered by his lecturing, though she certainly noticed that he was always happy to direct his knowledge at anyone nearby. Eventually, a little window into the future flickered open in her mind, a sort of a gut feeling that his particular brand of chattiness might wear thin, but she let it flicker right out. Solution: several years in, Jean simply stopped engaging in any conversation with Gordon that wasn't necessary for plan-making; she no longer made any casual comments that might provide him an opening. Dealing with Priscilla took just about all the emotional energy she had.

And so, by the time Jean met another man, some seventeen years later, you can imagine that she needed a little break.

JAMES, JEAN'S LOVER, IS a good man (although he has a history of depression that Jean is unaware of, for which he's long been treated with a combination of prescription medication and psychotherapy, which seems to work well). He teaches art at the public high school, and he, too, pays attention to Jean, but in a normal way; their conversations actually go back and forth. When Jean first met James, at her book group, she'd thought he was nice-looking, with his thick, tousled brown curls; there was something soft about him in general, a slight softness around his middle, a warmth in his eyes. She hadn't immediately wanted to take him on the floor or anything, that would happen much later, after she got to know him, not that she was a take-someone-on-the-floor kind of woman anyway. The main thing with James was that Jean felt something she could hardly remember feeling with Gordon. Seen? Was that it? She wasn't sure, but it felt right, in spite of the obvious wrongness of it. The group had begrudgingly read *A Confederacy of Dunces*, James's pick, and when Jean made a tentative comment—that the book had made her think about art and fate in a new way—James responded with a comment that was roughly equal in length and thoughtfulness, an opening for subsequent comments to occur.

Jean, of course, did not enter into her extramarital relationship lightly; neither did James. They were friends for a great while before becoming more; they talked a great deal about their feelings of guilt and shame, and had talked about ending it, but they never really came close to breaking it off. No one knew. No one would ever have suspected Jean of going outside the marriage, least of all Jean.

It had begun innocently enough, they'd gone for coffee after book group a couple of times, no big deal. Well, but who are we kidding, that's not really true, there were sparks, and they both knew it. They never told anyone they were going out for coffee on their own. It went on like this for a year before it became more: once a month they'd have coffee, and talk for a couple of hours about everything under the sun. Jean confided in James about the distance in her marriage and James told her of his own long-term relationship that had ended in heartbreak some years earlier—the woman had left him abruptly and moved out of state to be with another man, with little explanation. Jean couldn't imagine who would ever leave such a lovely man, felt something in her chest she could barely recall ever having felt, had a vague memory that she'd felt this way about Gordon when they first met, but couldn't quite grab on to it. She only knew that this feeling had been sustaining her more and more lately. She told herself that she and James weren't doing anything wrong, just having coffee, maybe sending a few emails every now and again, once every week or two, every couple of days, every day, a few times a day, until finally one day he wrote, *You are a beautiful, flowering tree and I am a tired bird looking for my nest.*

The day after that, James prepared a picnic for Jean; they went down to the lake. He brought his dog, Mott the Hoople, a giant brindle mastiff. Mott loved nothing more than to take one quick run into the lake after a bird, then come back and lie down with his long legs stretched out by James for the rest of the afternoon. They talked as always, about books and art and life, and James confessed that he could no longer hide how he felt about Jean, and they kissed and held hands, drank wine and ate cheese and figs, and she didn't have to hear anything about the provenance of the wine or the cheese or the figs, and they fell asleep for a little while, the three of them, and it was about as beautiful a day as Jean had ever had. They soon became lovers.

So, there's love here, this much we can't deny, some real true love between Jean and James, and no one knows, but it's a sort of bittersweet joy for Jean, who's abided Gordon and his information for a long time, and no one in her family is interested enough in her to notice. Well, except for Otis, whose observational skills are slightly above average for his age, but his communication skills are still at the third-grade level, so he doesn't say anything about it. And it's not like he knows what's going on with his mom, specifically. It's more like he's just noticed that his mom has been acting a bit weird for a while where his father and sister are too busy with themselves to bother.

two

The Copelands live in a small Midwestern college town where Gordon and Jean were both born and raised. Their house is a good-sized colonial, a hundred-plus years old, with a four-acre meadow and a goldfish pond, that had belonged to Gordon's grandparents when he was growing up. It's fairly close to the center of town, and is the largest property in the immediate vicinity. When the town was built, everyone had large parcels, many of them farms, but most of their neighbors had long since split up their lots. The Copelands kept theirs intact. When the grandkids and great-grandkids were young, those four acres were like their own private park, where they came for holidays, family reunions, and weddings, canoeing and fishing and running barefoot in the summer, ice skating and sledding and snowball fights in the winter.

There had been quite a bit of discussion between Gordon and Jean about moving into this house. At first they had lived in a split-level ranch, one they'd bought a year after they'd gotten married; the house still had bits of early-seventies décor (olive green wallpaper in the hall bathroom, shag carpet in the family room) that remained in place even after they left. Jean had always loved that house. It was hers. But the deal was this: Gordon's father, Theodore, had been diagnosed with Parkinson's several years before; his wife, Laura, was still alive and well then, and at the time he was still able to function easily in his own home. After he retired, though, Theodore and Laura had moved into his parents' home; the house had already been added onto twice, so there was plenty of room, and Theodore had wanted his parents to be able to stay in their own home and to help care for them for as long as possible. Unfortunately, Theodore's wife died suddenly about two years after the move, and Gordon's grandfather, Baron, had died around the same time.

So as Theodore and Vivian, Theodore's now ninety-eight-year-old mother, each grew more incapable in their own ways, Gordon convinced Jean to move into his grand-parents' home, to make it easier to care for them both. He promised Jean a kitchen remodel, and suggested a separate, handicap-accessible ground-floor efficiency for the elders. *Economically*, Gordon argued, *it won't affect us; they've both invested well, and they have more than enough funds for in-home care for the rest of their lives, if needed.* Gordon felt he'd had a privileged childhood and wanted to do the right thing by his family, as he believed his parents had. Jean couldn't disagree, but one of the things that Gordon left out of the picture was that she would undoubtedly bear much of this burden, that moving in would mean any shift to in-home care would be put off for as long as possible.

Jean also refrained from mentioning the palpable tension she'd always felt between Theodore and Vivian. For decades, Vivian had indulged in ongoing, though veiled, criticism of his choice in Laura for a wife (Laura had had a youthful marriage *annulled*, a word Vivian would linger on as though it were the ultimate scandal, before adding a comment along the lines of *Oh, but you know she is lovely*). She had also made no bones about her disappointment in her son's youthful pursuit of music and photography instead of taking over the jewelry store her husband had worked so hard to build. (Theodore *did* ultimately take over the business, which briefly raised her pride in her son, but when he later focused on the shop's optometry sideline, finally selling the jewelry part of the store after her husband retired, Vivian was displeased to no end.)

Gordon had seemed oblivious to the tension between his grandmother and his father, preferring to view his family life and childhood as idyllic, something out of the movies, and he chose to hope—against Jean's better judgment—that moving in with them wouldn't be a problem. Jean, as always, kept her uncertainties to herself. She had always adored Gordon's father, but his grandmother seemed almost as scornful of Jean as she had been of Laura. (Vivian found ways to be disapproving of a lot of people and things generated after about 1935, though her comments were always delivered with a lilt in her voice.) Jean, thus, had reasonable concerns about what it would mean to move into Vivian's home. Vivian insisted that she wanted them to feel that it was their own home, though it would soon be clear enough that this was not entirely sincere. Nevertheless, move they did. Jean knocked out the mudroom

to create a larger kitchen with a sitting area, knocked out most
of the back wall to create a huge picture window overlooking
the meadow and pond, and added a bright, airy efficiency
for the elder Copelands, fully outfitted for the handicapped
and with easy access directly into the main house. The efficiency has a kitchenette of its own, where they eat lunch and
breakfast many days, though most often they eat together as a
family in the main house.

In the years since they've moved in, Theodore's Parkinson's has progressed in a variety of ways. He can still walk,
but his balance is wobbly, so he prefers to shuffle around with
his walker or in his wheelchair. For about a year, he's been
wearing a device on a string around his neck that he simply
has to press in order to call the hospital should he fall down
or find himself hurt when he's in a room by himself. He has
some difficulty projecting his voice, so he talks quite a bit less
than he used to. He gets asked to repeat himself a lot, and he
gets tired of it, so unless he really feels like putting in the effort, he often prefers just to listen. His recall for things from
the distant past is still impressive. Theodore was always a big
reader and collector—of stamps, coins, old postcards—and
he's been a passionate amateur photographer since the age of
twelve, when he got his first camera, a Brownie given to him
by his mother (a gift she would later deny she'd given). He
still recognizes the family, usually. On occasion, he's mistaken his mother for his wife, but tends to pass it off as just
a slip, and the family is fine ignoring this progression for
the time being. One morning he asked Gordon what his father did for a living. *He was an optometrist*, Gordon said. *Oh,*

just like me! Theodore replied. When Gordon then pointed out that Theodore *was* his father, Theodore smiled wryly. *So your mother claimed, anyway.* His face is slightly stiffer, less expressive now than in the past, but his clear green eyes still sparkle with mischief. He had always spent a lot of time with Priscilla and Otis, reading them books, taking Otis fishing in his canoe, and both the grandkids adore him; he is pretty much the only member of the family that Priscilla would be described as openly adoring, though she rarely spends time alone with him now.

The big thing that's changed with Theodore is his lack of interest in the things that previously used to interest him, books being at the top of the list, followed by Westerns and certain corny TV shows. He's still engaged by some of his collections; he has a box of commemorative medals he likes to look through—they have famous composers on them—and he tends to forget he's shown you these things before, and so shows them again and again, and the family has yet to establish a consistent protocol for how to deal with this. Gordon, for example, says nothing at all, usually just walks away to do something else. Otis sits with his grandfather again and again, to the point where he's memorized all the faces of the composers. He'd usually rather be doing something else, like working on a crossword, but doesn't know how to excuse himself. If Priscilla sees her grandfather with the box of medals, she just tries to ditch the room before she even goes in. Vivian is the one person who'll flat out tell Theodore that she's seen the medals already, and makes little effort to hide the impatient puff of air that emerges from her nose.

In the past, Theodore would have reacted to his mother's impatience in one way or another, even just a word or two. Since his illness, though, he merely presses forward. *Even this one? The Monteverdi?* A simple *Yes, Theodore* is rarely enough to stop him from asking about the Mahler, and the Brahms as well, sometimes even the Chopin and the Liszt, at which point Vivian's discomfort overtakes her and she excuses herself from the room. Vivian operates at a pretty high level of denial where unpleasant things are concerned.

These days, Theodore's interests lean toward the lights around the fish pond, the ongoing nature show in their yard (the rest of the family also enjoys the occasional *Oh, look at the deer* moment, but Theodore can sit and look out the window for hours), and piles of rocks, in which he sees many things. Around the holidays last year, he discovered a rock that looked somewhat like Mary holding the baby Jesus (it actually does), and made it the centerpiece of a diorama he crafted out of an empty checkbook box, featuring a crèche of rocks representing Joseph, the wise men, and a sheep. All but the Mary and the baby Jesus are a bit of a stretch to anyone else, but Theodore is more than happy to point out the turbans on the wise men, the rock representing the frankincense (he's still searching for the perfect myrrh), and so forth. (This interest in the manger scene represents no special religious concern on Theodore's part. He just sees what he sees.) Studying, developing, and displaying this crèche has occupied more hours than is possible to tally, but it's hard to imagine anyone but Theodore, or maybe a geologist, taking quite this much interest in a box of rocks. If there's any upside to this for anyone, especially Theodore, it's that he truly seems no less happy than he ever did—and Theodore has always been a happy, contented individual.

VIVIAN, A SOCIAL BUTTERFLY, has a tendency to gossip and make sideways comments passed off as truth. *What?* She's just making observations. Well, she never. She's the 1912 model of Priscilla. Five-foot-one in her youth, she's now four-foot-nine, ninety-eight years old. Vivian likes to tell people how old she is, has been doing this since she was about eighty. (Before that, she would have said it was *improper* for a woman to reveal her age. After she turned eighty, she quickly realized how impressed people were with how fantastic she looked, how vital she still was, and how much mileage she could get out of it. It wasn't so much that she didn't look eighty—though Vivian didn't think that—just that she was as full of life and put-together as ever.) Loves, loves, loves attention, is used to getting it, has been since she was an eligible young bachelorette. Will leave the room if attention's not on her for more than a few minutes. Will pay attention to you for as long as it takes for her to determine if something about you reflects well on her. Say, if you're a person of some means, some social distinction. Tells stories, most about herself, one or two about others in the family. (She still beams with pride telling the one about a luncheon she'd held, after which she'd written in Theodore's baby book, "Theodore hilarious." At one time, the story included the actual hilarious thing he'd said, but after fifty years she'd finally forgotten it, and the story mutated into something that was more Vivian-centric involving the suit from Carson Pirie Scott she'd worn and what she'd prepared for lunch that day, though "Theodore hilarious" always remained its climax.) When Theodore went to college to study music and photography, Vivian spent four years telling people who asked that her son was just *having a little whim* before he went to work at the jewelry store. She had taken great pride in being the wife of a prominent jeweler, and after Theodore dropped the jewelry business for optometry, she took to beginning her sentences, *If you'd only gone into the jewelry business . . .* In Theodore's better days, he often finished it for her. *I wouldn't have been as happy, Mother.* Vivian generally replied with an uncomfortable chuckle. *Oh well, yes, of course, but still . . .*

So if Vivian's about to launch into a story about a member of the family, chances are it happened when that person was a baby. Priscilla, for instance, is way beyond tired of the story about how quietly and perfectly she laid on a blanket as a baby. (All Priscilla can figure is that her great-grandmother repeats the Priscilla Lays Quietly On A Fucking Blanket story because it didn't happen often. Even Priscilla knows that much about herself. But it's only partly the case. Vivian does repeat it because she's easily impressed by well-behaved children, and on that day, Vivian had found Priscilla laying on this baby blanket about twenty minutes after she'd exhausted herself screaming. Vivian hadn't witnessed that part of it, and was charmed by Priscilla's momentary fascination with a crystal paperweight and the reflections it was making around the room. Still, Priscilla thought, had she done nothing that her great-grandmother admired since lying still on a blanket before she could even walk? Not even fucking *walking*? *Gah*.)

Otherwise, Vivian's stories tend to be about Vivian. She has about fifteen stories in permanent rotation, and the grooves have worn deep. Was a minister's daughter, positively hated Sunday services, hated moving around, hated not knowing where they'd be from one year to the next, went to twelve schools in ten years. The year she was six, her father moved ahead of the family; she came home from school one day and her father was gone, and all she was told was that he'd been "called" and that they'd meet him soon. Never went to church again after she got married, never moved again once they bought their own home. Has wonderful memories of childhood, wonderful memories, oh yes, they didn't have very much money at all, you see, on her father's salary, but they made do, raised their own chickens, her mother taught her to bake. Only had one birthday party ever, her seventh. Was engaged twice before she met her future husband, Baron, gave the rings back, *of course*. Heavens. No proper young lady would keep such things. Was on the women's swim team in college. Was a teacher in a one-room schoolhouse. Jean has been seen mouthing the words to Vivian's stories along with her behind her back.

Despite her age, Vivian is as fast on her feet as ever. If she decides she needs something in the other room, she'll be there and back in a blink, as if she has her own little high-speed conveyer belt. She's a little slower with other things, like cooking, but still gets it done. Keeps her part of the house tidy, neat as a pin. Has a cleaning lady come in once a week to do the sweeping. Sometimes forgets that the word "Negro" is no longer in favor (*Oh, I can't keep up with that*). Watches her weight. Collects antique valentines and little windup toys, the kind that do things, ducks and penguins that waddle and flip over, bobble-head dolls, tops that open up and fan out when you spin them, finds them endlessly amusing. Not super interested in her great-grandkids now, hasn't been since they were toddlers. Thinks Otis is a little off, does not approve of Priscilla's: hairstyle, manner of dress, attitude. A little obsessed with a nephew who graduated from Princeton. Photos of him on her fridge. (Don't get Priscilla and Jean started about this.) Is always prompt for engagements and expects promptness from others. Always sends handwritten thank-you notes. It's just proper etiquette.

Oh, and one more thing: has never in her life driven a car. Oh, my word, no. Prefers to be driven. Her husband used to do this, then Theodore, but he hasn't been allowed to drive for several years now. That's fine. She's happy to call a taxi.

Review: difficult daughter, know-it-all dad, son sweet and okay if a little weird, mom delayed potential/having affair, great-grandmother bitchy, granddad losing it. So we know where we're starting.

three

Priscilla heads out, takes her mom's car without asking—a fairly regular occurrence—leaving her mother with no way to go back out and pick up anything she needs for tonight's dinner. *Where are you going*, Jean asks, and Priscilla tells her she'll be right back, even though she won't. She's on her way to meet some friends at the mall. Priscilla's in junior college but that's not likely to last; she's mainly there because her parents told her she'd have to move out if she didn't go. A weak ultimatum at best, unlikely to be followed up on, but somehow it worked. Priscilla would love to have her own place, of course, has fantasies about a modern, spacious loft in New York or somewhere, like on *Sex and the City*, but (a) spends everything she makes on clothes and (b) seriously has no idea how to go out and sign a lease and all that. Also, she's never prepared so much as one meal involving more than cereal and milk, never done one single load of laundry ever; even Otis has done laundry. Not that she's consciously added up the thoughts about moving out meaning cooking and doing laundry and paying bills, of course. It may sound like

Priscilla isn't all that bright, but that's not the case. Let's just say that she doesn't quite know what to do with the kind of intelligence she has. Like her mother, she has potential. This is maybe the one thing they have in common.

At the food court, picking at one Cinnabon, Priscilla and her three girlfriends, Ashley, Danielle, and Taylor, her BFF, go over some recent gossip. It is agreed that a certain girl they know is fat, and also that she is homely. *Busted.* A troll. *A severe troll*, Taylor says. It is probably not a coincidence that this girl has also recently taken Taylor's *sloppy seconds* in the form of her senior year boyfriend. It is not agreed that this certain girl is also a shady bitch, though Taylor adamantly insists this is so. *Well, I'd be bitchy, too, if I looked like that*, Priscilla says, and all three of her friends simultaneously think "You're bitchy anyway," and they glance at each other sideways, but no one says it. Taylor almost does—but then these two guys come over to them with clipboards, asking if they'd be interested in trying out for a new reality show.

Priscilla can hardly believe it. None of them can. Their eyes all widen, they all sit up a little bit straighter, try to pretend they're not smoothing down possible flyaways on their perfectly flat-ironed hair, but Priscilla especially believes this is her moment, believes it is absolutely fate; though she's never previously thought about fate, she knows now that she completely, wholeheartedly believes in it, and that this is hers. These two guys ask the girls a bunch of questions, nothing unusual, what are they interested in, how old are they, a little about their families. Priscilla feels sure that one of them is directing more of his attention to her than to the others, and at one point she even tries to lean forward over the table in such a way that Taylor and Ashley are behind her and thus less likely to be noticed. She asks what the show is about and one of the guys, whose name is Ted, says that they can't really say too much about it except that they're looking for one main person to be the focus of the show, that it would be sort of like those MTV shows about the friends, but more focused on one character instead of an ensemble.

Priscilla is doing everything she can to remain calm, but she is totally freaking out. It's seriously like her *destiny* has come to her *right now*, right here at the food court. She tilts her head and nods in what's meant to be a thoughtful way, a way that indicates anything but that she's freaking out, a way that says, *I think thoughtful things*, a way that says she's interesting. The guys leave applications with each of the girls and tell them that if they're interested in auditioning they should show up at this time and place the following week with the completed application and a headshot. *Do we need to, like, prepare a monologue or something?* Priscilla asks, immediately sure it is the dumbest question ever asked in, like, the history of dumb questions.

Before we proceed, we should probably mention that when Priscilla uses the word "like"—and she uses it often—it is invariably merged with the word that came before it, forming a compound word of sorts: *tolike, inlike, islike.* If we didn't know better, we might think she believed it to be a grammatical rule, and that, in her universe, the rarely used comma is reserved for sarcastic pauses only.

The guy named Ted smiles but doesn't laugh and says

No, all you have to do is just be yourself. Priscilla is over the moon. She is *so* good at that. She is going to spend all weekend practicing being herself.

Ted and the other guy leave and the girls agree that the time has come to go shopping, that for this auspicious occasion they will need new outfits. Priscilla gets a 50 percent discount at Express, where she works, so they head there first. It's not Priscilla's favorite store by a lot (her taste runs to pricier brands), so she buys and wears the minimum she can get by with to work there, but her friends all like it just fine, and she's happy to let them buy stuff with her discount and show them how to wear it, which all agree she has a knack for. *If you take that $19.99 knit dress*, Priscilla says about an item Taylor's looking at, *and splurge on one really badass pair of knee-high boots that you can wear with everything, it's like practically a fashion miracle.* All the girls nod at Priscilla's great truth.

IN THE END, ASHLEY and Danielle won't even show up to the audition, Taylor will, but she's really only sort of half into it. Taylor confides this to Priscilla the day of the audition, and Priscilla is for once silently outraged—silently only because they're in the waiting room and she does not want to call attention to herself in this way. *Well then why are you even here*, Priscilla whispers, to which Taylor says *I dunno, I just thought I'd see.* Priscilla makes a loudish huff through her nose. This is, like, her life's dream. She's wearing a pair of designer jeans with a tank top and a long cardigan sweater she found on sale by a designer whose name she recognized from another reality show. The only part of the outfit that isn't brand new

are her boots. The tank top by itself was sixty-eight dollars. Priscilla has put the entire cost of this outfit, minus the
boots, on her credit card, adding up to almost $370, or what
Priscilla might make in forty-one hours, which will take her
close to a month as she only works twenty hours a week,
and of course, she has been charging other things, and will
charge more things, and will not be paying off this credit
card anytime soon. Unless she gets this TV show. Which she
will, she's so sure.

Taylor goes in first, is in there for ten of the longest minutes of Priscilla's whole entire life. Have any of the other girls
been in there for ten full minutes? Priscilla wishes now that
she'd noticed. They're scheduled ten minutes apart, but some
of them have come out a minute or two earlier. Ugly ones,
Priscilla thinks. Beasts. She looks at the photo she's brought
for them. Is this what they want? Is it too sexy? It's not a
professional headshot, it's one that Ashley had taken of her
right before a party. She had bangs then, doesn't now, hopes
it doesn't matter but is thinking *Shit, shit, what if it matters?*
She tries to think about something else, anything, can't for a
minute, scans the room for more ugly girls she can cross off
the callback list. She's not wrong about these girls, not about
them being ugly so much as about them being not pretty or
stylish enough to be called back. *A plainer girl can go a long way
with a little style*, Priscilla thinks. *Why don't they know that?*

Finally Taylor comes out and she's making a face like
That was weird but kind of fun, and Priscilla is dying to grill
her about it, but her name is called, so she has to go in. *Don't
leave*, Priscilla whispers on her way in. She smoothes her hair

down one last time, shakes hands with Ted. The other guy from the food court isn't there. Instead there's a panel of four people: Ted; a guy Ted introduces as the casting director; and another man and woman he says are producers. Priscilla catches a weird vibe from the casting director, which may or may not be there, and smiles at all of them like she's never smiled before. All it is is, they just ask her a few questions about herself, what she's interested in, what she'd be willing to talk about or do on TV. *Oh, anything*, she says, a little too quickly. She didn't really mean *anything* like she'd take her top off or eat spiders anything, she meant more like flirt-with-cute-guys-and-drink anything. But she doesn't explain. That could have been a mistake. Probably not. But it could have been. But probably not. Probably not. Hopefully not.

four

At work this morning, first thing, Gordon's secretary presents him with a small plant, a bonsai she's picked up for Boss's Day. Support staff is encouraged not to spend more than five dollars on their bosses on Boss's Day, as their salaries are obviously much smaller. It's just supposed to be a gesture. Gordon's secretary, Doris, is a few years older than he is, and she's been doing this for thirty-five years. So she gives him this sweet little bonsai to thank him; the fact is, he's a decent boss, he doesn't make her stay late, has her birthday on his calendar, knows the names of her kids, and is generally friendly toward her. But, but, he's the same with her as he is with everyone, and so when she gives him the bonsai, he responds with the following: *Oh! A bonsai! Did you know that the bonsai dates back as far as the early times of Egyptian culture? Of course they're most closely associated with Japan, and the concept of wabi-sabi. You surely know about wabi-sabi—how best to explain that? Well, it's a sort of appreciation of the transience of things. On that account, it's almost surprising that the bonsai has gained any popularity in America, since we're well known for our throwaway culture. Do you know that there's a bonsai at the Tokyo Imperial Palace that dates back to the seventeenth century? Think about that! Often, copper wiring is used as a technique for directing the tree into a desired shape. And there are many different shapes.* Gordon holds it up and examines it from all sides. *I'm not quite sure whether this one is upright or informal upright, but it's clearly not multitrunk. I'll have to find a nice sunny place for this.*

Gordon means to include a thank-you in here some-where, but by the time he's done, he's forgotten. Doris nods and smiles, but about halfway through the bonsai talk she's begun to go through the morning mail, tossing out junk and handing her employer the letters he needs to see.

Now Gordon's day is about to take a weird turn.

At the deli counter at one of his stores, he's consider-ing a tabouli salad for lunch, providing some information on tabouli for the chef who prepared it. *Did you know tabouli was originally a Lebanese mountain dish, but that there are Turkish and Armenian variations of the dish as well, in which there is more parsley than bulgur? Also, interestingly, there's a common misconception that bulgur is the same thing as cracked wheat, but in fact it's usually just parboiled.* The chef is just listening for any part of Gordon's talk that includes the word "pound." Gordon is still talking about bulgur when a woman on line behind him recognizes his voice and peers around him to get a better look at his face. *Gordon!* she says, smiling. *I thought that was you.*

Gordon would swear he has never seen this woman be-fore. Gordon often claims he never forgets a face, which is usually true, although once in a rare while he'll forget a name, but this face and its name are entirely unfamiliar to him. *I'm sorry, do we know each other?* He figures they must have met at a party, maybe a corporate training event, that she's someone he knows casually. Gordon may be priggish, but he's a polite man, and is hoping that they did not date, that would be awkward. But, of course, that's exactly the deal. The woman introduces herself as Trudy.

Oh, Gordon says, *of course, of course*, except it's not *of course*. Gordon and Trudy had been in the same graduating class and had dated for the entire nine months of their senior year, and he does not remember her. It's hard to believe, near impossible to believe, and yet we can see from his face that it's one hundred percent true. And we can see from Trudy's face that she's having trouble believing it, too.

You're kidding, right?

Gordon, rarely at a loss for words, does not know what to say. He is not kidding. He thinks his mouth may even be hanging open, but he's not altogether sure.

Senior year? ___ Hall? Pitchers of beer and darts at the Rat? Frisbee on the quad?

Gordon certainly remembers these things, but not in conjunction with Trudy. She's an attractive woman, to be sure, he thinks, taking in her large brown eyes, the chestnut waves of hair resting on the tops of her shoulders, her slender waist, delicate ankles atop a pair of heels. She looks like someone he *would* have dated, without a doubt. But any memory of this woman is utterly unavailable to him in this moment.

For Valentine's Day you gave me a pair of red footed pajamas? I gave you a copy of 'Leaves of Grass'? We went to that little French place and then on the way back it rained and we ducked into that big cement pipe until it stopped? Trudy leaves out the part about how they kissed in the pipe, can't imagine just the pipe won't trigger his memory, but it doesn't. *You used to joke that our song was "Why Don't We Do It in the Road?" I lived on the second floor, you used to go down the fire ladder, you fell that one time, I had a roommate named Sheila?*

Sheila, Gordon remembers—curvy, sexy Sheila who was taking a belly-dancing class one semester. Sheila, he spent a lot of time fantasizing about. *Belly-dancing Sheila?* His face brightens a bit when he says it, which appears to displease Trudy. For a moment, they're both silent. *Okay*, she says. *Well, then. Take care.*

You, too, Trudy, he says, taking care to enunciate her name precisely, so much so that it's not only obvious, but weird-sounding. *Tru-dee. Truu-deee.* He hears this on a loop in his head for a moment, and then wishes he'd invited her to coffee, just to be polite, not as a date, of course, he's married. Maybe over coffee he'd remember.

Gordon will spend no small amount of time concerned about not remembering this. Back in his office following this encounter, he scribbles down a list of pre-Jean relationships to try to spark his memory:

- 5th grade kissing game disaster—Debbie Olsop
- 10th grade girlfriend Tammy Micklin, prom
- awful blind date w/ ferret lady
- regrettable personal ad date
- Ellen, visible thong above skirt, unrequited

But there's a noticeable and troubling hole between tenth grade and adulthood. He has not, until now, connected the fact of his father's memory loss with the possibility of his own fate, but now that he has, the corner he's turned is not one he'll easily turn back around. He will not talk to his wife about this, because they do not talk about previous (or current) lovers. He will begin, repeatedly, to pose a hypothetical scenario to coworkers, friends, anyone, really: *Say you were approached by a person who claimed they had a history with you, the details of which were specific and believable, and yet even when told these specific and believable details, you still have no recollection of that person and those things as being connected, due to the fact that you have no recollection of that person?* Gordon gets a number of different answers to this question, none of which he feels are especially useful. *Happens to me all the time. That's just CRS is what that is,* Doris tells him. *Can't remember shit.* (Doris loves that phrase, CRS, thinks it's the funniest thing ever.) *Nothing to worry about.* Priscilla doesn't understand the question. She looks up from her cell phone long enough to say *What are you even talking about, Dad?* but not long enough to wait for an answer. He becomes worried that his memory may be failing him in other ways he's unaware of, that his knowledge, which is pretty much the most important thing to him, could be slipping away in small bits and pieces, that what if one day he wakes up with complete amnesia, what then?

five

So, this part of the story is a bummer. Jean's lover, the other man, the good man James, he kills himself. There's no sense being delicate about it. He freaking hangs himself. It's not a delicate thing. Jean finds this out in the worst possible way.

She and James had a standing date every Friday for lunch at the cabin he used as a studio. They often met at this cabin, down by the lake, less than a mile from her own house, but Fridays at noon were a regular thing. James had no classes on Friday afternoons and Priscilla worked. So Jean arrives at the cabin as usual, but this day she finds a note taped to the door, a folded piece of paper, the outside reading CALL 911, WALK AWAY. At first her mind does not go all the way to the worst place, but it's a weirdly ominous message, and she doesn't recognize the caps as James's handwriting; the door is locked, he isn't answering her knocks and the blinds are down, so she takes the note down and looks inside. *I'm sorry.* That's all it says. Now she shoots off to the bad place. She's got one thought—that maybe he's breaking it off with her—because that's a slightly better thought than the other one, the one where *I'm sorry* and CALL 911 mash together into something she's utterly unprepared for. She tries to look through the blinds, but they're all down, which isn't completely unusual on the days when she comes, finally comes across the one broken slat, one missing six-inch length of slat where she can peek in. It's not at the perfect height, about at her chin, so she has to bend her knees a bit to see what she wasn't supposed to see: James, hanging from a support crossbar in the middle of the room.

The crossbar had been the subject of conversation between Jean and James on more than one occasion because of its distinct, yokelike construction—three wrought-iron bars coming together in an upside-down T-shape across the center of the room's vaulted ceiling, one suspended from the ceiling, one on either side of the two walls, all three hooked around a plate-sized ring in the center. Jean and James had always found something sort of lovely, but also amusing, about it; they'd lie on the single bed in this cabin, with its blue ribcord bedspread, stare up at the crossbar, and wonder together, *Was this the builder's best idea about how to keep the walls from falling down?* Jean, it's fair to say, will never unsee her beloved James hanging from the crossbar, his feet less than a foot from the floor.

Jean drops to her knees. She feels like she might throw up. She's too shocked to cry, feels like she was kicked in the stomach. Feels like she can't breathe, like she might vomit out of her eyes. How could he do this to her? Call 911? Walk away? How could he make her be the one to deal with this?

Could he have been expecting someone else? They had a date. How is she supposed to just walk away? Does she have a choice? She's not prepared to confess to Gordon, not prepared to break into the house, not prepared to figure out how to pull him down. She pulls herself up and looks through the slat one more time. Maybe it's not true, maybe it's not true. She takes one last look, closes her eyes, feels the tears coming, and does as he requested. She walks away and drives to a pay phone to call 911. Anonymously, of course. She makes up a weak story, she's too fraught to do better than say that she was a jogger passing by, that she doesn't want to be involved. She doesn't tell them what she saw, but stresses that it's urgent, and hangs up.

Of course, when someone goes and hangs themselves, it's often the subject of much gossip and discussion, and this is no exception. So Jean's kind of fucked right now, pretty much. In her head, anyway. She's a mess. But she's trying not to be a mess, because obviously no one is supposed to know she's a mess. She has to pretend she doesn't even know until the news hits the paper the next day. She does a good enough job hiding that she's scanning the paper specifically for this news, but when it appears, in a small item in the Metro section titled "Beloved Teacher Found Dead," she can't stop herself from bursting into tears at the breakfast table. Gordon asks her what's wrong, so Jean does her best to act as though this is the first she's heard of it. But it takes a bit of reframing in her head before she knows how to answer. *It's James, from my book group*, she says in a strange, slow voice that seems not quite her own. *He died.*

Oh no, Gordon says. *Well, that's terrible. What happened? He couldn't have been very old. Was he sick?*

Jean takes another pause, considers the various meanings of "sick." *It says an autopsy will be performed but that it appears he took his own life*, she says, shaking her head. Is this what grief for a book club friend looks like? She doesn't know. Everything feels wrong.

Of course the book group all knew him, so it's not surprising that the phone rings just as Gordon's about to get started with some extensive commentary. Her friend Margot has also just read the newspaper, and expresses her shock as well, and says to Jean *I know you two were good friends*, which makes Jean's heart rate speed up a bit, and she wants to hang up quickly, but Margot appears eager to chat about it, adding that maybe she shouldn't be surprised *given that 'A Confederacy of Dunces' was his pick.*

At first Jean doesn't get Margot's meaning at all. *What are you saying?* Jean asks her friend, feeling her face grow hot. Margot explains that she always thought it was interesting that James had picked a book by a guy who killed himself and *What do you suppose* that *means?* Jean raises her voice but stops a fair bit short of yelling. She's never been a yeller, but she is feeling something odd and churny in her. *Well, if you thought it meant something, Margot, why didn't you say anything about it at the time?* Margot tells Jean she was kind of just thinking it was interesting. Jean wants to make the point that when they read *The Bell Jar* no one had thought Alisa was suicidal, but finds herself hard pressed to go any further into the discussion without implicating herself. So she tells Margot she has to go and hangs up. Gordon puts a hand on her shoulder, seeing that she's upset, but she gets up abruptly and tells him she has to go take a shower.

IN THE DAYS THAT follow, Gordon provides several discourses on the nature of suicide, the relationship of James's profession to suicide (this knowledge gained during his time at the hospital working on the psychiatric floor), as well as a tangent on the pros and cons of certain meds. Jean tries to make a comment here and there, without crying, without too much expression that goes beyond general compassion, something that seems along the lines of what someone else might say about it, *Such a shame*, what have you, but she feels transparent.

Of course, Gordon says, *it's well known that there is a higher rate of suicide among artists. The corollary between depression and this field is well-documented. And they say there are always signs, if you know what to look for, like withdrawing from relationships and giving away possessions.* Gordon often does this thing with his hands when he talks—it's a little hard to describe, but picture: he has all five fingers on each hand spread as far apart as they can go, sometimes bending down all but the pointer and the thumb but not, not meaning to point but sometimes pointing anyway (a particular peeve of Priscilla's); the elbows are bent and there's a lot of wrist action, almost as though to wave the arms would be too dramatic, as though limiting the motions to the hand is somehow more dignified. This impassioned gesticulating is exactly one of those things you find engaging when you're first dating someone, *Oh, he's so expressive with his hands!*, that kind of thing, but which carries a high likelihood of becoming one of those things you'll later come to find weird, affected, or just plain annoying. Right now it's all those things for Jean, with *annoying* rising to the next level, a plateau just below rage. Jean opens her eyes wide, tries to go somewhere else in her head when her husband does this—Maui or Malibu, places she's heard about on TV that seem tranquil and surfy—because when she listens, she kind of wants to scream and run at him with a tenderizing mallet. There were no signs. She saw no signs. None. No signs. No, there was, there was one sign, when she arrived at the cabin and saw him freaking hanging. That was the sign.

six

James's memorial service is as small a service as Jean has ever been to, held in his brother's backyard, just his parents, a few students and colleagues, and the book group. Minus one. When Jean asks her friend Margot where Alisa, the missing friend, is, Margot reports back that Alisa had said she *wouldn't feel comfortable*. Jean's eye starts to twitch when she hears this, wonders how her friend got the idea that a funeral is for her personal comfort. She thinks of a thousand bitter things to say, none of them terribly clever. We're not going to a spa, she thinks. Out of anyone, Jean thinks, she would be the one with a right to lock herself in a bathroom.

James's younger brother, Hal, is the first one to speak. He sobs a great deal, off and on, talks about how much he had always looked up to his brother, talks about depression, the struggle James had had for years, his first suicide attempt, when he was in college, how his parents had done everything they could, or believed they did. Jean, needless to say, is stunned by this. James had never mentioned his depression to Jean, never seemed depressed, and to discover he had actually tried to kill himself once before is a complete shock. Jean begins to wonder, if she hadn't known this critical thing, if she'd really known him at all.

One of his students, a weeping sophomore girl who'd been in his class, talks about how encouraging Mr. D always was, even if your art kind of wasn't so hot, like hers, how his enthusiasm for art had inspired her, how he'd made her see how it connects people, and could, you know, change you. Mott sidles over to the girl and lays down at her feet while she's still talking, and she looks down at him for a moment, smiles sadly, says how much Mr. D had talked about his dog, Mott the Hoople, and how he was named after some band from when he was a kid, that he'd brought him to class once and how much they'd laughed when he knocked over a jar of paint with his big tail. When she's done, Hal stands up to mention that the dog needs a home, his wife is allergic, his parents can't take him. Jean knows right then that Mott the Hoople is going home with her today.

At the reception, Jean and her book group friends pay their respects to the family. Not being able to talk to the family about their relationship is crushing. She has a vision of an entirely different life she might have led, one with these people as her in-laws. It's easy for her to see where so much of what she loved about James came from, even if the sadness on them is creating new lines she can practically see forming in their faces. She hugs Hal for an entirely inappropriate length of time. He smells like James, a faint combination of turpentine and grass. They talk about Mott; she convinces him that her kids will love the dog (one-half true), that her husband won't mind (she has no idea, right now doesn't care), and she leaves her lover's memorial service with a 120-pound dog.

REACTIONS ARE PREDICTABLY MIXED when Jean arrives home with the dog. Otis is thrilled. Priscilla, eyebrows raised, says *Keep that drooly beast the hell out of my room.* Vivian says, *Oh my goodness gracious!* Theodore doesn't say much, but reaches out a wobbly hand; Mott comes over, sniffs it, and licks Theodore's face, which cracks him up. Theodore had had dogs as a kid, never one a quarter this big, and is tickled to have an animal inside the house. Gordon asks a question or two about why there wasn't someone else who could have taken the dog, but the incident with Trudy is still distracting him, which is just as well since Jean knows she's made an executive decision here, regardless of what Gordon wants. So he doesn't push the argument, he just talks at length about the proper care and feeding of a dog, and what he knows about mastiffs, and how as long as it doesn't sleep in their bed, it's fine.

The day after the service, Jean stops by Hal's to pick up Mott's bed, among other things, pausing none too subtly to deeply inhale Hal's familiar scent one last time. In fact, though Mott will often nap in his own bed, he will soon begin sleeping in Jean and Gordon's bed. It's not that there isn't room; they have a king-sized bed, and they sleep with plenty of room between them. (In fact, they have not had sex in several years—since quite a while before she took up with James, actually.) Gordon isn't thrilled about this arrangement and says so, to which Jean says flatly, *What's the difference.*

Gordon's actually stumped, she's got him there, and what he doesn't want to say—what's hardly more than a half-formed thought—is that he was hoping someday they would sleep together again. But the sight of Jean and the mastiff cozily spooning does not inspire confidence that this will ever happen, that he'll ever even get as far as spooning his wife again, which looks awfully nice, and on subjects relating to their own marriage Gordon remains silent. On this page, they're together.

seven

One day, shortly after this, Otis stays home sick from school. When asked what hurts, he says *I dunno, just everything*, which Jean knows is more or less the same as *not really anything*, but this day she's feeling a little lonely, so she lets him take a mental health day. Everyone needs one, Jean realizes more than ever. Jean herself could use a mental health week, month, life. She fixes Otis some tomato soup and a cream cheese sandwich on white bread, crusts cut off, cut into squares, puts it on a tray with a couple of Oreos and a glass of milk and takes it up to his room, where he's working on a new crossword puzzle in his bed, Mott curled up at his feet.

Otis has gotten pretty good at making crosswords, filling in words in patterns, and creating clues, although generally his clues are for the specific audience of his family and would not work in wide circulation. The clue for 21 across, "What I'm sick of hearing every stupid day," and its correct answer, "FREAK," are unsurprisingly of concern for Jean, and they begin a discussion that's essentially about depression, in which

Jean looks for signs, tries to discern whether Otis is suffering from anything more serious than the typical fallout from sibling squabbles, anything she needs to worry about, given what she's recently been through and—according to Gordon, her book group, and the entire local news media—missed. Jean's overall worry level has gone up by a lot recently, to where everything—even seemingly good things—now seems like a possible sign of suicide: a taste for bananas, a sudden appreciation for a terrible sitcom, silence from her daughter in place of a snotty remark.

Later in the week, on the way home from school, Otis mentions to his mother that he might sort of kind of maybe like this girl, but probably not. Probably not, but kind of. But probably not. But kind of. *Considering she's a girl and everything.*

Oh, that's wonderful, sweetheart. Tell me about her.

Otis doesn't quite have the words to describe the tumble-y sensation in his stomach when he sees her, really isn't at all sure yet what he feels. They've hardly spoken.

I dunno. She has two ponytails. He doesn't mention that they spiral into small shiny coils at the bottom, like perfect, soft little Slinkys, and that every day he has to resist the urge to gently pull on one just to see it spring back up.

You mean pigtails?

I guess. Otis takes a minute to contemplate what's different about the tails of a pony and a pig, can't quite translate it to girl hair.

What's her name?

Caterina. The slight lilt in the way Otis says her name, the way he takes care to pronounce each syllable distinctly (to make sure his mother doesn't think he's saying Katrina— he hears Caterina correct people almost every day) tells Jean everything she needs to know.

That's a pretty name.

Otis nods and shrugs at the same time.

Jean tells Otis about the first boy she ever liked, when she was around his age, and Otis perks up a bit, feels like perhaps the situation isn't hopeless (even though all signs point to hopeless right now: Caterina, the girl he sort of kind of probably likes, has never said much more than a word or two to him).

Apropos of nothing, Jean segues into some thoughts about love that are very clearly about her relationship with James. *Love is a—it's a thing, Otie, it's a thing that isn't always what you think it might be.* Not only is this far too abstract for Otis, it also leads him to believe that she's talking about his dad, which isn't exactly the case. She does mean to tell Otis the story of how she met Gordon, but before long the stories of her two lovers have begun to twine. *When I first met your father,* she tells her son, *I was truly in his thrall, as they say. He was so worldly and handsome in a certain way, I thought, and I was so young. Time has a way of changing things like love, and so what it means now is different from what it was then—stability, that sort of thing. That's a kind of love. James has reminded me of a different thing that love can be.*

Otis is clearly confused by the introduction of the name James. *James? Daddy's name is Gordon,* he says tonelessly, as though she truly has just gotten mixed up. Otis gets mixed up all the time. Jean takes a pause, looking at her son. She sees something, we don't know yet whether it's actually there, or whether maybe we shouldn't pass judgment yet or something, but she sees something in his eyes she reads as *I will understand and hold in complete confidence anything you tell me*. It's not that this is a misperception, either, it's just that what this means to Otis is somewhat different from what it means to Jean, and he knows next to nothing about sex or anything like that, and if he's expecting anything from his mom, it's probably just something like, *Oh, don't tell your father but the chocolate cake that he loves so much comes out of a box*.

Except it isn't. What it is is that Jean proceeds to tell her young son that she has met a man named James, and that he has died and that they had been very close friends and now she was very sad. That's what she tells him the first time it comes up. Otis offers a solemn nod. He had learned the meaning of "died" two years earlier when his pet turtle Bishop stopped moving, although he still does not have the clearest impression of what any of this really means—love, death, sex, none of it. Otis hasn't had his first boner yet, so the sex part of the equation, perhaps mercifully, is absent. Nor does he appear to be even slightly traumatized by the idea that his mother has been spending time with another man, that's how it appears to Jean, and she is correct. As of now, at least, the idea that this scenario could potentially remove his mother from his picture—or possibly create a second picture into which he and members of his family and some new man might enter and exit—has not yet occurred to him. Right now it's just a bit of information that, to Otis, seems only like a sort of free-floating fact, one with little direct impact on him. And, actually, he's kind of right in that way.

So, okay. Plus, on this day, what Otis is really waiting for is how this all relates to him, how this might help him with his interest in Caterina, the girl whose cubby is next to his. That information doesn't come now, and it may never come. Jean fixes dinner for the family. Gordon discourses on the difference between sweet potatoes and yams. Theodore gets up for a Popsicle before he's half done; Jean reminds him he's not done, so he shuffles back to the table. Vivian, as always, eats only half of what's on her plate. Efforts to put half-portions on Vivian's plate have resulted only in her eating half of that. This is how she watches her figure, you see. Priscilla slumps in her chair and texts during most of the meal, and Otis looks as serenely odd as always. Maybe slightly twitchy, because he's thinking about Caterina, and the way she chews the tip of her pigtail during science, when she's a little bored. He's unfazed, anyway. And of course Jean, as she has been since her secret lover's death, is somewhere else.

eight

Aside from meals, one of the few times when the family convenes (to describe their dinner conventions as interactions would be a profound misnomer) is when Gordon calls them all together to play games with their grandparents, about once or twice a week after dinner. Priscilla usually huffs but comes to the table anyway; she still has a soft spot for her grandfather. Otis actually likes these gatherings; he loves every member of his family, and in spite of their various distractions, he likes hearing anything they have to say about their day. Vivian usually finds reasons to quit early, but it's one of the few things they can all do together that Theodore's still decent at. Occasionally they play Dictionary. Priscilla particularly hates this game, it's way too hard, she despises writing and doesn't see why she should be forced to do it *like supposedly for fun*, seeing as how it isn't; she's always the last to finish and no one ever guesses her definitions. Otis loves it, thinks it helps with his crosswords, and Gordon loves it as well, although he's always been a bit confused about the concept of the game, tending to actually try to think of the real definition of each word, rather than trying to come up with a definition that will fool people. Lately, though, they've been playing a card game called Spite and Malice, the main object of which is to be the first player to get rid of all their cards by playing them essentially in numerical order one on top of another.

This is where everyone goes during Spite and Malice: Often the TV is on, so there's that. Anyone has the option to check out that way, and it's a popular choice. Gordon, before the Trudy incident, is as present as anyone, at least to the extent that he will find things to explain, as always, whether they relate to the game or not. Jean tries hard to stay present, but she sees James's image on all the face cards—there he is holding a scepter, or bedecked in a crown or a silly hat—and, since the game is played with multiple decks, there are a lot of face cards and a lot of Jameses. Priscilla sends texts between turns. Mott curls up under the table. There's barely room for him there, but he seems to like being right in the middle of things, equal distance to everyone. We suspect he misses James, even though he appears happy with the Copelands, but that's just a guess; we don't know how dogs think. Otis is usually engaged, unless a favorite cartoon is on. Theodore, well, sometimes he's in and sometimes he's out. If it's dark out and the pond lights catch his eye, he may go to that, and if it's light out and a ground squirrel walks past the window, he'll keep his gaze in the general spot where the squirrel was last seen, just in case it comes back.

Vivian, who may have been the one who passed the talking gene down to her grandson, is also the one who has the least patience for his information sessions. The fact of Vivian is that she has trouble if she's not the focus of attention, which at this point tends only to happen outside of the house or with strangers. Strangers love Vivian, and she knows it. She has her charms, but they're longer-lasting if you haven't heard her stories before. So these games are so much better for everyone when the occasional guest is over. Talk too long about something she's not interested in, something not-Vivian-related, and Vivian will find reasons to get up, go to the other room, come back five minutes later and say, *Oh my heavens, are you still talking about* books? Vivian will never say this out loud, but she misses her husband terribly. She doesn't like to complain, doesn't want anyone feeling sorry for her. It wasn't that her husband had listened to her one hundred percent of the time either, he'd been known to lower the volume on his hearing aid a time or two, but he'd never fallen out of love with her, always found her thoroughly charming, and she knew it. Would and did do anything for her. And he's gone. Vivian will often mention how long they were married, *seventy years!* But she'll never confess to feeling sad about it. *He lived a good life. We had a marvelous life together. When it's your time, it's your time*, she'll say.

Tonight they do have a guest: their neighbor Pete has stopped by with a coffee cake. He's a friendly guy, a little older than Gordon, sincerely gets a kick out of Vivian, and comes by once in a while just to be *neighborly*. The Copelands don't ever return this favor, but he doesn't mind. He has other friends. Anyway, he's heard Vivian's complete collection of stories more than once, but he's amused by her. Tonight she's chewing his ear off about the heyday of her *magnificent* rose garden, the one she'd kept up for forty years. *Forty years!* Vivian always says this twice. She had not wanted to let it go, but the burden of upkeep had fallen largely on Theodore after her husband and daughter-in-law died, and the garden had withered before Jean and Gordon moved in.

Anyway, Vivian had wanted to revive the rose garden, *which even had miniatures, Priscilla used to love those so when she was small*, or at least a smaller version of it, it would give her *such joy, and you can plainly see there's plenty of room*, Vivian says to Pete, pointing to the meadow in back. *What is it, five acres, Jean?* Vivian knows full well it's only four, but loves a chance to remind everyone that the property had even once had a barn that *at one time housed horses, you see. Anyway, someone doesn't think a rose garden is such a terribly good idea.* Someone knits her mouth into the little circle again as this is said, she's heard this more than once before. Jean had admired the roses, but knew what went into maintaining them, and who would end up providing the maintenance. *Oh well, at least I still have my African violets*, Vivian says. *Did you know that I used to attend conventions all around the country? Some of mine have won prizes, you see!*

Pete has heard this, too, but doesn't say so. *Wonderful*, he says, appearing genuinely impressed.

You must drop by sometime, dear, and I'll show them to you.

I'd be delighted, Mrs. Copeland.

I can even give you a cutting, if you like! Oh, those delicate blooms give me endless joy, I'm sure you'll see why. Of course, they're not terribly easy to care for.

Jean is well aware that African violets are not easy to care for, because she is the one who cares for them, mostly.

Here's a little game they play: Vivian asks Jean to come in and water the African violets, *Just the ones that are up too high* for her to reach. This accounts for about thirty plants; Vivian's bedroom and living room are essentially overrun with African violets, and a third of them are on high shelves (which number quite a few around here, considering Vivian's petite stature) or on plant hangers because they won't fit elsewhere. Jean smiles and says *Of course, Vivian.* Then, after Jean has watered these, Vivian will say, *Oh, well, these over here are getting a bit out of reach now, too.*

Jean will say, *No problem, Vivian.*

Vivian will tell the story of a certain *prize-winning* violet here, about how she'd had a new suit tailor-made *all the way from Marshall Field's in Chicago* for the occasion, about the particular *Mountbatten Pink* color of the blooms and the deep lavender of the underside of the leaves, about how this prize-winning violet, named for her, is still popular today.

Jean will clench her teeth, smile, and say, *Yes, I think I remember that story.*

Vivian will say, *Oh! Well, then. I suppose you do.*

At night, Jean will dream of going in and smashing every last one to the ground.

nine

At school the next day, Otis lingers around his cubby when he hangs up his coat, waiting for Caterina, hoping for some interaction. He'll take anything, get nothing. Instead, he'll act like he's doing something in his own cubby, retrieving some homework from his book bag, rearranging the décor—he's not really committed to a particular ruse; fortunately no one's paying attention right now—and so he has a few moments to make mental notes about the contents of Caterina's cubby and their possible meaning. He sees: a pink hooded sweatshirt on the back hook. An extra pair of sneakers for gym, neatly parallel on the bottom of the cubby. A plastic box, with an entire clean and folded outfit, just in case a change is needed. (Recommended for all students, but not everyone is so tidy about it. Otis has already worn his original set of extra clothes, stored not in a plastic box but in a plastic grocery bag, prefers not to talk about why they were needed, and has not yet mentioned it to his parents, nor has he been motivated on his own to replace them. You might think he would be, that it would call less attention to the undiscussed event, but he simply keeps forgetting. Ordinarily this might have been noticed by a teacher, but because Otis has taken pains to fold the clothes, making it look as though the clothes in the bag were simply the original spare set and not ones he'd already worn and, we assume, soiled in some way, although this is information we are not privy to. We know a lot, but not everything.) None of this provides him with any new information about his love, although it does inform us as to a bit of her charms for him. He's noticed a bit of a discrepancy between her tidy persona and some of her idiosyncrasies he feels he alone sees, and appreciates, and he may be right about that, not that it's going to help him with her at all. Not just the chewing of the pigtail but also the weird crossing of her feet under her desk, nearly wound around each other in a way that seems not quite possible. Also, the inside of her desk is straight-up messy, lousy with artworks, old homework assignments, and chewed pencils. All this together, the cubby, the desk, the girl, Otis finds to be magnificent. It should be said that Caterina is certainly very cute, her light brown hair is always brushed or in pigtails, and she wears colorful, coordinated stylish kid outfits, but she is not all that much more popular than Otis is. She's extremely shy, and she's got kind of a stone face, which makes her a little less cute than she really is. Except to Otis. To Otis it's all one big brilliant nebula of girl.

Something happens between Otis and Caterina this day, or something that Otis considers to be a something that Caterina considers to be a blip. At recess, on the playground, several kids are seated on a bench that's probably actually a railroad tie. Six of them are lined up, a couple of them are talking, a couple of them are just resting for a moment before they run back into the mix. Otis is sitting not too far away from Caterina; a couple or three kids could sit between them and totally mess things up, but no one does. Caterina has brought with her a tiny Tupperware serving of jelly beans. Otis feels sure he could easily fit anything that could fit into this Tupperware container into his mouth in one bite, with room to chew and swallow; this is to say, this is an absurdly small Tupperware container, a container that itself might well fit into an adult mouth, say, his dad's. After picturing this for a moment, he turns back to Caterina—and notices that she has been eating these jelly beans one by one, usually in three bites, three riveting bites. How could such a small thing be divided into three bites? Can you even taste that much of a bite? At what point of smallness of a bite can you even register flavor? Can you even chew such a third bite? Would your teeth even meet to chew this bite of a bite or would they just come down and rest on the tiny bit of a jelly bean, but not mash down on it? Is Caterina's mouth just so small that she cannot manage more than a third of a bite of a bean at one time? Does she just love the beans so much that she absolutely *must* savor them this way? These are the sorts of things Otis finds to wonder about Caterina.

Caterina has six jelly beans left in her container: two pomegranate-flavored, three birthday cake, and one jalapeño. *Want these*, she says to Otis, holding the container out over the space between them. It's sort of a question, sort of not, a flat question, and her face indicates only the smallest fraction of her displeasure with these flavors, but she's not about to expound on it. Otis reaches for the beans, which she spills into his palm, this moment, naturally, occurring in super slow motion for him. He sees each marvelous bean suspended in midair, each one glistening with a tiny but dazzling halo of light, these beans, every one, blessed by god, he is sure. Otis has never thought anything about god until this moment, but right now he is certain that god is shining his holy light on these beans. Otis says *Thanks!* with an exclamation point he immediately wishes he could take back, but if it registers with Caterina, it isn't apparent. She gets up to go back inside, expressionless. Otis watches her walk away and holds the beans in his hand, imagining that this is what Jack felt like, that his blessed beans are magic, and could surely sprout into a giant beanstalk solely on account of having been touched by Caterina's hand.

Now what to do? Eat them? He wants to eat them so bad. He could eat some of them and save some of them. If he eats them, it's like she'd practically be with him all the time, forever. (At least until he pooped. Could he somehow just hold it in forever after this? Is that possible? Why do we have to poop anyway?) Or, but, he could just save them and look at them. Keep them in a special place. Build them a shelf, or a pedestal. Or six little pedestals. With lights on each one, like in a museum. But he can't help himself. He has got to eat at least one of these jelly beans in three bites. He has three birthday cake. He will eat one. If he eats just one of the birthday cake, he will still have two left; he could even eat two birthday cake and one pomegranate and still have one of each kind left to keep, to say, *These are the flavors Caterina gave me.* So he starts with the birthday cake. He bites down on what he imagines to be a third of the bean. He notices that you do not get a huge burst of flavor with this much of a bean, but it's enough for him to discern why Caterina has rejected this flavor. It sounds like it'd be great. Birthday cake! But it isn't. It's something he can't quite name, and it's not bad enough to spit out, but he knows it doesn't work. He remembers now about that birthday cake Sno-cone he had that one time at the beach that didn't work, either. He had cried and cried because he didn't want to eat it, and Priscilla had called him *Baby! Baby Freak!*, which made him cry even harder, so Jean bought him a new Sno-cone, reliable blue raspberry. Still, he tries to keep this bit of bean in his mouth for as long as he can, until the slight, sugary mass melts away. He takes another third of a bite, and, like some kind of wine expert—or, to be more exact, his dad—rolls it around in his mouth for subtleties of flavor, then takes the third bite. Yes, Otis thinks, this is not very good. Otis imagines all the things he will now be able to discuss with Caterina based on this birthday cake jelly bean. This one birthday cake jelly bean will lead to endless conversations about crossword puzzles, about caterpillars and math problems and does she have a mean big sister too. It is the key to their future.

On the ride home from school, Otis reports to his mother about Caterina and the beans. *She eats jelly beans in three bites.* Jean nods, she does think this is interesting, but is not indicating this strongly enough for Otis's satisfaction. *Not the big ones, Mom,* Jelly Bellies. Otis emphasizes these two words by raising his eyebrows and sticking his neck out toward his mother. *Jelly Bellies.* Now Jean gets it, that this is not about Jelly Bellies, nodding more solemnly so that Otis knows that she knows, even though he kind of thinks it really is about Jelly Bellies, in the sense that he's not stopping to think that if some other kid ate their Jelly Bellies in this way, he might never have noticed.

His mother, in turn, reports to him more of the details of her love of James. She begins a story that relates to Otis's in her mind, but we'll see if that's the case. *When I first met James, I noticed that he had organized all his books by the color of the spine. I'd seen things like this on design websites before, books organized in various unconventional ways, but never in person, and I was so impressed with how each color was arranged from light to dark on the shelf. It was so beautiful, like a work of art. I always wondered how he ever found a book he was looking for if they weren't alphabetical or anything. He had a lot of books. I spent a lot of time contemplating this, Otis. I could probably have asked him about it the first time I noticed, but I got all up in my head about it and even after we started sleeping together, I was never able to bring myself to ask.*

Otis is lingering, in his mind, somewhere between *up in my head* and *sleeping together* and imagines these things literally. Sleeping together as an idea troubles him far less than *up in my head*; actually, it doesn't trouble him at all. He has had sleepovers. *Up in my head* he can't quite picture. He pictures himself, on a chair, sitting inside a skull.

And now I'll never know, Jean says. Otis doesn't really hear this, thinking about himself inside himself, which is just as well. Jean begins to cry, though she tries to keep from sobbing in the hope that Otis won't notice. At first he doesn't, but then she inhales in a way that catches his attention; she sounds kind of like a sheep. Fortunately Jean knows that Otis doesn't know why she'll never know, although he doesn't ask, doesn't even ask why she's crying, so she lets it go.

ten

At home, Otis runs up the stairs, eager to examine the beans again, brushing past his sister in the hallway. He's barely touched her. *Geez, look where you're going, Baby Freak*, Priscilla says, giving him a shove on her way down. Ordinarily he'd notice, not that he'd do anything much about it, but today's events have invested him with the temporary power to overlook his sister's abuse.

For his first few years of existence, Otis had shadowed Priscilla. It may have been nothing other than her relative height that intrigued him, her general big-sisterness, but wherever she was, he wanted to be. Once, when Priscilla was in seventh grade and Otis was four, he came upon his sister and her friend Taylor having a fashion show, begged to be in it, and the only reason Priscilla agreed was that Taylor liked Otis and plus also thought it would be funny to see him dressed up like a girl. *Pleeeeeeze*, Otis said. Priscilla rolled her eyes about it, *Fine-nuh*, she'd said, two syllables, and, *Gol*, and so they styled him in a denim mini and a pale blue ruffle top, threw on a necklace. Taylor insisted on some lip gloss, blush, and a headband with a bow, which thrilled Otis, so much so that he'd left the room briefly to show his mother but found only Vivian, who'd come over with Theodore and Laura for dinner that day. (Vivian, of course, would express concerns to her granddaughter-in-law about *where this sort of thing might lead*, but Jean remained unworried, hoped, futilely, that where this might lead was to Priscilla and Otis spending more time together.) Otis had sashayed down the upstairs hall "runway" the way Taylor showed him, beaming, both at the fun of it and at the prospect of more times like these with his sister. Unfortunately, the opposite would come to pass: even if Otis hadn't broken his sister's favorite necklace when he'd hastily pulled it off, even if he hadn't smeared his lipstick on her blouse, this moment would mark the official banishment of Otis from Priscilla's room.

Today, Priscilla and Taylor are frantically texting each other. Priscilla is actually on her way to pick up Taylor. They have both been called back for a second audition for the TV show. This time they are going to put the girls on tape. Priscilla is using exclamation points; she is not usually one for such overt displays of enthusiasm, but right now she can't help herself. The texting and driving is doing nobody any favors, but fortunately Taylor only lives a few blocks away. *Ohmigawwd!!* they screech when Taylor gets in the car. Taylor's a little bit excited now, too, not quite as excited as Priscilla, but remember, they're both nineteen, and Taylor doesn't have any much better ideas about what she's doing with her life than Priscilla does.

Priscilla is called in first. This time they've slotted twenty minutes for each girl, and there are three additional people present, more producers, in addition to the four from last time.

Okay, Ted says, *so we're just going to ask you some general questions, to get an idea of how you look on camera. There are no right or wrong answers, so don't worry about that. We really just want you to be yourself.* Priscilla is smiling hard, which is already her not being herself. Priscilla is not a big smiler. No one in her family is. Or maybe it is her being herself, but a new weird version of herself where she's actually excited about something—that combined with trying to be likable. Priscilla has never given headspace to being likable before, insofar as she has always assumed she is. Suddenly she's not sure. Suddenly the questions. Lots and lots of questions. Priscilla is so not prepared.

Do you have a driver's license?

Oh, yeah, I drove here!

Great. What famous person reminds you of yourself?

Oh wow, I don't know, maybe Jennifer Aniston, no, wait, she's old, oh, I know, Kristin Cavallari! I get that all the time. We hesitate to mention our knowledge of the televison series *The Hills* here, but for those of you who don't know, Ms. Cavallari is a character who is considered to be bitchy, but who Priscilla thinks is just misunderstood. She's hot, though, that's the main thing.

All three make notes. Priscilla hopes that's a good sign.

List the three adjectives that best describe you.

Oh, wow, um, cute? Awesome? No, just kidding. Um, hm, can

we come back to this one? Priscilla can't believe she's got nothing for this. She should have something better for this.

Sure. What is your biggest pet peeve?

Ugh, my freak little brother.

Could you be more specific?

He's just weird. Pulls the legs off caterpillars. Plus sometimes he tries to get me to like, play with him and stuff. Priscilla rolls her eyes. *You know, he's* nine.

Nods.

What is the worst thing that's ever happened to you?

The worst? Priscilla has to think about this one. She'd been pretty bummed when she hadn't gotten hired at J.Crew and had to settle for Express. Was that the worst thing ever? Do they expect one of those stories like on *American Idol* or something where your dad was killed like three days before the audition? She's got nothing like that. Getting dumped by Kyle had sucked, but she was so over it. But maybe that's the way to go. It's all she's got right now. *My ex broke up with me in a status update. Douchey, right?*

Nods. Like, totally unreadable fucking nods.

Do you get sea-, air-, or carsick?

No—well, I don't think so. Why?

In case we have location shoots and have to travel. Priscilla's head spins when she hears the word "travel." This could not possibly get better unless they told her one of the guys from *Glee* was going to be on this show. She doesn't even like that show that much, but those guys are so hot.

What is your level of education?

I'm in my first year of junior college. But I kind of hate it.

What are you studying?

I haven't picked a major. I'm thinking about dropping out. Priscilla actually thinks this is a right answer, that her willingness to drop out is a sign of her commitment to being on a reality show.

More expressionless nods and note-taking from the panel, nods that Priscilla cannot read, so many freaking blank freaking nods. So she covers, just in case.

Well, I mean, but maybe not. I don't know.

Name three of your favorite hobbies.

What do you mean, like, stamp collecting or something?

Yeah, like that.

Priscilla thinks hard. She definitely has no hobbies. *Is texting a hobby?*

Not really . . .

Shopping?

Well . . .

Oh, okay . . . what about reading magazines? Priscilla loves magazines, has an expanding file full of pages she's torn out with outfits she admired, and a separate folder for accessories. She's never thought of this as a hobby. She'd started it as an idea file. Ideas for what, she'd always been unsure of. She reads everything from *InTouch* to *Elle* to *Teen Vogue*. It fits in her purse. She almost says this.

No, more like—maybe games you like, or keeping a journal or something?

No, not really, I guess. Priscilla is getting worried now. This is not going well. Why does it suddenly seem like she has no life? She's never thought that before. But saying this stuff out loud makes it all sound so . . . she can't think of a word. Pathetic. Wow. She's feeling a little tear come up into her right eye. Not good. Swallow. Swallow.

Do you have any phobias?

What?

Any phobias? Fears?

Oh. I don't think so. I mean, I probably wouldn't like it if there were like snakes or bats hanging around my house.

Have you been treated for, or experienced, any physical or mental illness within the last ten years?

What? No! Ten years ago I was like, nine.

Nine-year-olds can have mental illness.

Maybe that's what's wrong with my brother. Ha!

Polite smiles and blank faces. Augh, why does she keep mentioning him? She sounds like she's twelve. Priscilla feels that tear coming up again.

Have you ever been arrested?

No! Jeez, no.

Have you ever been on television before?

Nah, not really. When I went with my family to New York once, we stood outside the 'Today' show, but we were kind of way in the back. It was lame. So we don't have to repeat it, you should just go ahead and assume that most times when Priscilla makes a negative judgment, she also rolls her eyes.

Have you ever appeared in a publicly released film or video of any sort?

I wish!

What is your favorite TV show?

Oh my god, I love 'America's Next Top Model,' I love 'Gossip

Girl'—well, for the clothes, mostly, the story lines are kind of lame. 'The Hills.' I die for Rachel Zoe. I love 'GH' . . .

Blank stares, nods.

'General Hospital.'

Nods. Is this like some kind of a total mind-fuck, some super harsh joke being played on her? How could these all be the wrong answers? Because, seriously? It's working. It's an effective mind-fuck. Her mind is very effectively fucked.

What is your favorite movie?

She has an answer for this! *'Say Anything'! Totally. I know it's super old school, but you know, Lloyd Dobler! You have to love Lloyd Dobler. I don't even know how many times I've seen that movie. I like know half the lines. The boom box!* Priscilla puts her hand to her heart in the most genuine display of emotion since the interview started, allows herself a half moment to imagine having her own Lloyd Dobler, drifts back in to see the panel, everyone doing that sort of "no, nothing wrong with that" face/shrug thing that also means there's nothing really right with it, either.

What is your favorite music to listen to?

Priscilla does not really listen to music. She doesn't dislike it really, she just doesn't think about it much.

I don't know, I guess I like popular music. Or—dance music! I love to dance. Is that a hobby?

Sure. Notes.

Describe your perfect day. Cool, she can do this.

Well, I'd get up around eleven, I guess, eat a waffle, meet Taylor and my friends at the mall and go shopping. And then come home and try on everything we bought and have a fashion show and then post photos online and then go to a party where we're the only girls, or at least the only cute girls—well, that's usually the way it is, but you know what I mean, and the rest of the party is all super hot guys—TV stars, maybe!

The panel members crack a smile, finally. Jeez.

What was the most exciting moment of your life?

Priscilla has enough good sense to refrain from mentioning that *this* is the most exciting moment of her life, this one right now, wonders how they could not know that, but she does not have an alternative answer.

God, I don't know, I don't know, huh, I don't know. My life isn't very exciting.

Wait, what? Did she mean to say that? That wasn't exactly what she meant. She should probably explain. But nothing else is coming out of her mouth. Dammit!

How do you blow off steam?

Priscilla has somehow never heard this phrase before. She imagines this literally, but that can't be right.

I don't think I know what that means.

Like, when you're angry, or frustrated, what do you do?

I scream? Priscilla is often angry and frustrated, and has no real, useful outlet for it. She slams doors, rolls her eyes, shoves, huffs, calls names. These don't seem like the right answers. They might actually be right answers, but they don't seem like it.

What is your primary motivation for being on TV?

Christ, these questions are so hard! College is easier than this. Priscilla knows "to get famous" can't possibly be the right answer, but it's the only one she has, and trying to think about why she wants to get famous, she draws a blank. *Gol, I don't know, doesn't everyone want to be on TV?*

Not everyone. What is the accomplishment that you are most proud of?

I don't know. This last *I don't know* will double-dutch into her mind with *My life isn't very exciting* until her eyes practically bleed.

eleven

t's been several weeks now since James's death. Almost everything Jean sees now is filtered through a hazy lens of James hanging from the bar in their cabin. Imagine: you're making microwave popcorn, and on the door of the microwave is a transparent film with an image of your dead lover hanging from a beam overhead, his belt around his neck, his feet just a foot from the floor, eleven inches actually, according to the coroner's report, eleven inches from salvation. Or imagine driving to school to pick up your son. On the windshield, a projection of the same. James's pants hanging loosely, beltlessly around his hips, worn work boots pointed slightly down, hovering over the windshield wipers, eleven inches from the floor. Your husband, delivering a speech about the history of clowns, behind a husband-sized image of your lover, his thick, shiny black hair hanging over his face, probably a good thing, that, since it hides a bit of his eyes, which are only half-closed. Watching the nightly news, the field reporters, talking about traffic backups, slightly visible behind your hanging lover, hoping day after day to hear that this was

all a terrible mistake, that it was some doppelgänger of your
lover, that though this means your lover left you, at least he's
not dead.

Very few days have gone by where Jean has had any relief
from her thoughts about what happened to James. She sees
things in eleven-inch measurements now. *Hm, this drinking
glass is eleven inches tall. If this drinking glass had been underneath
James, he could have lived. This candle could have saved James's
life. That pile of books. This lamp is about eleven inches. This
folding umbrella. If I had been there, and just put this little folding
umbrella under his feet. A Barbie doll is about eleven inches. This
vibrator or this ruler would have saved him by a whole inch.* And
so on. Accordingly, this is what Jean hears repeatedly when
people talk: *eleven inches from the floor.* It's like that thing where
you open your fortune cookie after you've had Chinese food,
and you read it out loud and then you say "In bed." Or, like
with Otis's version, "In your butt." *Pass the butter eleven inches
from the floor. Caterina eats jelly beans eleven inches from the floor.
Baby Freak eleven inches from the floor. Mom tell Priscilla to quit
it eleven inches from the floor. Mom tell Baby Freak to stop being a
Baby Freak eleven inches from the floor. Did you know that, in the
Deep South, nutria is often served in gumbo, along with okra, eleven
inches from the floor? I heard that on 'Paula Deen' eleven inches from
the floor. Eleven inches from the floor, eleven inches from the floor.
Eleven inches from the floor.*

Today, Jean is looking at the note again. She has already
spent entire days on analysis of the note, the piece of paper,
folded in two, written with a black grease pencil. *I'm sorry.*
Just like that, with a period. Jean has reviewed, is reviewing,

will review the few details of the note in her mind many, many times. Sorry? He's sorry? Sorry is for *I broke your coffee mug*, not for *I wrapped a belt around my neck and jumped off a chair.* The single period after *sorry* will receive mental scrutiny the likes of which no lone mark of punctuation has ever known. Could it have been the beginning of an ellipsis? If it was, what was that drifting off meant to indicate? A sigh? Sorrow? Regret? Hesitation? Could he have cut some lengthy explanation, something that could possibly have justified this terrible, terrible choice? She can't think of what that could be, unless he found out that he carried a flesh-eating disease that would kill millions of people, or that he was radioactive or something. Jean keeps coming back to the ellipsis theory because she can't attach any possible meaning to the period by itself. She had never doubted his love. But why on earth would someone do such a hateful thing to someone he loved, why would he leave her, why would he make her see this, why? Could he have been cheating on Jean, and that's why he hung himself? Why no explanation? Was there any possibility that his love wasn't true? No. No way. No way. No way. No.

Jean doesn't have a lot of close friends, certainly not one she'd talk to about this. She has not told one soul about the affair. Not one soul.

She had believed what James told her about himself, about herself, about everything. She also believed he held nothing back—which was, of course, where she went wrong. Jean has a small envelope with his love notes and Polaroids they'd taken of themselves, which she keeps hidden inside a copy of

More magazine in her nightstand. Gordon never looks over there, and if he did for sure he wouldn't look at *More* magazine. Jean goes through the Polaroids one by one, lingering in each precious memory: the time they went for a hike and she'd gotten poison ivy and he so lovingly daubed her ankles with calamine lotion, the time they almost took nude photos of each other but giggled too much to go through with it, the time they pretended they were in Paris wearing berets. They both look so happy and content in the photos. Is there any bit of tension near his mouth, around his eyes? She sees nothing. She wipes away tears before beginning an online search for information about suicide. Maybe she'll get some answers.

After skimming over a lot of information she's mostly familiar with, she comes across a blog full of horrifying photos. They're not photos of James, thank god—not that it would make any difference, imprinted in her mind as that image is—but photos of suicides, a chronicle of crime scene photos under the title Gruesome Moments. The masthead design features a Precious Moments figurine with a noose around its neck. Not funny. Jean's stomach turns over. Who in the name of everything good would do such a thing? She knows she should just move on; she's seen it in real life and hasn't forgotten. But she's burning right now thinking about the sick mind that would do something like this; she's on fire to find this horrible person and destroy him. Jean drafts a lengthy comment. *These people were in pain, you evil motherfucker.* Jean has used the word "fuck" about four times in her life before this, three of them usually referring to something someone else had said, and in those times, were uttered entirely awkwardly. *I will find you and hang you and take your photo and post it online, you sick fucking psycho. May god have mercy on your soul. No. I take that back. May god have no mercy on your soul.* Jean begins to cry again. She has no idea where this rage is coming from and she doesn't like it, wants it out. Maybe it's time to get some help, she thinks.

twelve

For his seventy-fifth birthday, the family had thrown Theodore a party. Vivian had not been thrilled about this idea—a birthday party for a grown man, such a fuss. But the grandkids made a big sign, decorated the dining room with streamers and balloons even, and finally Vivian agreed to bake a chocolate layer cake with fresh strawberry filling, his favorite since he was a boy. After the cake was served, Theodore had stood up to read "Sailing to Byzantium," a poem that he said had been a favorite of his since he was a child. But he choked up on the phrase "a tattered coat," and passed the poem to Jean, whose reading was so lovely she seemed born to do it. Gordon had held no small admiration for Jean in this moment, noticing an elegance he hadn't seen in her before, how poised her posture was, how present she seemed, though he failed to mention any of this afterward. Theodore sobbed loudly through the remainder of the reading, and when Jean was done he stood up once more for a toast.

I just want to say how much I love every single person in this family, he said, raising his glass, *even those who aren't present.*

My beloved wife, Laura, he said, taking a big gulp of air as tears began to pour down his face, *who I miss so much and who took such good care of me all of our life together.*

Everyone at the table squirmed in their seats. Vivian desperately wanted to get up at the first mention of Laura, opened her mouth to ask if anyone wanted more coffee, but withdrew when Gordon shook his head in her direction. Gordon, no more comfortable than anyone else, distracted himself thinking about an upcoming work retreat. Jean, at least, had a slight tear in her eye.

Theodore took a huge gulp of air and continued.

My wonderful, generous son, and Jean, my lovely daughter-in-law—well, Gordon, you chose very, very well. My beautiful grandchildren, you have given me precious memories. And my loving father and mother . . . Theodore trailed off, sobbing too hard to continue.

Unilaterally, the family was stunned. Jean found Theodore's speech sweet, even got a little misty herself, but the rest of the Copelands froze. Priscilla was so uncomfortable that she volunteered to clear the plates, just to give her an excuse to get up from the table.

Vivian knew she should have been more vocal about the whole party from the start. Not to restate the obvious, but we might mention again that Vivian hadn't had but the one birthday party as a kid, which she'd repeatedly claimed had not bothered her. *It wasn't the popular thing in those days, you see,* she always said, though that wasn't altogether true. Baron had always made a point of taking her out to dinner on her birthday, giving her flowers and jewelry, even taking her to

Europe, but had never in all their years together given her a party, at her request. He had not known it was a request she'd wished he'd ignored, just once.

A TYPICAL THEODORE DAY now:

Much of Theodore's daily life is as it always was. Here's what's the same: He gets up early, still in his pjs, brings in the paper, fixes himself breakfast, usually cereal, followed an hour later by a low-fat ice cream pop, followed every ten minutes by some small treat, a piece of chocolate, a cookie, a handful of nuts, a low-cal Popsicle. He sits at the table with the paper, turns on one of the morning news shows, maybe CNN or one of those. Works on the cross-word. Goes to his desk to do some work there for an hour. Couple hours later, goes in to take a shower, get dressed. Jean might come in to see if he wants his lunch fixed, but if she comes in after 10:30 A.M., it's likely he's already fixed and eaten it himself. Not that there's anything wrong with two lunches now and again. Changes channels on the TV, maybe to a channel playing old Westerns, maybe to an *Andy Griffith* marathon. A classic. Takes a short nap. Putters around (his words) for a while, an hour or two or three at his desk. Continues to snack. Goes into the main house for dinner with the family around 5:15, which Jean will usually prepare, and the evening news at 5:30. He has watched the *CBS Evening News* for more than fifty years, even though he still misses Cronkite, hated Katie Couric, doesn't even know the name of the new guy. After this, maybe a game; after this, bed. In the years before he retired, you would have added in work, but really, a lot of the content would be remarkably similar.

What's different now: Okay, so Theodore has always had a sweet tooth, and as the years have progressed, he's started eating sweets earlier and earlier in the day. Now, however, there's a combination of things going on. His sweet tooth hasn't gone away, but because of his memory issues, he sometimes forgets that he's already eaten a piece of chocolate and starts to yearn for another one. There's some gray area here, of course, as Theodore was always inclined to consume a fair amount of chocolate throughout the day. But now, as often as not, he eats another piece of chocolate because he's forgotten about the one he ate ten minutes earlier. If Jean's in the room, she'll gently point it out, and he'll protest weakly, but this will only shave off maybe two or three extra pieces of chocolate in Theodore's ten-to-twenty-piece day.

He scans the paper, but no longer reads it closely. That's different. Theodore used to read a great deal of the local paper. He cuts articles, coupons, and ads out of the paper, just as he always has, but these days he tends to nick himself with the scissors, as his hands are pretty shaky.

Subsequent to this, he puts the clippings in piles. Piles that only grow. Efforts to reduce the size of the piles have been made by both Jean and Gordon (Vivian does not like the mess, but won't have anything to do with it), but any lowered piles are quickly built back up taller than they were before, or they get sifted through and moved around to generate entirely new piles. This, too, has been going on for years, but now Theodore cannot say what exactly any given pile means.

Also: whatever's on the TV doesn't get watched all that much. Often Theodore nods out briefly (in large part because of the medications he takes every four hours), or turns his attention outside. He may add a few words to the crossword before getting distracted by whatever's outside, but will say, as he always did before handing it over to someone else, *There may be a wrong word or two in there.* In fact, the few words he adds are usually right, but there are more wrong words now than there used to be.

As regards *work* and *puttering*: These activities, once distinct, are basically synonymous now. They primarily involve the aforementioned paper-moving, but also include the careful examination of rocks, the careful observation of critters, another look at his box of medals, and taking things apart.

Theodore has written a draft of an academic paper on optometry that he claims he's still working on, but it's been a while since he's changed more than a word or two. In the years before his illness, he had lectured on the subject at numerous colleges and universities, had always been well-received at these events, somehow managing to inject humor as well as insight into his subject matter. He reads his intro to the sitter. She doesn't know much about optometry, doesn't really know whether it's any good or not, nods and smiles, says *Sounds great!*, goes back to dusting. *Of course, it hasn't been accepted yet, but I think it's some of my best work yet.* The truth is that it hasn't been accepted because he hasn't submitted it. Theodore hasn't sent an email in months, and doesn't go to the post office alone, isn't allowed to go anywhere alone now, and until recently

Jean's been trying to keep on top of the paper situation so he doesn't embarrass himself.

Other things added to the day: a wheelchair, a walker, and a sitter. The sitter, who also does some light housecleaning, is an older lady from down the street, though not as old as Theodore; she comes in for a few hours each day, cleans, and makes sure Theodore doesn't hurt himself. But that's about the extent of it. If she gets the house clean, she watches TV to fill up the time, maybe fixes the elders a snack. Sometimes she'll set up a table with a five-hundred-piece puzzle before she leaves. Theodore always used to enjoy a puzzle, but cannot get two pieces together now. He'll try though. For an hour.

Something else he used to love but no longer does at all: read. Theodore used to read about a book a day, Westerns and mysteries were his favorites, but also the occasional *highfalutin* titles, a Bellow or an Updike. At some point, his ability to focus, to move from sentence to sentence, fell away, and he lost interest; now he doesn't even think about it. It's kind of the same with the TV. Theodore used to highlight his week's programming in the *TV Guide*. He had his favorite shows, and always looked forward to the New Fall Season issue in the hopes of adding a new one or two. Jean dropped his subscription a year ago, knowing he hadn't been looking at it, and Theodore hardly seemed to notice.

What's in Theodore's mind? We think it's something like this:

I'm hungry. (Opens freezer.) Ice. Peas. Frozen dinners. Ice cream pop. (Retrieves chocolate-coated ice cream pop from freezer. Struggles with wrapper.) These wrappers are a little harder than they used to be to open. (Eats ice cream, opens newspaper on table, gets bits of chocolate on chin, paper.) Local teen. Complications. Iraq. 20 percent off. Cinema. Dilbert. (Looks up, out window.) Oh, look, there's a ground squirrel, carrying a nut. Or maybe that's an acorn. And a cardinal. I wonder if the cardinal sees the ground squirrel. Op, there goes the cardinal. Oh, there's a little frog on the edge of the pond. Op! In the pond. There goes the ground squirrel, under a bush. But he dropped his nut. Or acorn. Maybe he'll come back to get it. I should go get my camera. (Gets camera, comes back. Waits. Falls asleep for a minute. Wakes up, sees squirrel again.) Op, there he goes, there he goes! (Sits and waits for twenty minutes.) This is where we have to admit we don't have complete access. We imagine these longer silent periods are just blank. We wonder when, if, he thinks about his wife, who he had loved so. We just don't know. But the rest of it, we're sure that if it's not exactly like this, it's close.

thirteen

Today Vivian has a bridge game with two of her oldest friends, and a fourth who's eighty-five. They call her The Baby. Vivian, Berenice, and Flora have been friends since college. The Baby is Flora's cousin. They're in the middle of a lively discussion about Berenice's great-granddaughter, who's expecting and *unmarried*. Berenice is, predictably, all aflutter about it.

Well, it's just a different time, Flora says, shaking her head.

Go ahead and assume there's a lot of head-shaking going on around the table here.

I'll say, The Baby says.

Yes, but the poor child! Berenice says.

No father! Flora says.

Well, now I hear they live together, Berenice says.

Oh dear. Oh dear, The Baby says.

And apparently he's Catholic, Berenice adds.

Oh dear. Oh, The Baby says.

Wears his hair long, says Berenice. Long, we should note here, meaning it brushes the top of his shirt collar.

Oh!

Flora, Vivian's partner, plays her hand. *Oh!* Vivian says, letting out a not-subtle huff of displeasure. *You trumped my trick! Well!* Flora says nothing.

Oh, well, I don't know if that's true, says Berenice. *He may have cut it since I saw him. But it was long then.*

Well, it's just a different time, Flora says again.

I suppose, Berenice says.

If you ask me, women's lib just ruined everything, Flora says.

Ordinarily, Vivian would relish this conversation. Ordinarily, Vivian would dip into her story bank and pull out the one about the girl she taught at the one-room schoolhouse who'd had an illegal abortion. It's not one she tells often, she doesn't like to say the word "abortion," has actually told it many times without using the word at all, but it's a good one, always gets rapt, shocked responses from the girls, even though they've heard it many times.

But today she's distracted. Last night there was a lady on *Nancy Grace* who'd swerved to avoid an oncoming car and instead plowed into a homeless man on the sidewalk. Vivian imagines the crunch of every bone, the terrible *mess*; imagines herself in that situation, trying to apologize to police officers, saying she had no idea what happened, truly she didn't, the car just swerved, it was an accident; imagines them gruffly whisking her off to the slammer, like in the movies; pictures herself in jail, weeping, misunderstood, alone. And so now, in this bridge game, she's not only missing a terribly juicy story, she's losing.

Since childhood, Vivian has had a fear of hitting a pedestrian with a car. It's the reason she doesn't drive. It's an event that simply can't happen, yet it is one she has recurring nightmares about. She's never been afraid to get into cars as long as someone else is driving; nor is she afraid of crashing into other cars. She would much prefer to crash one car into another car. With two cars, there's more protection, Vivian thinks, and more places to distribute blame. Hit a pedestrian and you're a murderer. Her fear is very specific: that she herself will be the driver, the pedestrian-killer. The nightmares and the anxiety are worst just after she's seen a news report about this type of accident. As far as we know, Vivian has had no similar experience that engendered this fear. It's a thing that got wedged in her brain when she was a kid and cars were still pretty new, seemed almost as exotic and hard to believe in as rocket ships; in those days stories flew around madly about cars running over people, and it spooked her. She'll tell you she simply never wanted to drive, that she thought it was the man's job, but that's not entirely true. In fact, it's completely false.

Now and again, Vivian dreams that she's behind the wheel of a red convertible cruising a winding mountain road, her silver curls blowing in the wind. No one walks in front of her car. On the mornings after Vivian has these dreams, she's genuinely nice to everyone around her, for about an hour. *What a splendid day it is*, she'll say.

Vivian, Berenice says.

Hm? It takes her a moment to snap out of her mountain-top reverie.

It's your turn, dear.

Oh! Vivian looks at her cards, shuffles them around in her hand, embarrassed to have lost her composure. *Oh well yes of course it is. Of course it is. Of course.*

fourteen

An Internet search of Trudy has yielded Gordon a defunct business profile and a sad—in his opinion—page on a social networking site. First of all, she has twenty-nine friends, which seems like an exceptionally low number, at least compared to the other profiles he looks at. Gordon's not on any social network, so it hasn't occurred to him until now that people might use these networks differently. Maybe it was just her very closest friends? Maybe she doesn't really even use the site? How many good friends does anyone have? Does Gordon have twenty-nine close friends? He doesn't. Gordon *knows* a lot of people. Some of Trudy's info is blocked, but there are the requisite sets of photos: tropical vacations with middle-aged girlfriends, holding up speedboat-sized umbrella cocktails; Trudy as one of five identically dressed bridesmaids; adorable, semi-adorable, and less-adorable nieces and nephews; faded, yellow-and-red-tinged scans of old photos, including one from college, a photo of Trudy, him, Phil, and Sheila scrunched together on someone's top bunk, Sheila half out of the frame, likely because she snapped the photo.

Gordon can remember most of this moment—Phil's holding a bong, and Gordon got high exactly three times in college, so he remembers them all pretty well—but the inclusion of Trudy in this photo mucks it up for him. He thinks it was the time Phil had to talk him down because he was convinced there was PCP in the pot; how else to explain why Sheila's spider plant had been waving its arms? Phil had tried to reassure him that it was Sheila, not her spider plant, whose arms were waving, and Gordon vaguely remembers this, but Trudy's presence in the photo only serves to convince him that something is terribly, terribly wrong with his brain. But then he gets an idea: What if it's brain damage from the pot, or the possible PCP? Or maybe even chemicals in the plastic of the bong? Gordon wonders if there have been any studies on that. Searching "bags, plastic, chemicals," turns up a wiki that indeed says that toxic chemicals may be released in such circumstances, possibly associated with cancer—but there's no mention of brain damage. Is this good news? (He also learns that "bong" is an adaptation of the Thai word "*baung*," meaning a bamboo tube, something to remember for a relevant conversation someday, although ordinarily he would continue to study the history of the bong and gather quite a bit more information than he's bothering to do today.) He types in "bong, brain damage," gets a headshoppy site with a lot of info on different types of bongs that says that the paint from an aluminum-can bong can cause brain damage. Shit, did he ever do that? He can't remember. That can't be good.

A search on memory loss only concerns him further. Tumors, medication side effects, and depression are known contributors. He already knows quite a bit about the memory loss associated with Parkinson's. He has listened carefully to every doctor's report about his father, taken extensive mental notes. He spends any number of hours taking "memory tests," though the scientific basis for any of them seems dubious at best.

One test gives him pause. The questions:

> 1. Do you have difficulty remembering people's
>   names or phone numbers?

Up until Trudy, it's been a great source of pride for Gordon that he never forgets a name and has recall for a great many phone numbers as well, even though both his office and cell phones have had numbers programmed in for years, he still dials many of them out of habit. So Gordon marks this one *rarely*.

> 2. How often do you find yourself trying to remem-
>   ber the location of everyday items (keys, glasses,
>   cell phone, etc.)?

That's a *never*. Gordon has a valet in his bedroom; all these things go there as soon as he comes home. Has always wondered why they only have these for men, when some women and children he knows could make good use of their own.

> 3. How often do you have to replace passwords be-
>   cause you've forgotten the original one?

Also a *never*. Even though he keeps these on a list on a zip drive in his safe-deposit box, Gordon thinks, he's yet to actually have to use it. Almost a funny question, he thinks.

> 4. How often do you find yourself asking questions like, What was I about to do next?

Never.

> 5. How often do you end up double-booking yourself because you forgot you had previous plans?

Never. People do this?

> 6. How often do you have difficulty remembering where you parked your car?

Never!

> 7. How often do you have to ask someone to repeat instructions or a story because you can't remember what was said the first time around?

And here's the reason he didn't get a perfect score on this test: the one *rarely* and the *sometimes* on question seven. This is where Gordon gets a little tripped up; he answers sometimes, because on the occasion that Gordon isn't the one talking, he's waiting to talk, and when he's waiting to talk, he's just not listening. He thinks he can do both, but as you can imagine, he doesn't do it well. So his struggle with this is clear: if he acknowledges that he doesn't always listen, then he's acknowledging a character flaw, but if he says it's because he doesn't remember, then this problem may actually be a problem.

In this moment, though, looking at this quiz, it's not quite coming to him that that's the reason. He's just trying to bring up some instances. He remembers a time, just the other day, when Jean asked him to pick up a few things at the grocery store on his way home and he had to ask her twice. Then again, he's got this Trudy thing on his mind. Maybe he could round down to a *rarely* on this one. But he's nothing if not honest, so he marks it *sometimes* and he gets a 93 on the quiz—which, according to the summary at the end, indicates that Gordon has little difficulty with his memory. The summary includes a reminder that fatigue, stress, and poor diet can contribute to the decline of cognitive functions with age. Gordon scribbles these things down, along with suggestions for improving memory: mnemonic devices, visual associations.

Gordon takes several more tests, one involving a series of words he has to remember, another involving photographs. He passes all of these tests with almost perfect scores, but this does nothing to reassure him that there isn't some diagnosis, some obscure condition he hasn't heard of, that is causing his past to tumble out of his mind, one ex-girlfriend at a time.

fifteen

Jean goes to the first grief support group she finds a listing for online. As support groups go, there aren't a lot of surprises here. Everyone is sad. Everyone wants to know why. Why these good people, why now, why cancer, why. Good question. Some of them talk about angels—how their loved ones are angels now, or with the angels. Jean would like to believe such a thing, but would have preferred one fewer angel and one more living lover. Plus she's not sure how to talk about her grief without naming her lover, without giving herself away. So she straight-up lies. When her turn comes to talk, she says *My husband killed himself.* There are minuscule gasps from the others. It's an unspoken thing that loud reactions are best kept to a minimum. But Jean hears the gasps and finds herself oddly energized. None of these people know her; does it matter? Sometimes she wishes it were true. She doesn't wish Gordon ill, doesn't wish the father of her children to be taken away, but of the two? Why James? Doesn't the world need art more than it needs *effective point-of-purchase representation* and other bombastic nonsense coming out the ass? Jean is almost entirely unaware that the thoughts in her head carry any ire; she thinks of herself as a nice person, she *is* a nice person, all she's thinking is that they're true, that she's never known truth like she knows it now. Maybe for a fragment of a second she'll become aware that she's got some anger or something, but she believes it's entirely justified, and then the next random thought comes and takes over any deeper consideration about it.

The fantasy is an easy one for her to construct. Just a few tweaks to the details, a slight merging of elements of her two relationships in order to best keep it straight. In this fantasy, James is named Jake, and Jean and Jake were married for the same length of time as she and Gordon have been. They have two children, Priscilla and Otis. There's no Gordon in this scenario, never was. In this scenario, Jean met Jake in graduate school; he was getting his MFA in printmaking, she was getting a masters in books. Wait, what? Education. They married in their backyard, just family. She wore a knee-length yellow shift. Jean taught first grade. Jake was a professor. They were a loving, tight-knit family, excited to sit down for meals together, to play games, take family trips together. Jake was an attentive father and husband. He listened to Jean. She listened to him! He complimented her all the time, said her beauty was *astonishing*, that she was his *beacon, his lighthouse.* James had actually said those things and more. *My love bee*, he called her. He brought her gifts, books he thought she'd like (based on conversations they'd had or other books he knew she'd liked, as opposed to books he thought she should read, like someone else who'd given her books on occasion), made art for her. True as well. Nothing was wrong, everything was right. But.

Here Jean takes a pause. The real story contained in that "but" is one Jean will probably never know. She only knows how it ends.

He shot himself in the head.

Wow, did she really just say that? She did.

Yes, he shot himself in the head and I found him, there he was in his office at school, backward on the floor, flopped half on, half off his desk chair, blood and brains splattered on the window, blood, beginning in a pool, funneling into a line across the floor from one end of the room to the other, which had a slant to it, toward the door.

It's hard to say who's more shocked by this part of the story, Jean or the support group. Heads shake. A mouth or two remain open. Tears fall. The group abandons its effort to conceal its gasps. Jean takes their reactions in. She wishes she could say the real truth, that he'd hanged himself, that she'd seen his beautiful eyes half-open with no life in them, couldn't say that the image of James suspended from the crossbar might as well have been branded onto the backs of her eyelids, such was the likelihood that she'd ever unsee it. She thought it best to create a whole new grisly scenario. The group is silent. Jean is the winner. She hadn't wanted this victory, but finds herself leaning back in her chair to accept. The people here have lost: parents, beloved aunts, grandparents. Those people died naturally. Those people are supposed to die. Well, aren't they? If there was someone in the group who'd lost a kid, well, that would be another story. Jean hasn't lost her ability to empathize with other mothers. But no one here has lost a lover. Isn't all grief the same? No. It's not the same, not at all. Hers is the worst.

sixteen

Gordon creates a page on Trudy's social network so that he can leave a message for her. He takes some time to create his profile, listing every possible means by which he can be reached—work number, home number, cell number, email address. Now to upload a profile photo. But which one? He could just use his work photo, it certainly looks like him, but that's not really what he's going for here. Which one says what he wants to say? What *does* he want to say to Trudy? Is there one photo that conveys *I am a serious and intelligent person, but I am also lighthearted, fun to be around, and sorry I don't remember you?* Gordon isn't really all that much fun to be around, as we've established he's a bit boring at times, so there aren't really any photos of him that capture this quality that he doesn't have, not any recent ones anyway. There is a photo of him from the time he hit a single in the company softball outing; that doesn't convey serious and intelligent, but maybe athletic and fun is good enough? Also, Gordon is only looking through the photos on the computer, photos that were taken in the last five years since they've had a digital camera (*there's no sense investing the money in something that was designed to be obsolete; until they come out with one that has eight or more megapixels, you might as well take the time to make a pointillist painting*), photos that were taken long after Gordon was last connected to, you know, himself. Might have to look back to childhood photos for that. There are a dozen photo albums from which he could choose one in which he at least *looks* like himself; also in these albums are photos of Gordon holding each of his children when they were first born, rare genuine moments, many of them snapped by his dad. That's maybe neither here nor there. We're just saying it's been a while. But it may be just as well that he's not thinking about the photo albums right now, because if he did, he'd find a lot of photos of people he doesn't remember. Finally Gordon remembers the built-in camera on his computer. He will take a self-portrait. It will take him only ninety-seven attempts before he gets one that seems right. It's our observation that the differences in most of these ninety-seven photos are visible only to Gordon, that it's the visual equivalent of the sounds that only dogs hear. Gordon has a "photo face," but he doesn't seem to know it.

There's a box on one side of his home page that suggests "people you may know" to add as friends; it does indeed list some people he knows, a few work associates, a few college friends, Priscilla. Unfortunately, it also lists a half dozen people Gordon does not know. Or he knows them but doesn't remember them. Gordon understands that it searches your email address book, but also feels that he knows who's in his email address book, although he's forgetting that he'd set it up so that anyone who emails him is automatically included in his email address book, and as such, this little box of people he may know only strengthens his concern that there may be any number of people besides Trudy whom he doesn't remember. He quickly puts in friend requests to all of them, as well as to Priscilla. He has no idea that won't happen.

Now to compose a message. ~~Dear Trudy,~~ ~~Trudy.~~ ~~Trudy~~ ~~Trudy~~ Trudy, ~~I am so sorry~~ It was nice seeing you again the other day. I hope you will accept my sincere apology for ~~having forgotten our entire relationship~~ ~~for not remembering you~~ ~~our relationship~~ ~~time together~~ the other day. Would you be ~~available~~ ~~willing~~ available ~~to meet me~~ for a cup of coffee ~~to discuss this matter further~~ at your ~~earliest~~ convenience? I would like to try to make it up to you. ~~Gordon Copeland~~. Gordon. ~~C.~~

This last line is almost completely insincere. He does feel a little bit bad about it, but mostly it's just there because Gordon has the good sense not to write *I would like you to help me remember why I don't remember you and hopefully reassure me that I am not slowly losing my mind.*

Gordon becomes distracted by a series of quizzes he discovers are popular on the social networking site. Fairly preposterous, he thinks, that anyone would waste their time on such things. Don't most people know the answers to these questions without taking the quizzes? Even the silly ones? Doesn't everyone know what Greek god/goddess best describes them? Obviously I'm Prometheus, Gordon thinks, god of forethought and crafty counsel, I don't need a silly quiz like this to tell me that. But according to this quiz he's a Harpy. Nonsense. He'll prove his point with another one. What era are you from? He's obviously from the 1950s, when life was so much simpler. But this quiz says he's from the seventies. Oh, pff. So *literal*. He'll do one more, What fairy tale are you? So many good choices; he could be the prince in just about anything, maybe a knight. Snow White? Oh, come now. What Hogwarts professor are you? Could Gordon be anyone but Dumbledore? Lockhart? Lockhart's nothing but a pompous buffoon! Which movie love story is your life? Oh, *Desk Set*, possibly *My Fair Lady. Unfaithful*? For heaven's sake, that makes no sense, that's about a *woman*. These quizzes are clearly skewed, asking the wrong questions. One more and he'll be back on track. What kind of dog? Surely a German shepherd. A Labradoodle? What could that possibly mean? Why is the Inquisition after you? Without a doubt they want to censor him. But wrong again. Freemasonry? He is no Freemason. Which *Family Guy* character? Brian, of course, but no, wrong again, he gets Peter, the oafish dad. All right, that's just absurd. Which *Wizard of Oz* character? No-brainer. The Wizard. This one he gets right, but doesn't realize it's for the wrong reasons. Thinks it's because he's smart, when in fact it's because he's afraid. What Smurf? In the bag—Brainy. But no . . . Papa Smurf. What opera character? Eugene Onegin, maybe, perhaps Werther. Canio? The sad clown? Oh, for Pete's sake. One more, just one more. What Beatles song are you? "Paperback Writer" maybe? "All You Need Is Love"! Huh. Well, ordinarily it might be hard to argue with that, but under the circumstances this answer just strikes Gordon as being as arbitrary as the rest.

Under normal circumstances, he'd have had no problem dismissing these quiz results as wrong and thinking no more about it. Unfortunately, because everything is wrong for Gordon right now, he finds his inability to match up who he is with who these quizzes thinks he is is rather disturbing. As Gordon discovers that he's wrong about so many of these quizzes, a thought passes through his mind—half a thought, perhaps—that there might be some small insight to be found here, that perhaps his idea of himself is too fixed.

Maybe I'll try one more, Gordon thinks. Are you happy with the one you love? Of course I am, he thinks. Finally, the quiz results match up.

Convinced he's back on track, he takes one last quiz: Why were you born? He has never wondered why he was born. He doesn't even think about it. He was born to be a productive member of society like everyone else, and to share his knowledge. Which is going to be a little difficult if all that knowledge drops away, as it seems to be doing.

Gordon's answer: You were born to be in love.

Gordon has no idea what to make of this, but surprisingly, he doesn't hate it. He's already in love, he thinks. Wouldn't it be nice if that were all he needed to worry about? Clearly, Gordon and his wife have different ideas about love. He thinks of himself as romantic because he remembers Jean's birthday, their anniversary, gives thoughtful gifts like books and perfume. He tells her he loves her. Maybe not often enough—a lot of times he drops the *I*, so it's just *Love you*, and to Jean that missing *I* is an important one—but Gordon doesn't know this. He believes she knows he loves her whether he says it out loud, or with an *I*, or with no *I*, and believes in saying it only as it comes to him, like when she undresses herself before bed, always after they've turned off the lights, the slivers of light between the blinds highlighting the outline of her still-beautiful form, unknown to her. He makes no distinction between *considerate* and *romantic*. Gordon's idea of love is practical. It's what grown-ups do. He's attracted to her; she's a good woman; she's beautiful; she's given him two children and she's a good mother. He knows they haven't slept together for a while, chalks it up to "marriage," tells himself it will change, and that it doesn't mean they don't love each other. But without a doubt this childish quiz has planted a seed. We'll see if he reaps it.

seventeen

For three days, three interminable days since the day Caterina gave him the jelly beans, Otis has been hoping to find himself close enough to her to say something—anything. He has tried to make this happen by lingering around his cubby to no avail, by sitting on the railroad tie at recess every day in case she sits down near him again. He knows she doesn't sit there every day, that sometimes she plays with other kids, or swings (and oh, what a thing to behold that is, Caterina on the swing, especially when her hair is in pigtails tied with colored ribbons, streaming behind her in the wind like kite tails of the most perfect kite in existence), but she does sit there often enough that he feels the odds are best in this location. He has been wanting to tell her that he didn't like the birthday cake flavor, just like her, but worries that she'll ask about the other flavors he hasn't tried, and ask him why wouldn't he have just eaten them. He knows nobody saves five jelly beans to eat later. He could just say thanks again for the jelly beans, but would that just shut down the conversation?

Just before the bell rings, Caterina does come over and sit down, but she's got that girl Bethany with her. Bethany talks really fast, nonstop, about nothing, if you ask Otis, and so he knows that there's not much chance he'll be able to add anything. Bethany's talking about some doll she got for her birthday that supposedly looks just like her, and about all the outfits that came with it, and about how she's hoping to get some matching outfits for Christmas. Caterina is only a smidge more interested than Otis is, but she's also unable to redirect, because there are nearly no breaths, or at least very unenterable breaths, between Bethany's words. Once, Caterina thinks she sees a pause coming, and she opens her mouth to leap in—but it isn't a pause, it's preparation for more about this doll and her outfits, and Otis and Caterina meet eyes for maybe one fraction of a fraction of a second, a moment in which Otis knows that Caterina knows that she would also like to say something, that Bethany should shut up already, a moment in which Otis is sharing something real and true with Caterina, a transcendent moment, a moment for the history books. Then, of course, the bell rings. Caterina jumps up and Bethany follows. *Wait up, wait up!* She has more to say about the doll. The girls are gone.

On the car ride home, Otis tells his mother about Caterina looking at him. Her son's first love! How have these years passed so quickly? She glances over at her son, wishes she could capture the light in his eyes somehow, keep this moment for her son so he'll always know what love is when it seems far away. She nods, a lot. *James and I had moments like that all the time. We had wonderful conversations, but half the time we didn't even have to talk. We could just sit there together.* Otis finds this very heartening news indeed. He and Caterina could just sit there. Already, they have sort of a foundation in just sitting there. This is good. Maybe he doesn't need to worry so much about talking. He likes to talk, though. He wants very much to tell Caterina about all of his interests. He almost feels like, if he could just start talking to Caterina, he could tell her everything and she would contain his thoughts and they'd be preserved for a later time in case he forgot them.

And when we—Jean catches herself—*laid down together,* she continues, *for the first time . . . Oh, well! It was like—well, it was just like all of your favorite things in the world swimming around in a goopy, soupy, delicious . . . oh, love is a beautiful thing, Otie. Someday you'll come together with a person and a very—almost spiritual thing will happen. I don't know how else to say it. Hopefully your lover won't kill herself.*

Okay, this is where we wish there could be a photograph, or a series of photographs of Otis's changing expressions as his mother talks, a moment of contemplation on *laid down together,* another moment on *spiritual,* another moment on *goopy, soupy, delicious,* and the last, the last moment on *kill herself,* Otis's changing expressions as he puzzles through these descriptors and lands finally on *kill herself,* a scowl settling into his face as this idea takes shape. All these pairs and trios of words bring numerous images to Otis's mind, and he doesn't have nearly enough time to work through each one before *kill herself* comes up, which is the easiest to picture but the hardest to understand. Why would Caterina kill herself? Is that just what happens, eventually? Will I kill myself? Accidentally or something? He tries to think of some reason this might happen. He hardly thinks he or Caterina would kill themselves of their own free will. Plus, he can think of only so many ways for someone to kill someone, or themselves. Things he's read about in books: guns and magic swords, poison apples, cannons. A cannon. How would that work? He can't picture how you'd kill yourself with a cannon; you'd have to light it somehow and then run around to the front before the cannonball came out. Probably he can't run that fast. Perhaps his teacher would say, "Okay, class, everyone take out your compasses and begin stabbing yourself in the stomach until you're dead." But why, though? Or what if his mom and dad handed out guns after dinner one night? "Priscilla, Otis, instead of ice cream tonight we're all going to shoot ourselves." But no, Mom seems too sad about James; she probably wouldn't want all of us to kill ourselves, too. Unless, if we all killed ourselves, then maybe no one would be sad—maybe that's the idea. Jean is driving, so she doesn't see Otis's thinking hat and at this point she's far past worrying that she's said too much. Otis doesn't ask any of the questions in his head, he just continues to generate more questions, and more erroneous answers.

eighteen

Gordon's heart is not in his discourses lately. He's upset that he hasn't heard back from Trudy. And he's not completely aware of it, but he's not getting much more than one or two short sentences out on any given topic lately. You'd think his family would notice, Jean in particular, but everyone is tripping out on their own shit right about now. Priscilla has picked up the slack a bit—not in terms of proffering information, but at least in terms of conversation. She doesn't feel that the family has adequately recognized the significance of what's going on in her life at this moment, even though she's been talking about it nonstop, every meal. *Do you guys even understand what this could mean for me, getting this show?* Gordon says, *There are those who believe that Shakespeare would be writing for reality TV if he were alive now*, then goes back to sopping up a runny egg with a piece of toast. Everyone is waiting for more from Gordon, but nothing comes, which brings the conversation (or, more accurately, the talking) to a dead stop. They have all officially noticed, but they're so used to him talking that they haven't tried hard to come up with anything to add in years. Gordon wipes his mouth, gets up, pats Jean absently on the head, which is totally odd, and leaves for work. Did he mean to pat Otis on the head? Mott? Even we're not sure.

Gordon goes to see his GP, ostensibly for the checkup he's due for, but wastes no time mentioning his memory loss. *Could it be dietary, do you think? I've read that there can be a connection between certain foods and brain development, these so-called super-foods like wild salmon, nuts, seeds, and such. Perhaps the converse is true—that if you don't eat enough of those foods, your cognitive decline is hastened? I've always considered myself to have a well-balanced diet, and, I might add, a sophisticated palate, but perhaps I overlooked some-thing.* His doctor doesn't seem the least bit worried, but makes a casual comment that is of no small concern to Gordon.

Perfectly common at your age.

Gordon does not like either part of this sentence. In fact, it's hard to know which part is worse, the "perfectly common" or the "at your age." Ordinarily "perfectly common" would tip the scale, because we know he considers himself anything but, but this "at your age" business opens up all kinds of things Gordon doesn't want to think about. He knows he's well into middle age, but he's always thought of himself as being above anything as pedestrian as a midlife crisis. (Common indeed.) Even if he had the urge to drive a Ferrari or something, he'd surely recognize it for what it was and squash it on the spot. But he's getting off-track. *At your age?* He's not middle-aged. He's old. He's old, probably near senile. Near death. No—death would be a blessing. Walking dead. That's what's com-ing. Gordon says one or two of these things out loud, realizes that he can't be helping his case, asks for a referral to a shrink.

nineteen

A little more about why Vivian prefers to be driven: The story she's been telling herself for seventy-some years is only part of the story. Her fear of hitting a pedestrian is fully real. But it was one she had hoped to surmount when she met her husband, who had discouraged her. He had known about her fear, and didn't see any reason for a woman to drive anyway, so he simply said he'd drive, and it wasn't discussed again. And so, though Vivian had maintained a tight control on her household throughout their marriage, on this one point she had, regrettably, capitulated. He was the man. She hoped, for a while, that someday he'd soften, imagined that he would finally teach her, that he'd move her hand over the gearshift, tell her she was doing swell, that no one was going to get hurt. She'd envisioned them on long road trips in a shiny new coupe, a Buick or a Chevy, sharing turns, he asleep in the passenger seat while she drove; they'd stop to go camping, as they'd done a time or two before the kids were born—perhaps you haven't heard the story about how Theodore's sister Patricia had *most likely* been conceived, picnicking on the banks of the Colorado River one afternoon after a hike. It wasn't in heavy rotation for obvious reasons, it being a bit scandalous to talk of such things, but it was a story, perhaps the only story that everyone was amused by, and Vivian told it once in a while because it spoke to her youthful allure, and she knew that in the context of marriage such things were acceptable.

The story holds particular interest for Priscilla, the one time she hears it. At dinner the word "stream" comes up, which is as much of an entry as Vivian needs to endeavor to steer the conversation her way. Never mind that in this particular conversation the word "stream" was referring to videos on the Internet. Vivian is perfectly happy to latch onto things that hardly exist in order to change the subject back to more interesting topics, topics that involve Vivian. In her mind, Vivian links "stream" and "river" and says, *Oh! That reminds me of the time Baron and I went camping. We made a picnic on the banks of the Colorado River, you see, and well, oh, I could never resist your great-grandfather.*

Priscilla's eyes go wide when she hears this. She's a little bit grossed out, because she can't picture them anything but old and wrinkly. It's near-impossible, not to mention freaky, to imagine that her Grandma Bibbie was once a young person who had sex, like, for fun. But this one thing makes her rethink Bibbie entirely—enough to engage her mother in a conversation about it, albeit a brief one.

So, you think Grandma Bibbie, like, liked sex? she asks the next morning over coffee. *Like, if she was doing it outside and stuff?*

Jean smiles and tells her she supposes she had. *That surprises you?*

Well, yuh, she's old.

She wasn't always old.

I know, but I mean, I guess I thought that back in those days you didn't really do it . . . Priscilla doesn't want to finish the sentence because she knows it might imply what she thinks sex is for.

For fun?

Yeah.

Yeah, sweetie, sex has always been fun.

The conversation is moving rapidly in a direction Priscilla does not want it to go; the idea of her own parents having sex, which is possibly even more disconcerting than her great-grandmother having sex, is not one she cares to have in her head. Plus, Priscilla doesn't personally think sex is all that much fun. In theory, maybe. But her two partners haven't done much to convince her. She thinks she might have had an orgasm once, but she's not totally sure. She likes that she has a certain sexual power, but isn't much interested in using it toward that direct end, mostly just likes that she's been able to use it once or twice to get something she wanted. But the last thing she's interested in right now is a relationship. What she's seen of that in real life doesn't entice her. What she wants is to get what she wants on her own merit. She just doesn't really know what she wants.

Priscilla makes a dramatic gesture of shaking off what her mother's just said.

Oh honey, when you're with the right person, it'll be better, I promise.

Who am I going to meet here anyway, Mom? In this town?

I met your father here.

Okay, look, Priscilla loves her dad, but this isn't really the best way to make the case, and Priscilla doesn't do much to hide her skepticism.

Well, that was a long time ago, Mom. Before status updates.

Jean has no idea what her daughter has just said.

It's an online thing, Mom.

Jean's still not following. Until now, Priscilla has not told her mother the story of how Kyle decided to break up with her: by posting "Kyle Woolrich dumped Priscilla Copeland's tired ass" on his social network page.

Oh no! Who sees this?

Only everyone, Mom.

That's horrible! Why didn't you tell me this?

Priscilla doesn't do much to conceal her look of "Do I ever tell you anything?" She's also not in the mood to get into the fact that her mom has obviously been somewhere else for, like, a while—definitely since before the Kyle thing.

I'm very sorry that happened to you, Priscilla. I wish you felt you could tell me things.

We know you see the moment that could be here. But it's just not going to happen right now. Priscilla's not there yet, and we're not sure Jean is either, even if she thinks she is. Priscilla does, for a second, think about spilling it all to her mom—telling her how sweet Kyle had been at first, showing up to their first date with flowers (from the grocery store, but she didn't mind), how he always paid when he took her out, gave her that silver bracelet with the heart locket with their pictures in, and, like, told her he loved her on their one-week anniversary. But then, too, how everything changed over-night when she gave him what he wanted, and how he never took her anywhere after that, and how he only wanted to stay in and drink beer and play video games, maybe watch a DVD if she was lucky, and then do it, and then suddenly he didn't even want to do that, and then they had a fight, one fight, and then the status update. Her mother couldn't imagine the amount of damage control she had to do with her friends. Seriously, if she hadn't been popular, she'd have been ruined.

I'm over it.

They're not all like that, Priscilla. Just try to trust me on that.

Priscilla would like to believe her mother. It's that word "trust" that's tripping her up.

twenty

There is no class Priscilla enjoys less than English Comp. She has never understood why anyone should be required to take a lesson in the language they already speak totally fine. She doesn't want to be a writer, can't imagine any job she'd want to have where she'd have to either write or do math, the two least fun things she can think of. So, as the professor is going on about something, *thesis statements* or *effective organization*, or some other boring-ass shit, she's zeroing in on only enough of the example on the board to start scribbling notes for a paper about her relationship with Brody Jenner.

    I. Brody Jenner & me meet at a big party of reality stars.
   II. Brody Jenner flirts with me even though Avril Lavigne (or whoever) is there. Realize BJ is a douche.
 III. Tim Riggins & me meet at a big party of famous people. Looks greasy. Blow TR off for *Boardwalk Empire* guy. Also greasy.

    a. why is greasy a thing?

    b. greasy should so not be a thing

IV. Blow *Boardwalk Empire* guy off for hot Asian dude from *Glee*. Blow HAD off for young British Darth Vader. (Hott, also looks smart & maybe is not so douchey)

V. How I get Darth Vader away from Rachel Bilson (or whoever)

    a. wear something super-hot

    b. eye contact, flip hair, ~~tongue on drink stirrer~~

    c. hook up

VI. ~~Wedding.~~ Relationship

    a. Us pretending we don't like paparazzi when really we do

        i) covering face with oversized designer satchel

        ii) going to Hawaii for a private getaway but oops I mentioned it to a couple people, whatevs

VII. Big fight, Darth Vader really doesn't like paparazzi after all

    a. *You're full of shit, No you're full of shit, I'm not full of shit, whatevs, you knew they'd be there when we went to get the tattoos*

    b. hot makeup sex

VIII. Romantic proposal in English countryside

    a. Reservations

        i) suspect he's private tweeting RB

        ii) not crazy about ring/doesn't know me

IX. Wedding.

X. Divorce.

All this amounts to, really, is that Priscilla realizes she has nothing under "wedding" except for "divorce," not even a beautiful dress, because she's not really interested in getting married—not anytime soon anyway, not from what she's seen of it—plus she doesn't want to coast on somebody else's star. Really can't even think of even one famous guy she's super into, anyway. All guys are assholes. Her mother has no idea.

She crumples up her outline and starts over with the tentative title "Anna Wintour, Role Model." She knows what a lot of people think about Anna Wintour, but what Priscilla knows about Anna Wintour could probably fill a book, if she were so inclined. She feels a certain kinship with the misunderstood fashion editor. She's known for being cold, but her love of fashion began so young. She read *Seventeen* magazine as a kid! *Priscilla* read *Seventeen*! Anna hemmed up her skirts in junior high school! Worked at a boutique! Does just fine without a man! Priscilla has seen *The September Issue* half a dozen times, has a file folder full of articles about Anna Wintour. Screw boys.

Plus, as much as she's always hated her name and wanted to change it to something normal, like Madison or Olivia, she suddenly realizes there are no famous Priscillas except for that lady that was married to Elvis and that was like a hundred years ago.

Priscilla will be the first Priscilla to be super famous with her own last name.

Priscilla wants her own separate star.

twenty-one

Vivian comes into her kitchen this morning to discover Theodore, dog at his feet, taking apart the electric can opener. This is another thing that Theodore likes to do lately, take things apart. He doesn't necessarily want to fix them, he mostly just wants to see how they work, although in this case the can opener wasn't working, and now it's in about as many pieces as there are pieces of it, all spread out on the kitchen table.

At one time, for Theodore, this practice might have been about saving a few dollars. He used to be decent at fixing things, but he doesn't really know he's not anymore, and these days he's mostly only interested in the mechanics of the thing. His intention is to put it back together—that's always his intention—but it never happens. The parts that look like they go together do not go together, not at all. It's just like the puzzles. But he will keep trying. If he turns this one thingamajig a centimeter to the right, he knows it will lock right into the doodad and be as good as new. Never mind that Theodore's hands no longer operate on the centimeter level. Lock into place. Just a little to the right. To the left. To the right. Lockintoplace. Boy, this is sure making Theodore hungry. He'll get this back together, he knows he will, if he just looks at it long enough.

The repeated taking apart of appliances drives Vivian crazy. It almost makes her sorry that he seems to be past the crying, sentimental period he was in before his mind got a little worse. It was unseemly, just not manly. Her son had not shed a tear in front of her since he'd been about six, was always—well, not stoic, but certainly composed, a well-behaved boy, and there he was now so undignified, mushy, suddenly weepy at the drop of a hat, at dinner, during card games.

Anyway, it's not just that his hands wave wildly now, even on the meds, causing him small injuries on a regular basis. Gordon took away his father's beloved pocketknife only recently, after a pretty serious stabbing to his left hand sent them to the ER for three stitches to his palm. It's true that the can opener wasn't working right, but for heaven's sake, it was from the seventies. That's what Walmart's for, Vivian thought, you throw these things out and go get a new one. She'd go out right now and get one herself if she didn't have to schedule rides so far in advance with this family. Theodore's thumb is perilously close to the little circular blade now, and though it's coated in thirty years of gunk, as of yesterday it was still sharp enough to open a can of soup.

Theodore. Vivian says.

Theodore doesn't hear his mother at first, is contemplating a tiny screw and trying to locate the corresponding hole.

Theodore!

Theodore looks up at his mother with wide eyes. Vivian feels a mix of things right here, flashes back to Theodore as a small boy, always curious, always interested in how things worked, finds her irritation softening just a bit. *Dear, it's broken now. For heaven's sake, we can well afford to get a new one.* She knows that's not really the point for Theodore, but it's something to say. *You're going to hurt yourself.* She should stop here. She knows she should stop here. She should really just not say another word. *Again.* Vivian takes the piece with the blade out of his hand.

Theodore's face turns into as much of a frown as he's got anymore. He looks down at the dog. *Whole lotta people around here telling me what to do these days.*

All right, well, please don't throw it away, Theodore says to his mother. *I'm sure it can be fixed.*

Vivian goes to look for a box. She's learned that sometimes it's easier to appease him. Hopefully he'll forget, and she can throw it away soon enough.

twenty-two

Jean's book group has decided to convene as scheduled, in spite of their recent loss, as a "tribute" to James. They tell themselves it's what James would want, though the truth is, none of them besides Jean had known him well enough to know what he'd want, and we know now that even Jean didn't know everything. The fact was that Margot had picked an atrocious book, *The Bridges of Madison County*, one James would never have read on his own. Jean had read it when it came out, long before she'd ever even imagined she'd be unfaithful herself, hated it beyond words back then—the story unbelievable, the writing so dreadful she remembers feeling embarrassed for the author, had only ever hated one book more. (*Conversations with God*. She'd found it almost beyond comprehension that so many millions of people had purchased and found meaning in this book—it was all well and good, she thought, that some guy talked to god, but paying money to read these absurd conversations seemed like paying money to hear someone's conversations with E.T.) So she didn't plan to reread *Bridges* this time—not before James died and especially not now. To Jean, it had seemed chosen as a direct response to James's last pick. Everyone wanted something romantic. Something *easy*.

Today Jean is in no mood to socialize, but she's choosing between staring out the window with Theodore and getting out of the house, so she grabs her copy of the book, which she hadn't even been able to unload at their last garage sale for a quarter, and heads out the door.

Four of the remaining five members are completely captivated with the book, so excited to talk about it. Each takes a turn reading some of her favorite lines. Most of the ones they single out are lines Jean would have chosen to demonstrate how bad the writing is. Margot reads: *"My life . . . lacks romance, eroticism, dancing in the kitchen to candlelight, and the wonderful feel of a man who knows how to love a woman . . ."* Jean wonders what on earth had convinced her to get together with this group in the first place. She thinks it was mostly that they asked. You'd think she'd identify with this character, but on hearing these lines she can barely suppress a gag reflex. Bad writing trumps potentially interesting story every time. Maybe *she* should write a book. Couldn't she write a better book along similar lines? She should write a book about a lonely woman who takes up with a man who kills himself because his book group picked the worst book ever written. She knows these people aren't bad people, but are they really this shallow? How did she not notice this when James was alive? Oh, right. For a while, Jean sits mostly in silence listening to the group *ooh* and *aah* about Francesca and Kincaid's love— even the only remaining male in the group, Duncan, who isn't usually such a sucker—about how surprised they were to find that they empathized with her even though she'd betrayed her family. Jean can't help but wonder how empathetic they'd be if she confessed her own secret right now. Having listened to their gossip for years, she doubts that they'd swoon over her story the way they are for these flat, fictional people. She can't decide what she's more upset about: their attraction to this story, or the fact that they can't seem to recognize that this book is a blight on mankind.

Finally Margot notices that Jean hasn't said anything. *You're awfully quiet tonight, Jean. Didn't you like the book?*

As is customary, Jean leans toward being polite, in spite of what's in her head.

To be honest, it's been a long time since I read it.

Okay. But you must have loved it then, right?

Jean is polite, but she's also a bad liar, when pressed.

Well, not so much, no.

Surprised reactions from the rest of the group. They can't believe it. They should be able to believe it; she'd loved *Confederacy* and always picked *difficult* books herself, but they can't believe anyone wouldn't love this book.

You didn't think it was a beautiful love story?

Not really.

But why?

Jean tries to work around what she really wants to say, that she has some experience in this area, but that even when she didn't, it still hadn't rung true. She tells them she just thought it was poorly written, takes a deep breath and flips through the book to find an example.

Okay, here: "I am the highway and a peregrine and all the sails that ever went to sea."

The group practically swoons in unison.

All right, what about this: "In a universe of ambiguity, this kind of certainty comes only once, and never again, no matter how many lifetimes you live."

I was blown away by that line! Alisa says. *So completely true!*

Don't you just dream of that kind of certainty? Margot asks. *I've been married for seventeen years. I don't even think I felt like that on our wedding day.*

Okay, here's another one: "Here I am walking around with another person inside of me." I mean, I dunno, don't you think that's kind of creepy? What Jean had loved about James was that she'd always felt he was walking around next to her. No one gets the difference, and Jean sees that they're not going to. This effectively ends this month's group on an awkward note. Jean waits until the last few *Well-I-loved-it*s to leave, but she will not go back to book group.

twenty-three

Gordon's shrink, of course, suggests therapy. Gordon is not eager to rush into anything of the kind, but he is desperate. He's always thought that psychology was a branch of quackery, or that it was for the truly disturbed, that everyone else should just buck up and think their way out of their problems. But right now Gordon is willing to explore all avenues—hoping for the ideal scenario, that the doctor and the shrink will each make the same crisp and clear diagnosis, something to the effect of "There's nothing at all wrong with you."

Gordon tries to push the shrink to explain various causes of memory loss, whether or not this is the beginning of a long slow or swift decline, whether it could be Alzheimer's, Parkinson's, dementia, a stroke, a brain tumor, what? The shrink tells him he'll have to have tests to determine whether or not he has anything along those lines, but that since the short-term memory usually fails first, and real memory loss would likely be accompanied by many other symptoms, he doesn't believe it's necessary at this time. This is a brief bit of relief for Gordon—until the shrink adds, *It's really very normal to repress certain painful memories.*

Painful memories? With Trudy? How painful could they have been? Even if that were true, wouldn't he remember *something*? Wouldn't he remember Trudy herself? Her face? Even if he couldn't put it into context? How was it that he remembered Sheila but not Trudy?

The brain has a remarkable ability to maneuver its way around trauma.

Trauma?

Sure. For example, the connection between horrific trauma and fractured—that is to say, split or multiple personality—is well-documented.

Gordon rolls *horrific, trauma,* and *multiple personality* around the tumbler; he knows there would have to be other symptoms if he were some sort of Sybil, his family would surely notice, he'd probably have blackouts, nothing like that has been happening. But horrific trauma? What could possibly have happened between him and Trudy that would fall under that header, that would be so unthinkable that he'd literally have unthunk it? Could she have drugged him, done something like that while he was unconscious? The shrink admits that's a stretch, suggests maybe a more subtle trauma—maybe something that relates to Gordon's mother or father somehow, or another family member, a childhood trauma, that something about their interaction connected to some long-forgotten ordeal.

You may have had a good family life, but often such experiences occur with family friends, babysitters, other relatives.

This is where Gordon veers off. He knows he had a good childhood. He *thinks* he knows. He used to know. Unless what the doctor says is true. Which it isn't. There's no way. No, really, there isn't. We're telling you. It's just that, from now on, Gordon will never be more than 98 percent sure. The remaining 2 percent is troublesome, to be sure, but not so much that he can't deny it. Something else is causing his memory loss, he is certain.

Do you suppose there's any possibility that Trudy is lying, that she's making the whole thing up, that she was some kind of crazy stalker? Someone I maybe dated once and then she became obsessed and fabricated all kinds of stories she believed, but that weren't true?

I'm not sure how that follows. Gordon isn't really either, but even a *Gaslight* scenario would be better than a defective mind.

Don't stalkers usually hunt you down, follow you around? He'd only run into Trudy once, but could she be such a good stalker that she made their meeting seem accidental, that she might possibly be stalking him as we speak? That she's so furtive a stalker that she would deny his online friendship just to make it look like she wasn't stalking him? Gordon is warming to this idea, even though it means his life could be in danger. Given the choice, he prefers the idea that someone is interested in killing him to the idea that he's losing his most precious resource. Who would he be without his mind? He doesn't know, and he does not like not knowing things.

Gordon finally thinks to call his college roommate Phil to ask what he remembers about Trudy.

That was the year you blew me off most nights to be with her, Phil says.

Gordon explains how they'd run into each other recently. *Except I simply could not remember her at all.*

Really? You sure were into her then. You don't remember me bitching to you guys when she spent the night? God, the noises still haunt me. I always thought something was wrong with you guys. Phil makes a fake shuddering noise; Gordon is silent. *But, you know, we're old now, man. Don't sweat it. I mix up my wife and my dog's names all the time.*

That is not the same thing at all, Gordon thinks. Not at all.

twenty-four

Priscilla has just gotten a text from Taylor. *OMG 3rd callback today!!! What 2 wear???* Priscilla cannot believe Taylor is being so insensitive. Couldn't she have texted someone else? Priscilla has not officially been rejected, nor has she heard anything more since her last meeting. She sends a text back, *White jeans*, the ones she knows Taylor loves but which Priscilla thinks make her look severely slutty. Her thong always sticks out the top. Like, entirely on purpose. Slutty *and* tacky. Priscilla would never. *With what top???* Priscilla would totally smash her phone right now, but she did that once and her parents wouldn't buy her a new one and it took her two wretched text-less months to save up the money for a new one. *WhatEv!* Priscilla texts back—the capital E indicating her irritation—then turns off her phone with a grunt and a sharp, unsatisfying poke of her index finger. This was her one chance, and Taylor has taken her spot, and now all the spots were taken, and she doesn't even have a BFF to commiserate with. She totally wishes she were the type of girl who would kill herself. Well, not, like, permanently, but it could be super great to be able to kill herself briefly so everyone would realize what a huge mistake they were making in not immediately casting her on this TV show.

She spends a minute or two thinking about how she could actually fake this, like in that old movie from the seventies her mom always loved with the old lady and that bug-eyed young guy. How great would it be if she could make it look like she stabbed herself in the neck, with, like, a big freaking stiletto heel or umbrella or something and a bunch of fake blood? Maybe not so believable. She could just spill out a couple of pills on the floor, lie down next to them. But what if Otis were the one who found her? She doesn't hate him that much. She actually doesn't hate him at all, he's just severely annoying. That would suck ass, actually, her poor little brother. Plus, whoever found her, how would this news get back to the TV show? Following this thread, P imagines that Taylor finds her instead, that starts out being a genius idea, like, "*Now* do you get how important this was to me? Are you happy to have this show over my dead body? I bet not," but then her imagination goes in the wrong direction and the show in her mind follows Taylor in her grief, giving it a layer of depth it might not have had otherwise. Either way, Priscilla realizes that it'd still really be about Taylor. Fuck. She would have to make sure it was her mom who found her.

Priscilla has no idea what has been going on with her mom lately—like, she has seriously been on a mental bender to Outer Mongolia or somewhere. This would snap her back to. But it would also suck pretty hard. She doesn't really wish that on her mom. Even just a fake suicide, that would be a suck-ass two minutes before she sat up and revealed herself to not be dead. Does she wish that on any member of her family, really? Fine-*nuh*, she doesn't. It would be nice if any of them noticed her, is all. She thought Taylor at least had her back, but now she wonders if anyone does.

twenty-five

Jean is wandering around the mall today. She's gone there to pick up a new book she's heard about, even though she hasn't been able to read a thing since James died, is still barely able to flip through a magazine without seeing James on every page, every black-and-white perfume ad of muscled lovers is James and Jean (though nothing particularly "muscled" ever came into the real life picture), every recipe with an ingredient once eaten by Jean and James in some dish, every article somehow reminding her of James, every title with James in it, somewhere.

Slaves to James

Products for You: James Tested, Wife Approved

Your Most Secret Sex Question: How Can I Get
    James to Watch Porn with Me?

10 Positions James Has Never Heard of but Needs to
    Try

How to Find James in 30 Days

How to Leave James at Work

How to Meet James at the Grocery Store

How to Dress for Yourself but Make James Think
  It's for Him

What Does Your James Mean?

Why Women Are Obsessed with James

Six Ways to Get Over a James

Why James Loves Power-Hungry Women

James's Best Masturbation Tips

The Body Language of James

DIY: Make a Festive Centerpiece out of James

Signs of Menopause James Might Not Know

Should People Be Allowed to Buy James with Food
  Stamps?

Best James-Removal Gadgets

Four Easy Ways to Get Healthy James

The Tough Stuff: "James Is Taking Over Our
  Lives!"

Is James's Dress Too Slutty?

Know How We Always Say to Wear Spanx Under
  Your Spandex? This Photo of James Shows You
  Exactly What We Mean by That

James Is the Hot New Lunch Meat

Style Secrets from James

Five Steps to Planting a James Garden

Beware of Jameswashing

One Thing James Keeps Private

Wandering through a department store, Jean mindlessly fingers various cosmetics, tries on a lipstick in a bright shade of red

that is decidedly not her. It's unflattering, but it is bold. For a second she thinks of leaving it on, as a little screw-you to the world. Huh. Screw you? Is that really what she's going for? She's about to wipe it off when a saleswoman bounces up from under the counter and tells Jean it's fabulous, pulls out a few samples and creams, directs Jean to sit on the tall chair right in front of her, she'll give her a free makeover. A makeover! A super idea. She hasn't updated her look in forever. If this were one of those TV makeovers, it could go either way. She could be one of those who end up looking kind of generically shiny, not improved so much as just different—but if they get it right she could be a knockout, walk in the front door for the reveal and watch as Gordon somehow finally notices her, sees both her outside and inside, such is the power of a TV makeover. In fact, Priscilla could probably help her mom out, make her look like herself but better, fresher. But no one's thinking of that right now. That's not what's happening here. She's in a mall. Jean doesn't expect this will change much of anything, thinks maybe it will be a little pick-me-up at best, and for the first moment or two she's able to tune out the saleswoman's pitches, feeling only the woman's gentle touch on her face, drifting away for a brief moment in which these hands belong to James, a moment where James is lovingly touching her face as he once had. But as the saleswoman dabs on an under-eye cream, Jean drifts back in on the word "anti-aging."

I'm sorry, Jean says, *what did you just say?*

I was saying that this is one of the best products on the market right now for anti-aging, an incredible value. I swear by it myself.

Jean looks at the jar of cream. Miracle Worker, it's called.

Miraculous anti-aging moisturizer. To witness a miracle is to know yourself, vital, brilliant, heavenly in spirit. It's all right there on the label.

This is the promise of the cream? Seriously?

Why is this the big thing, anti-aging?

Oh, you know, we all just want to look our best, right?

*I don't think you understand what I'm saying. Anti-*aging, Jean says.

I'm sorry . . . I . . . guess I don't?

I think you're selling me a lie.

The saleswoman is doing everything she can to maintain her poise, somewhat concerned that this woman means this personally against her, that she is lying. *Oh, but ma'am, I swear to you, this is a fabulous product.*

So you say. But you see, it can't possibly do what you say it does.

Stunned saleslady silence now.

It says anti-aging. *This is the big thing. You see it everywhere. Everywhere. But really, why not just say what it really is? Don't we really mean* anti-death?

What?

Seriously, what is anti-aging all about, really? We think it's because our culture is obsessed with youth, but think about it: at the bottom of it, we're all obsessed with death.

Ma'am, I don't know what to say. I've been using this product for years. It literally turns back the clock.

No, it doesn't literally *do that.*

The saleswoman pauses for a moment, can hear the hostility ratcheting up in Jean's voice, but doesn't want to lose the sale. *I'm sorry?*

It doesn't literally do that. Do you know what literally *means? It means something actually happens. So what you're trying to tell me is that by using this product,* all of time *will move backward. Which is not possible, literally, or otherwise.*

Oh, well, I just . . .

I truly wish that it were. I truly wish that this anti-aging cream would literally turn back the clock so that I could beg my lover not to hang himself.

Jean jumps off the chair, with one eye made up and the red lipstick still on, and leaves the store.

twenty-six

So Theodore's been working on his paper. Over the years he has given and published many papers, and his audiences have generally been quite enthusiastic. As optometry papers go, Theodore's always made good use of his sense of humor, where those given by others tended to be on the dull side. Over the last year, though, as his cognitive powers have declined in this odd way, he's in a sort of a nether place, mentally, where he believes he can do anything, that everything is as it always was, that the only thing different about him is that his body doesn't work quite as well as it used to. Which is a pain, but it could be worse; it's not like he was ever into athletics or anything like that, he's always been an *indoorsman* (it still makes him chuckle to think of it this way). And so what that means here is that he's been working on this paper, which he genuinely believes he will be presenting at an optometry convention. The thing is, in the months since Theodore got an early (two-page) draft written, "working on" has come to mean "looking at," sometimes for hours, and reading it for anyone nearby. Today he's gathered the entire family. An unspoken pact to humor him about the content and the future of the paper has clearly been established. The family seems to understand that, despite his intentions, he'll never get as far as submitting it for anyone's approval. Jean has already heard the paper several times before, as has Otis. Gordon has not, and the timing could not be worse. But everyone recognizes that, in Theodore's mind, these pages are as brilliant as anything he's written before. He beams with pride as he reads them. He knows exactly what he means, even if no one else does.

Here's a snippet from the beginning:

Sight vs. Seeing: Optometry, the Long View: Myopia vs. Hyperopia

I first became fervent with visions as a child. My father was an optometrist, and was also in the jewelry business, as these commerces were often conjugated together at that time. I loved to sit in his chair, loved the things of it, the click of the giant eye piece, the blurry letters. But what has always most convoluted me about optometry is perhaps esoteric and not why most people go into this courtyard. What I am interested in is the adherence between sight and seeing. We cannot see if we have no sight. Or can we? That is what I am here to obtain today.

Everyone in the room is doing his or her best to nod in an interested fashion, while avoiding any eye contact with Theodore that might give them away. His hands are shaking considerably; one might wonder how he can even read a piece of paper that's waving about quite so much, but our guess is that he very nearly has it memorized, given the amount of time he claims to have spent on it.

Hold it still, Vivian says.

Vivian! Jean whispers.

What? Vivian says to Jean, looking aghast.

Theodore doesn't have much of a stern glare in him at this point; his expression has a few variations, but the endeavor to produce a stern glare at his mother is plenty clear. *I can't.*

Oh! Well, I didn't know.

Theodore takes a rather long pause here. It's hard for us to speculate about what's in his head. In his better days, he would have spoken back to her. Their fights were never big blowouts; generally Theodore spoke his mind fairly directly, Vivian denied that she'd intended anything unkind by whatever criticism she'd put out, and after an hour in separate corners, they'd go back to pretending nothing had happened. Theodore always promoted a cheerful philosophy; he met apologies with *No need*, thank-yous with *Not to mention*. If he'd held on to any resentment toward his mother, that was probably Laura's secret. What's different at this moment is that his mother has called direct attention to his limitations. It's a bubble no one wanted to see burst—least of all, we're guessing, Theodore. On the outside, at least, his existence is similar enough to what it once was, that we imagine it's easy for him to tell himself nothing has changed. Until people go pointing it out.

Theodore, go on, please, Jean says.

Theodore reads the rest of the paper. It's not much longer than the two pages he began with; nor has it changed in any substantial way. It's more of the same. He lifts his eyes from the paper, nods to indicate that he's finished. Everyone claps; it's the only thing anyone is sure about doing. Their uncomfortable smiles should betray them, but this doesn't register with Theodore. Vivian is the first one out; Jean kisses him on the head; everyone pats him on the back, tells him it was great and mumbles their various reasons why they have to leave the room. He believes they approve.

Otis is the only one who stays behind. *Great job, Grampa! Yeah, you think so?*

Otis nods, hadn't planned a follow-up answer, just wanted to keep his grandpa company.

Theodore nods back, smiling. He believes his grandson. His paper will be a huge success at the convention, he is sure.

twenty-seven

Twelve unanswered social network messages later, Trudy finally answers one in the hopes of getting Gordon off her back. *Meet me at Uncommon Grounds Monday at noon and do not be fucking crazy.*

Monday comes and Gordon arrives at Uncommon Grounds at 11:30 A.M., doesn't want to miss her, downs two espressos and a latte before she gets there. Just in case he wasn't janked enough without it.

Trudy walks in, sits down at Gordon's table. He thanks her for coming. She glares at him. *I've got five minutes*, she says.

All right. All right. All right. Well, well, well, Trudy, ever since we ran into each other I can't stop thinking about you. I mean, not about you, about us. I mean, not about us but about why I can't remember us. I've been to doctors, shrinks. His hands are shaking from the coffee.

Well, that's good, I guess, Trudy says.

But they all say nothing's wrong with me.

Trudy's eyebrows go up.

So either they're just missing something, or you're stalking me. Gordon has no idea how abrupt this transition is.

Well, then for sure they are missing something, Trudy says. *That is a very interesting math equation you've done in your head there, Gordon. And how am I stalking you, exactly? Have I phoned you even once?*

I believe you are stealth, that you may perhaps be so good at it that you're able to make it seem like it's not happening at all, and that what's really happening to me is an extravagant game designed to mess with my mind so that I'll be at your mercy.

She holds up a hand. *I'll speak now,* Trudy says.

Gordon nods vigorously, though he plans to speak.

You need to leave me alone.

Please, Trudy, I just want to have a conversation.

Here's the conversation, Gordon. You will stop sending me messages.

Please, Trudy. You're the only one who can help me!

Do. Not. Contact. Me. Ever again, Gordon. I mean it.

I'm losing my mind! he shouts after her.

Yeah, no shit, Gordon. She's gone.

twenty-eight

With regard to caring for Vivian and Theodore, Jean's in a bit of a lose-lose situation. The sitter bears a good portion of the burden, at least theoretically—minding Vivian and Theodore during the day, making sure no one falls down, keeping Theodore from wandering. But much of the balance of the responsibility falls to Jean; the facts of Vivian being Vivian, and Vivian being in Jean's house, have contributed exponentially to Jean's emotional exhaustion. There's always been friction between them. Vivian has a way of insulting you with a smile while leaving you uncertain of what was just said. (*Oh*, she'll say, fingering Jean's sweater, *I suppose this is what people are wearing now, well, that's fine.*) It doesn't matter whether Gordon picks up some of the slack, at least in terms of helping out physically, which he often does. In the evenings he steps up, helping Theodore get changed, getting him his meds on schedule and such, and has been attentive (if recently his mind is elsewhere—like everyone else) and eager to spend time with his father and grandmother. He's always believed in family, and though he's always been a bit deluded about how close they all are, in this way, at least, he's suiting up.

Vivian is much more capable than her son is, in terms of dressing, showering, using the bathroom—basic daily activities. She can do all those things. Still, there are moments when Jean wishes that she could replace the one Vivian with three Theodores. This is one of them.

Today, Jean needs to go to the market to pick up a few things, but she has failed to put it on the calendar. We may have forgotten to mention the calendar. When the family moved in, Vivian had requested a calendar of everyone's planned comings and goings. Vivian likes to know where everyone is at all times. Even if Jean conceded that it might be useful in some way for Vivian to know the family's comings and goings (and with Priscilla, this is fully impossible: her work schedule is on the calendar, but otherwise she refuses to participate), errands like grocery shopping and dry cleaning Jean tends, like most people, to do on an as-needed basis, and therefore she does not always remember to mark them on the calendar. Jean has never quite understood that, for Vivian, managing the calendar comes under the heading of *things she can control*, a category that has drastically dwindled in her later years. It's a need she's always had, but one that has gathered steam since the family moved in. It's so simple, she thinks, to mark the calendar. It prevents so much worry if she knows when people are coming back. If they're coming back. You can imagine how well this has gone with Priscilla, but in fact it has always bothered Jean the most, and her solution has often been to fabricate things for the calendar, just to pacify

Vivian. This was especially necessary while James was alive. Jean had a lot of appointments when James was alive. Lately, though, Jean has not really bothered.

Oh! Vivian says. *I see! What time shall I expect you back?*

Jean sighs. *I don't know, Vivian, an hour maybe.*

Vivian looks at the clock. *Oh, all right then, I'll look for you at eleven-thirty.*

Jean suddenly understands her daughter's tendency toward eye-rolling. Her version of this is just to widen hers while simultaneously clenching her jaw. Part of the thing with Vivian's relationship to the calendar is that she calculates the amount of time she believes any given appointment should take, so that she can anticipate their safe return, and know when to begin worrying. Not worrying isn't an option, though it's been suggested. Jean wants to ask Vivian what she thinks will happen if she doesn't return promptly at eleven-thirty, but she's asked this question many times before, and the response tends to be *Oh! Well, nothing, I suppose*, because it would be improper to speak of possible car accidents or such, and then Jean says, *Right, nothing, Vivian. Nothing will happen, the world will not cease to exist as you know it*, but then later Jean feels bad about being sarcastic to a ninety-eight-year-old woman, realizes that without the calendar Vivian's world very well might cease to exist, and eventually Jean apologizes. A lose-lose deal. It doesn't matter if the ninety-eight-year-old woman is bitchy and controlling. It's just not nice to be mean to the elderly. Jean's better than that. But. Things are a little different right now.

Jean picks up the red pen that's tied to the calendar with a string, marks on today's date MARKET, and walks out.

EVER SINCE THE FAMILY noticed Vivian's interest in mechanical toys, they've been a staple of her Christmas stocking. At ninety-eight, she's accumulated quite a collection—a drawer full, actually—and she likes to take them out now and again, just one at a time, and demonstrate to the family what great fun they are. One that she's had a particularly enduring affection for has been the Furby she got about a dozen or so Christmases ago, whenever it was that they were popular. This one she keeps out on her dresser. Vivian believes, wrongly, that it responds directly to what she says, that it repeats her words much as a parrot does. She thinks it's just darling, just a marvelous thing, even though she's never seen half of what it can do, although we suspect that if she ever saw it interact with another Furby she'd freak out completely. What this one does is quite enough. It says *Sun up!* in the morning, every morning, which cheers her to no end; it says *Tickle!*, which she does; it says *Again!*, and *Whee!*, and it dances, and says *Boo* when it doesn't like something. But Vivian's favorite thing of all is that it says *Love*. When the Furby says *Love* to Vivian, she very nearly believes it loves her, and we know for sure that she loves it. It has appeared, at times, that Vivian loves the Furby more than she loves her own family, more than her beloved fancy college-going nephew, more than just about anything. Vivian has always been forthcoming with use of the word "love" toward her family, and in fact even says it with a certain amount of warmth, but pretty much everyone can tell the difference between how she says it to them and how she says it to the Furby. Theodore in particular. Plus, she never says anything snarky to the Furby, which tends to cancel out some of the nicer things she says to the family.

Today is not a good day for the Furby. Vivian's out with her friends and the Furby has started to scream. This particular Furby has never screamed before. Theodore goes into Vivian's room to find out what's going on, quickly locates the source of the scream, and brings the Furby to the kitchen table to see what he can do. Unlike Vivian, Theodore has always understood that the Furby is a piece of machinery, one he can surely stop from screaming if he just opens it up. Unfortunately, with the fur covering the entire thing, Theodore is unable to locate the screws so that he can start taking it apart. He spends a good long time poking and pulling at it too, probably an hour, before he decides to take more serious measures.

Vivian arrives home to a dreadful whirring noise but doesn't add it up until she finds her son at the kitchen table with the power drill. She's much too late. About an hour ago, he drove the drill into the back of the Furby's head. This, unfortunately, is the exact wrong place to do this; it's where the sensor is located. It's hard to know whether Theodore has any ulterior motive in doing this. His interest in taking things apart may be masking a separate but equal interest in destroying something his mother appears to treasure more than she does him. It's entirely possible that Theodore himself doesn't know.

Now, the kitchen table is strewn with tiny pelts of fur, little wheels and springs, a beak and a bare pair of eyeballs.

As with the can opener, the parts of which are now in a box on his desk (having been retrieved from the trash by Jean, who knew Vivian had thrown it away, and knew how upset Theodore would be about letting it go, even if he never did get to it again), Theodore is sure this will all work out just fine. Vivian is beside herself. *Oh! Oh, Theodore, what have you done! Where is anyone when you get into these things, I swear!*

She scurries into the main house. Otis is at the kitchen table doing some homework. Vivian is unable to conceal how distraught she is. She stands in the doorway, looking around for Jean.

Where's your mother, dear?

She went to the store.

I don't think that was on the calendar.

What's the matter, Gramma Bibbie?

Vivian has never cared for this nickname, it sounds too much like Libby, the name of a runny-nosed girl she'd known in elementary school. But *Bibbie* had been bestowed on her by two-year-old Priscilla, whose Vs and Bs were one and the same, and the name had stuck around even after she worked that out.

Oh! Your grandfather destroyed my Furby!

No one has ever seen Vivian cry, because she doesn't. Not even alone. Ever. Hasn't since she was a small child. But in this moment, there's a feeling moving up into her throat and close to her eyes that she does not like one bit, and is working hard to overcome. But not before Otis sees it.

Oh no, Gramma Bibbie, that's terrible! Otis gets up and gives Vivian a hug. She's a bit frozen. She's usually fine with hugging, but presently feels unable to respond in kind. It feels to her as though her arms at her sides are containing all of her, that to release them would be to let loose something she's not prepared for, that perhaps what's been happening to her son is worse than what's happened to her toy, that sons are not supposed to go before mothers, that life without her husband *and* her son would be unendurable. So she continues to stand there for as long as her grandson hugs her—the longest hug of her life, she is sure—in the hope that the moment will pass.

This is one of the worst days of Vivian's life.

twenty-nine

Gordon's up in the middle of the night thinking about his problem. He frankly can't understand why Trudy would think *he* was the stalker. He was simply trying to get to the bottom of his memory loss. For a moment he tries to put himself in her position, to imagine what it might be like for a person you were once intimately entangled with to hear that they have been forgotten, that they were not memorable to you. Oh. Hm. But he doesn't have time to take it further than that. His is the more serious problem, the one that needs immediate attention.

Lately, he's been doing puzzles and memory games; he's heard these can improve one's memory. He's even taken a bit of interest in Otis's crossword puzzles, though he sometimes finds them more difficult than, say, a *Times* puzzle. As you might imagine, Otis's puzzles, which often use words drawn from his life, tend to leave Gordon mystified—which only serves to confirm, of course, that his mental problem is real and may be worsening.

Earlier today, Gordon sat down with Otis and a cross-word he'd recently created. Examples of clues Gordon gets stuck on:

a. 3 across. "Talks too much," seven letters. Ironically, Gordon is not thinking of a person—which in this case would be Bethany—and has no self-awareness about how much he himself talks; instead he tries to think of seven-letter synonyms for talking too much. *Rambling?* Too many letters. *Garrulous?* Also too many. Never mind that he's sure Otis wouldn't know the word "garrulous." *Verbose?* No, there's an F in FREAK where the B goes that he's fairly certain of; even Gordon couldn't miss that clue.

b. 21 across. The clue is "Up in your head." The correct five-letter answer is CHAIR. Gordon can't imagine it's anything but BRAIN, and he already has the A and the I, but trying to make BRAIN fit practically makes Gordon's brain swell right out of his head.

c. 7 down. The clue is "They kill themselves," six letters. Gordon's mind, of course, is nowhere remotely near the correct answer, LOVERS, even though OVER is already right there for him. Nor does he add up that these very personal clues in his son's puzzle might indicate some issues that needed addressing. He has a vague memory that there's an insect genus that kills itself after mating, but he can't think of it. He plugs in the S at the end, since he knows from the clue that it's a plural, then tries a series of letters to make actual words: COVERS, MOVERS, ROVERS, HOVERS, LOVERS. Gordon vaguely recalls that he may have mentioned *Romeo and Juliet* a time or two; could that be it? That must be it. Though he doubts he'd have said "kill themselves" to his young son. Could Otis have overheard the news about that teacher friend of Jean's? What would that have to do with lovers, though? Does he want to know? He doesn't. Needless to say, the fact that he can't think of something he usually has within easy reach is extremely disturbing.

So now he's awake in the middle of the night, going over the puzzle in his head, concluding that he's royally screwed, mentally. Perhaps he hasn't been paying enough attention to his kids or his wife; perhaps he actually *has* repressed traumas, as his shrink suggested, or has suffered some kind of brain injury, as his doctor hinted. He goes downstairs for an extra pint of blueberry juice, one of the superfoods he's heard can improve memory, and sits down in front of the TV to try to get his mind off his mind. He passes over several channels he's ordinarily quite interested in. The History Channel is showing a rerun of *Swamp People*; Gordon silently laments that the History Channel has lost its focus on history. PBS is showing *This Old House*, which he loves but which isn't quite the ticket. Usually he'd watch any episode of Paula Deen more than once; he loves cooking shows and secretly finds her sexy. But what he's hoping for right now is an episode of *Nova*, or something about the brain, specifically about what if an ex-girlfriend comes around and you can't remember her. No such luck. Changing channels, he finally lands on something better: an infomercial for something called *Stop Memory Loss*. The product itself is not immediately identified, but in his present state Gordon would order this product if it involved strapping himself to a rocket and blasting himself to Mars. One caller on the show describes his experience with the product, claiming not just that his memory improved, but that he felt imbued with a renewed sense of purpose. Gordon is on the phone, credit card in hand, faster than you can say *This is a very misguided idea indeed.*

thirty

I t's been weeks since Priscilla's heard anything about the reality show. She hasn't completely given up the delusion that something will happen, in spite of the fucked-up fact that Taylor's gone back in several times. Until Priscilla gets this text from Taylor: *O. M. F. G. Flying 2 LALA!*

Oh, please let this be some weird family vacation, Priscilla thinks (even though Taylor's family's idea of vacation is spending a night at the casino boat in the next town over), and not what she knows is true. Priscilla calls her up immediately.

What the fuck are you even talking about, Tay?

Priscilla has to hold the phone away from Taylor's squeals. *They're flying me to Hollywood! Hollywood! This is it, P! Fucking Hollywood!*

And you're going?

What? Of course I'm going, what are you talking about?

What are you talking about? Last week you didn't even care that much.

Well, I care now! I'm going to Hollywood!

I can't believe you'd do this without me.

What?

If it was the other way around, I wouldn't go without you.

Oh, that is bull fucking crap. Get over yourself.

I wouldn't. It is, of course, the biggest bunch of bullshit ever.

You're out of your freaking bitch mind. Nobody wouldn't go to Hollywood.

I wouldn't. Not without my supposedly best friend.

Why are you being like this? You should be happy for me!

You should be sensitive to me.

Oh my god, get a fucking life!

Of course, this is exactly what Priscilla needs to do, but exactly what no one ever does because someone tells them to do it.

Well, I would—but somebody fucking stole mine right out from under me.

I didn't steal anything from you!

You knew how much I wanted this.

Priscilla, you're being a fucking cunt pill! This isn't about you!

Well, I feel how I feel. Have a great trip. I hope you get the fucking show and become a superstar of reality TV and have Brad Pitt and Tom Cruise's fucking stupid foreign babies and live happily the fuck ever after.

Taylor is in the middle of screaming *Tom Cruise doesn't have foreign babies!* but Priscilla hangs up on *doesn't*. This actually isn't even the worst fight they've ever had, but it's for sure the one Priscilla will hold on to the longest.

Priscilla remembers the Great Dollhouse Disaster of 1997, when her mother gave her that godawful cracked vinyl suitcase of a Barbie house and tried to pass it off as the Barbie Mansion she'd asked for, the one that Taylor did get. Priscilla has been wondering, since about the age of six, why her parents so misunderstand her. She always felt she was stating her needs perfectly clearly, and yet time and again they went unmet. How could her mom not see the difference between a Barbie mansion and that creaky plastic thing she'd gotten instead? Jean, of course, so excited to hand down her Barbie house, should have realized the reaction she'd get from Priscilla, should have at least given a thought to giving her daughter both the one she asked for *and* her own old one. Instead, she'd seen this as a chance for them to share something, for her daughter to know who she had been at Priscilla's age— that she *had* once been Priscilla's age. So she wrapped it up and gave it to her for Christmas, and Priscilla had not hidden her displeasure. *This is* not *what I wanted*, she'd said, pushing it away without even looking inside. Jean opened the doors and laid the furniture out, hopeful that Priscilla would change her mind. *Look, sweetheart, here is the sofa and chair for the living room, and there's this neat little chandelier over here, I thought this was the coolest thing when I was your age . . .*

That's not a chandelier, that's a picture of a chandelier.

Well, honey, you have to use your imagination.

No, I don't!

Look, sweetie, here's the bedroom over here, I had so much fun playing with this, here's the bed . . .

But it's orange. Priscilla said the word "orange" as though it were the color of poop. *And it looks like a soap dish or something.* She pushed it away.

Here's the little closet . . .

That's not a closet! It's flat!

You have to pretend, honey, it's pretend.

We can't lie. It may have seemed pretty radical when Jean was a girl, but this dollhouse was pretty weak. Even the earlier, cardboard model was way cooler than this.

No! I don't want to pretend! I need the mansion! It has real little hangers. I can't hang clothes in that. The clothes hangers were key because the clothes were key. Surely her mom knew how important clothes had already become to young Priscilla. She hadn't been old enough to consider detailing the finer points of why the mansion was preferable, and was too young to appreciate what her mom had been trying to do. She'd felt like a forgotten old dress in the back of the closet.

Just after this, Priscilla went to Taylor's house for a playdate—where Taylor proceeded to show off the very same mansion Priscilla had so wanted. Priscilla could hardly hide her jealousy, though she was eager to examine and play with it. It was three stories tall, all pink, and had bathrooms and real furniture and everything. All Priscilla had gotten, besides the *used* house, was a few new outfits for her Barbies. Taylor began to point out each and every feature of the mansion and was showing her the closet when Priscilla couldn't take it anymore.

Look! Taylor had already hung up some of her Barbie's clothes on the tiny hangers, laid a dozen pairs of her little plastic shoes in a row on the floor.

Priscilla ground her teeth, stood up, and pushed over the entire mansion on her way out.

Theodore had seen his granddaughter's reaction that Christmas Day, and he wasn't proud of her, but he loved her, and wanted her to be happy. So he built her a dollhouse. Jean was not thrilled about the idea of encouraging her daughter that way, but she knew she'd miscalculated, and Theodore said that grandfathers were allowed, and she knew it would give him pleasure. The house he built was four stories tall, a foot taller than Priscilla herself. It had four bedrooms, two baths, a fireplace, and electricity; at Jean's suggestion, it even had a closet, with a working door and a real bar across it. He set in parquet floors, made most of the furniture, fixtures, and fittings, built bookshelves and beds, sofas and tables, using wood or things around the house (regular dollhouse furniture was not Barbie-scale), and convinced Jean to sew curtains and linens and even make a real hook rug with a punch needle. It took Theodore three months to build, and it was spectacular. Priscilla's initial reaction: unusually silent. It was bigger than Taylor's mansion by a lot, that was a plus, and it had real working lights. But it wasn't plastic. Dollhouses were supposed to be plastic. The best she could do was say thank you and give her grandfather a limp hug, and he didn't appear to notice her seemingly underwhelmed posture.

In fact, though, Priscilla had been entirely conflicted by her grandfather's gift. In her heart, she'd been completely blown away by it; it was like nothing she'd ever seen, all the little details he'd put into it incredible. She wished she could step right into it. The whole thing was way better than Taylor's mansion. By this time, with thousands of Saturday-morning TV commercials wedged into her little brain, Priscilla had already learned what had value in the world—things you could *buy*—and this wasn't one of them. Luckily, the envy of her friends would turn things partway around; every time Ashley and Danielle came over they *ooh*ed and *aah*ed, and Taylor was noticeably jealous, though she made a point to say that it wasn't a *real* Barbie mansion. And it was a point that was duly noted by Priscilla.

ON HER WAY OUT to meet her friends, Priscilla passes her father on the stairs. He says her name, but she doesn't stop. Why would she. Gol.

Priscilla! Priscilla, Priscilla. Priscilla.

Priscilla spins her head around as though her father has just said "Fuck you! Fuck you, fuck you. Fuck you." *What?* She pronounces "what" as though it has two syllables, to where the T becomes its own syllable. She doesn't even want to say "Dad" out loud right now because of the implication— that he is. Her dad.

Hey, do you go online very often? How come you haven't ac- cepted my friend request?

Priscilla rolls her eyes, as though the question deserves an actual answer. Apparently it does, but if he can't figure it out on his own she's not going to be the one to tell him.

Wow, like, really right now? Seriously?

Of course I'm serious.

Okay. Whatever, Dad. Shit, she said it. *I'm late. 'K, bye!* Priscilla puts an exaggerated uptilt on her "K, bye" here, at- tempting to leave things on an up note, but never has a "bye" been less sincere.

PRISCILLA, ASHLEY, AND DANIELLE meet at their favorite club; the plan is for them all to get shit-faced. Before long, Priscilla is more than halfway there.

She has no qualms about dissing Taylor behind her back. It's what she does. Well, it's what they all do, but P does it the most. By a lot. She leans in to her friends, yells over the booming bass, *I mean, I wouldn't do that to her if I knew she cared as much as I did.* Ashley and Danielle both say *Totally*, both look into their drinks and sip through their cocktail straws. Priscilla would totally do that to Taylor, and all three of them know it. Four, if you include Taylor. The reality is, each one of them would have gotten on that plane just as fast as Taylor, had the offer come their way instead. It's just that Priscilla is the only one who perceives it as a slight. *It's just like her. Like, she didn't even care. You guys didn't go. Why did she have to go? Fuck her. Right?* Ashley and Danielle say nothing. *Fuck her.* Priscilla's pretty drunk by the end of this. *Fuck* comes out *Fup.*

Priscilla's ex-boyfriend, Kyle (of the fucked-up status update) is there. She's long over him by now, at least in the sense that she no longer cares about him. The damage from the incident, of course, has far outlasted her feelings for Kyle. He publicly humiliated her *and* broke her trust, and her solution to this problem has been to put guys on an indefinite back burner—and/or, with a few drinks in her, to tease them as she sees fit. Tonight she wants to be noticed, so she's dancing provocatively on a speaker, although the only reason she's dancing on the speaker is because there's no pole, and we have to be thankful there's no pole, because if there were a pole, Priscilla might be doing more than just dancing.

Priscilla shakes it to "Bootylicious," mouths a few of the words she knows in Kyle's direction (*I don't think you're ready for this jelly*). Ashley yells up to Priscilla to get her to come down, but she waves her off—she's in a zone. Kyle goes over to the girls, leans his body in, and says, loud enough so that Priscilla can hear: *Your friend's a fucking slut.* She closes her eyes, unwilling to let him have the satisfaction of any little response from her, though it does sting for a second. Nothing another swig of her mojito won't fix. Priscilla's hardly surprised that Kyle's being a dick again, and she knows she's not really a slut, that she's an adult, and tonight what she wants is attention, someone's attention. She's gotten Kyle's attention, at least, and for the moment that'll do.

Shut up, Kyle, Ashley says. *You're a fucking dick.*

Kyle, also intoxicated, says to Ashley, *What did you say?*

Kyle, of course, heard Ashley. *You're lucky I don't hit girls.*

Danielle tries to push Kyle away. *Kyle, just leave her alone, get out of here.*

Priscilla gives Kyle the finger and incorporates it into her dance.

You're a fucking slut, slut!

Priscilla smiles, twirls, looks away, looks back at him, tries to make her dance extra-slutty just to egg him on, almost loses her footing as one ankle wobbles, not really so super sexy as she thinks, but she recovers. (In case you were wondering, Priscilla isn't any kind of slut. As noted, she's been with exactly two guys, Kyle and another boy she dated her sophomore year for a couple of months. She'll tell you there's no one really worth giving it up to in this town, which may or may not be true. For sure the guys she's met aren't, but we don't know that there aren't one or two nice guys out there that Priscilla might not run into.) For a moment she closes her eyes again, and as she rotates her hips and runs her hands along her own pretty slammin' body, she forgets about Kyle, the TV show, everything. It's all about this moment, up on the speaker. It's a great night.

Tomorrow she'll remember none of it. No, that's not true. She'll remember one thing: *Slut.*

thirty-one

All kinds of misses at dinner tonight. Jean had spent the afternoon in the kitchen making a gumbo recipe she found online, hoping to take her mind off things. She gets compliments on the meal—it came out fine—but as for the success of the recipe erasing her obsessive grief, no such luck. At the moment, she's back on the idea that James was just so close to life, that if she'd just gotten there a few minutes earlier . . . She feels her chin trembling and clenches her jaw to stop that from taking her over.

Priscilla is the only one doing much talking tonight. She's still hung over from the night before at the club, but she wants to talk. *Uch, it was so messed up. Kyle was there being a total douche. He has no business. Like, no business. Like, who even asked him to get in my face?*

Vivian says, *I was engaged twice before your great-grandfather, you know.*

They do know.

Honey, Jean says, *true love is a very rare thing.*

Mom, what are you even talking about right now?

Nothing, nothing, Jean says.

Is Kyle your lover? Otis asks.

What? No, Priscilla says, *Otis, where did you—*

Gordon flashes to his son's crossword puzzle—it was LOVERS, he was right—

Anyone want some more gumbo? Jean jumps in before they go down that road. *There's plenty!*

—and now, observing his wife's oddly cheerful effort at diversion, Gordon's synapses start firing, a few of them at least, but then Theodore pipes in—

Remember when we used to go out in the canoe, Otis, when you were small?

I do, Grampa, can we do that again?

Sure! Theodore says. Jean shakes her head in Otis's direction. That's not going to happen.

—and just like that, Gordon is back in the present. He hadn't liked those last thoughts anyway, not at all, was sure there was nothing to it anyway. *Maybe I'll take you in the canoe, Otis.*

We can all go! Otis says.

Jean shakes her head again, to no one in particular this time.

I just still can't believe Taylor up and went to L.A. like that without even asking me how I felt about it, Priscilla says. *Who does that? I've never wanted anything so much in my life.*

What's that, dear? Vivian asks.

The TV show. The one I auditioned for. The one I've been talking about for ten minutes.

Oh! Well. Vivian thinks it's all so very unseemly. Proper

young ladies don't go to lounges like these unescorted. And television! If Priscilla intended to go to law school first, Vivian supposes, like that Nancy Grace, then maybe, maybe—but she doesn't suppose that's what her great-granddaughter has in mind. And for heaven's sake, the girl's knees are showing in that skirt she has on, and her hair is hanging down in her eyes. Vivian reaches over to push Priscilla's hair behind her ears. *Do you like your hair like that, dear? You should let me take you to my salon.* Priscilla's eyes nearly bug out of her head. Gramma Bibbie's hair is like, just this side of violet.

Yuh, thanks, Gramma, Priscilla says, moving her head out of the way.

Now, how is school going for you, dear?

Uch, Priscilla says.

Theodore's med schedule was a little off today and currently he's asleep, with his spoon, precariously loaded with gumbo, still in his hand. He wakes up when Mott licks his ankle, giggles, lifts the spoon to his mouth as though pauses for naps between bites were only necessary.

Your cousin graduated from Princeton! Vivian says.

Yuh, I heard, Gramma Bibbie.

With honors!

Remember when we used to go out in the canoe, Otis? When you were small? Theodore says.

Otis nods, doesn't know what to say when his grandfather repeats himself.

We should do that again.

Listen, Gordon says to his daughter, *just be grateful you can remember what happened last night.*

Priscilla looks at her father like he's on crack, looks around the table. These people are seriously stroking out right now. Priscilla has no idea what anyone's talking about. Has it ever been this bad?

Eleven inches from the floor. Jean just about smacks her own head with the heel of her hand to get the thought out.

Why they decide to stretch this out and play a game as well is anyone's guess.

After the table is cleared, Otis hands out papers, pencils, and a pile of books he's picked out for a game of Liebrary. It's a variation on Dictionary that he'd played recently at school—it's his suggestion. *Except instead of writing a definition, you write the first sentence of the book*, Otis says. *We each take a turn being the "reader"—that person shows the book title and writes down the real first sentence, and then collects everyone's made-up sentences, and reads them out loud.* Priscilla volunteers to be the reader for the first round because she doesn't want to write. *And then we go around the table and we all guess which one is the real one, just the same way we do with Dictionary. It's fun!* Priscilla rolls her eyes, holds up *A Confederacy of Dunces*.

I don't know what confederacy means, Otis says.

An association of sovereign states or communities, Gordon says.

What's sovereign?

Well, son, sovereignty is when you have supreme, independent authority over a geographic area, such as a territory.

Seriously, it's like Dad memorizes Wikipedia entries, Priscilla thinks. In fact, that's exactly what he does. He doesn't intend to, he just has a good memory for things most people in his family find useless.

Otis is still confused.

It's like a group, Baby Freak.

Everyone works on their sentences, then one by one hands their slips of paper to Priscilla to be read. She hands Theodore's back to him for a second, says she can't read one of the words, points to it. He erases and tries to rewrite it more legibly. His handwriting was never good, but it's full-on wavy now.

You have to shuffle them so we don't know whose is whose, Otis tells Priscilla. *Because of if anyone was watching you collect them.*

No one was.

Okay, Priscilla says. *Here we go.* She shuffles them and reads the first one.

Once upon a time, there were some guys who were not so smart, and one of them was in love with a lady named ~~Caterina~~ Mary.

Otis has actually won this game one or two times, but the tell here, aside from "Once upon a time," is the word "lady."

Janet believed that her lover had been healed because she believed that she had been healed, that they had healed each other; she was wrong.

At first, Gordon is certain this one is Vivian's; she reads a lot of paperback romances. For a second, he flashes back to LOVERS from Otis's crossword, then pushes out the implication of that unpleasant thought as quickly as it comes in. It's Vivian's, he's sure. Otis is the only one who will guess this one correctly. But, really, he won't even know why. It's an instinct, but he doesn't make much of it.

~~Sebastian Montgomery~~ A man woke up to realize he had forgotten everything.

Jean has no idea this one is Gordon's. She's still entirely unaware of his concern about his memory. Like Jean, if he's talked about it at all he's done so in the abstract. Gordon had the good last-minute sense to cross out his giveaway, Sebastian Montgomery.

A green hunting cap squeezed the top of the fleshy balloon of a head.

A lot of them think this one is Gordon's.

The dunces were getting really tired of the corner.

Everyone knows this one is Theodore's, and it provides a welcome moment of laughter. Theodore has to wipe his eyes with his hanky from his own joke.

A slim, elegant woman in a timeless suit sat behind the wheel of a magnificent driving machine with the top down.

Gordon has gotten his wife's and his grandmother's mixed up. He's now sure that this last one is Jean's. It's nicely written, he thinks, and believable.

Gordon's first line wins the round.

Priscilla so doesn't want to play again, but the light in her grandfather's eyes makes her stick around for one more.

She huffs. Vivian takes her turn as the reader this time. She's not much fonder of writing than Priscilla is. She put about all she had into that last one. She holds up the book, *Catch-22*, writes the first line down, notices it's time for Nancy Grace, changes the channel on the remote, turns the volume up loud. When Vivian and/or Theodore are in the room, the volume tends to be up to unbearable levels—unbearable, at least, for Jean. She sneaks it down when she thinks they're not paying attention, puts on the closed-captioning. Priscilla grumbles while writing, Otis writes and erases several times, Theodore chuckles.

They all hand their papers back to Vivian.

Don't forget to shuffle them, Gramma Bibbie, Otis says. Vivian shuffles, reads.

~~She~~ *He wondered if ~~she~~ he would ever make sense of what happened.*

It was the most magnificent work of art anyone had ever seen.

It was love at first sight.

Gordon and Theodore guess Priscilla on this last one; Jean guesses Otis. Priscilla rolls her eyes. Gol, does, like, one person at this table know her? No one guesses that this is the real first line. Most of them think Jean's is the real one.

The fisherman was sad.

Something ~~big huge~~ big was ~~totally~~ about to happen.

He was hoping to catch 24, but 22 was the best he could do.

Most of them giggle, they all know this one is Theodore's, but a few guesses are made; some of the lines are more convincing this time, and no one is close to guessing the real one—everyone thinks the real one is Jean's, *He wondered if he would ever make sense of what happened*—so the game starts to fall apart before they cast their final votes. Priscilla has sent twenty texts, can't pull herself away from her phone. Theodore is distracted by the dog, gets up to get him treats, comes back, gives him one, falls asleep. Mott licks Vivian's ankle. *Oh! Goodness, that dog.* She gets up to clean herself up. *Honestly.* Game over.

thirty-two

Gordon has been taking the memory loss powder from TV for about a week. He has no idea what's in it and he doesn't care. He's got a strange energy, upbeat but strange—like when people are interested in you but, you know, *too* interested in you? Gordon was never glum, but nor was he chipper like this, smiley and wide-eyed. Seriously, it's weird, ask Priscilla. Suddenly at meals, when anyone says anything even remotely personal, her dad is all up in their grill. Like when she mentions Taylor's Hollywood trip again and how she's super bummed that she never got called back, her dad nods, like a lot, like he's got this weirdo look in his eye that's supposed to be concern but really just makes her concerned for him. *Oh, oh, I see*, Gordon says, *well no, that doesn't seem fair at all, not fair at all.* Or when Otis mentions he needs money for his school trip to an apple-picking farm, Gordon says, *Apple-picking! Doesn't that sound like fun! How much do you need?* At this point, the entire family falls into stunned silence, because they've heard many different talks on the subject of apples over the years, and no one can believe

that Gordon has made what seems to be an appropriate response, one that vaguely opens the door for a response back,
even if given in this bizarrely eager fashion.

Also, he's begun making paintings. He's moved everything around in the garage, always more of a storage space
than a place for cars anyway, and made it into a haphazard
studio. After he started taking the memory loss powder, briefly uncertain about what to do with the extra energy he had,
gazing at a favorite Matisse print in his office, he got it in his
head to pick up a paintbrush. The idea had seized him seemingly out of the blue, but once it popped in, it seemed to him
like it had always been there and he was in the car and at the
craft store dropping hundreds of dollars on supplies. He is
worrying less and less about his memory loss, caring less and
less about anything but painting. Several of the paintings are
so large that they won't fit out the garage door unless he takes
them off their stretchers.

Outside of one class in college, Gordon has zero training in art, although as can be expected, he claims to know
a lot about it from having visited the Art Institute and the
Prado. He's taken art in high school but only as required,
and he's never taken a figure drawing class of any kind, so
his figures are minus any sort of naturalistic dimension or
proportion. They look kind of flat. There's one of Trudy that
shows her face absent of any features; in the background is
Sheila the belly dancer. Sheila has a fully-featured face. The
paintings are not terrible at all, they actually have a sort of
outsider art feel to them, like maybe if you thought this guy
had spent his childhood locked in a cabinet under the stairs

you'd think they were brilliant; there's something compelling about them, in an awkward sort of way. Technically, of course, he *is* an outsider, but somehow this seems too elevated or legitimate or something to apply right now. Maybe later. He's not thinking past this moment right now, for a change.

Mostly, so far, he's been doing self-portraits. In one, Gordon is standing with his fists clenched, arms down but sort of out to the side by his hips, with a sort of constipated look on his face, his brain floating over his head. It's the first in a series he's started of the family. Right now he's just sketching; he's got five more life-sized canvases set up next to his, life-sized meaning each one is the exact height of the family member plus a foot on each side to leave room for the figure to pose however they might pose. At the moment, he's got nothing more than their basic body shapes penciled in. He sits down to contemplate what to do next. For the third time this week, Gordon is late for work. It's possible, today, that he won't make it in at all. He feels brilliance coming any minute.

thirty-three

Priscilla has been asked to mind her grandfather for most of a day when everyone else has other plans. She agrees, probably because she just got out of bed and can't think up an excuse quickly enough, and even though there are numerous requirements for the job, including helping him get around the house, making sure he doesn't leave the house on his own when he spots a squirrel (the last time he did that, he came very close to falling into the goldfish pond), and changing his bedsheets and/or his adult diaper and/or his clothes. He's somewhat able to do all these things on his own, but he has better and worse days.

Priscilla's day is a worse day.

On Priscilla's day, she and her grandfather sit down to play a round of Spite and Malice. The family had played several rounds the week before, and Theodore had won two rounds, as he often did. Today, Priscilla's grandfather repeatedly tries to lay down cards completely out of sequence—a seven on top of a four, a nine on top of a jack, and so on. The first time or two, Priscilla just figures he's distracted by a pretty bird or something, but as it happens again and again, her concern begins to grow. A few times, she tries explaining his mistakes.

No, Grampa, that's a four, you can only play a five there.

Oh sure, he'll say. From where Priscilla's sitting, it's impossible to tell whether he actually gets it, or whether he minds even if he doesn't. He seems unruffled. Eventually it becomes clear that they can't really continue to play this way, around the same time that she begins to notice an especially gnarly smell coming from his direction.

Do you need to get changed, Grampa?

This is one of the only things Theodore ever makes any complaint about—it's humiliating, and he doesn't like to admit that he's soiled himself, or that he needs help.

Mm. He shrugs. *Maybe.*

Priscilla wheels him toward the bathroom. He can get his pants down, easy enough to remove his suspenders from his shoulders, unzip and drop trou, but needs help getting the diaper off and his bottom cleaned.

Priscilla is not prepared for this. Like, not even. Nor is she prepared for this in herself: she steps up. She's completely grossed out, don't get us wrong, the smell is awful, there's a giant shit in a giant diaper and it's for sure the grossest thing she's ever seen. She would rather do a lot of things besides pick that diaper up off the floor, wipe her grandfather's ass, and see his droopy balls, which are nearly down by his knees, no lie. But in this moment, she actually kind of wants to cry. Like, for *him*. Like, what she wants to cry about is not how severely gross this moment is for her, or her fear of death or anything like that (which frankly she's never understood, because if you're dead aren't you just *dead* and pretty obviously not worrying about much?). What she feels is genuine sadness for her grampa. That's way new.

thirty-four

Jean goes back to the support group one last time. She's tried everything she can think of to stop her brain, and nothing's worked. But the support group is the same as it was the last time. A bunch of mopey, touchy-feely types who believe in angels and think things happen for a reason. One has the audacity to say that she's sure god gave her a parking space right out front of the building today because she was about to be late for group. Another woman actually says that she believes her mother died so that she could make room for her to *shine*.

What the hell are these people even talking about? *Shine*? The anger that's risen in her lately, her odium for the dead-angel speak at her support group, has grown into a rotten bile. Jean can't help herself. *You believe that?*

Fair to say this comes under the heading of what the social worker calls *crosstalk*, a no-no. The group is supposed to be a place where you can share your feelings without judgment among people who understand. A *safe* place. That's rich. Nothing's safe.

Yes, says the woman. *I do.* We're not sure she really does, though we can see that she wants to.

God has a plan for you, says the parking space lady. *A good one.*

Jean, for a millisecond, wishes she believed that, shakes it off. *Evidence shows otherwise* is what she says.

More will be revealed.

Do you all really believe this is helping you?

The group is collectively stunned, for the most part, too stunned to speak.

Jean, the social worker says.

No, seriously, what are you all hoping to get here?

Support, Jean, they're here for support, the social worker says. *Everyone feels the same way here.*

Don't tell me how I feel. Do you feel like the person you loved with your whole heart punched you in the face with a spiked boxing glove, while you were still wearing your glasses, and then told you everything you thought was true was a lie? And then handed the glove over to you so you could finish the job yourself? Because that's how I feel. Her chin trembles and her eyes well with tears for the first time since she started coming.

Jean, why don't you tell us what you have been hoping to get by coming here? the social worker asks.

Okay, I'll tell you exactly what I've been hoping for. I've been hoping that I would stop wondering what I should have done differently, what I could have done to prevent this, how if I were a better person, none of this . . . I've been hoping for it to bring my husband back so he can explain to me what happened. I've been hoping for it to bring my husband back so I can ask him what he could have been thinking about, what was so wrong that he wouldn't tell me about, so wrong that he would steal himself from the people who loved him, that he would just leave the world, that he would leave me, why he would make me wonder what true love was all over again after I thought he'd taught me everything I knew about it, if someone could do this to someone they loved, I want it to bring my husband back so he can tell me why the fuck he would make me see what I saw. I want it to bring my husband back. Jean notices, for a hair of a hair of a second, that when she says the word "husband" this last time, she's actually thinking of her real, living husband. But she has no idea what to do with a thought like that, hasn't had a thought like that since long before James came into the picture. *I want it to bring my husband back,* she says again, sniffling. The group nods.

We can explain it, one woman says, timidly handing Jean a tissue.

Tell me, Jean says. This should be good.

It wasn't about you, the woman says.

But it was.

Jean, the social worker says. *No person has that kind of power over another. This didn't happen because you weren't a good person. Your husband made a terrible choice because of the way his brain worked, and no other reason.*

Mmf, Jean says. She shakes her head. *You don't know. You don't know what kind of person I am.* She shakes her head, wipes away tears with her sleeve.

He was mentally ill. You couldn't have done anything even if he had told you. You told us before that some of his family members knew, right?

Yeah.

But they couldn't help him, either.

But I should have been able to. He helped me.

It doesn't work like that, though.

Jean sits with what the group has said for a few moments. She's obviously not making herself clear. She understands parts of what they're saying. In her head, she understands the meaning of the words "mental illness," when said together in this way. But what it feels like to Jean is in battle with what actually makes real sense. James had given parts of her back to herself, she had thought, and when he left the way he left, he took those things with him. But these thoughts aren't fully formed in her head, they're just information fragments mixed with feelings that she isn't able to get out of her mouth. *It was about me. It was about me,* Jean thinks. It had never been about her, not ever, not until James. *It was about me.*

thirty-five

Theodore is sitting at the kitchen table considering some new rocks for his crèche when Mott comes in and licks him on the face. Theodore giggles and opens the door to let the dog out, but he doesn't go, turns around to look at Theodore like he wants company. Well, sure he does. Theodore gets up from the table, hooks the leash that's by the door onto Mott's collar, fumbles with this a bit, it's tricky, doesn't want to stay open long enough to hook on to the loop—*Op! There it goes*—and heads out into the meadow with the dog. He's still in his slippers, and before he makes it to the fish pond, one of those will be gone. No big deal. Oh, isn't he a good boy, this dog! What a wonderful companion, it's been just terrific having him around. *Let's go see the fish, what do you say, Mott?* Theodore's last trip to the fish pond hadn't gone well, he doesn't remember it that way, but so far no spills.

At the edge of the pond, he peers down. *Oh, they look hungry!* he says. We're not sure what the fish are doing to indicate their hunger, but Theodore seems to. *We better give them something to eat.* He plunges his hand into a small covered tub beside the fish pond and pulls out a handful of flakes for the fish, tosses it in, and the fish quickly swim to the surface. *Oh! Oh that's a good photo right there.* He's got his camera with him, and he used to be a decent photographer, but at this point if he gets something that's not entirely out of focus, or half out of the frame, it's kind of just random, though very often there's a certain abstract beauty to what emerges. Theodore lifts his camera, snaps a few photos of fish mouths at the surface, an orange-and-white Richter-esque blur. May as well head on down to the wildflower walk and see what's going on over there. *Op! A vole!* Mott bounds after it, thankfully the leash drops out of Theodore's loose grip rather than pull him to the ground. Theodore snaps a few more photos, though the vole is in none of them. Phooey. Of course, the vole makes it away from Mott safely, and the dog ambles back over to Theodore, who tells him not to *pull that funny stuff again.*

The wildflower walk provides all kinds of discoveries. Critters, flowers, rocks. *Forget-me-nots! Oh, those were a favorite of Laura's, Mott. Oh, these would have pleased her tremendously.* Theodore snaps a few more photos, streaky cerulean swoosh- es. He spends not a few minutes examining and rejecting rocks before pocketing one to bring back for his crèche. *Ooh, this one has a bit of lichen on it, that's pretty.* He's about to pick up a small greenish rock and put it in his pocket when he dis- covers it's actually a toad. *Op!* He chuckles, not sure how he couldn't tell a rock from a toad. He snaps a few more photos but it's gone. Oh wait, there it is! He snaps one last photo as it jumps out of the frame, an unidentifiable green streak.

Theodore will obtain a few scrapes on his feet and arms from uncut branches, but will return to the house with the dog and no one will be the wiser. Oh, this has been so marvelous, Theodore thinks. What a wonderful companion Mott is. *Tomorrow I'm going to mail my paper off, Mott. Would you like to come with me to the post office? Well, sure you would, sure you would.* He pats Mott on the head. The meaning of *tomorrow* as relates to Theodore's current world has variables; in his mind it still means the day after the current day (though it may help to know that the current meaning of *yesterday*, to Theodore, is now sometimes *any* day prior to the current day), but when said aloud to family members, it can mean anything on the scale from later today to never, way more likely toward the never end of the line.

By the time he returns home, he'll have snapped a hundred and forty-eight photos, parts of hemlocks and bittersweet, leaves, rocks, a fat little wren in a bush. That one is almost in focus, though not quite centered in the frame. *These are fine*, Theodore thinks. *Just fine.*

When Jean asks Theodore about the scrapes, he says *Oh, I don't know. Someplace. S'fine.*

thirty-six

Otis is in his room, preparing for the field trip. His jelly beans, for the time being, are displayed on a Scrabble tile holder, but he does still plan on creating something more permanent. Probably they shouldn't just sit out in the open air like that. He doesn't have any ideas or thoughts about what the shelf life of a jelly bean is, packaged or otherwise, but doesn't want them collecting dust or bugs or anything else gross he can't think of. He's seen some clear little bead boxes about an inch in diameter in his mother's craft stuff that might work.

He has chosen this moment to eat one of the pomegranate beans so he can have two flavors to discuss with Caterina. The pomegranate, unsurprisingly, isn't a whole lot better than the birthday cake; kind of tart, not what you'd expect of a red bean, knowing how good cherry and strawberry are, but thinking about it, the pomegranate bean has that marbled-y look to it that can go either way, like chili mango, which is straight-up nasty, or tutti-frutti, which is outstanding as jelly bean flavors go. If Caterina would one day share a tutti-frutti bean that would be a magnificent day indeed, but Otis will not make room for the thought that's about to creep in, that Caterina may have shared these beans with him because they were bad, and, or, that if that were true, that she was making some statement about what she thought of Otis by giving him the bad beans, and, or, that she only gave them to him because he happened to be there. He grabs an image of the moment when they looked at each other. The memory of this moment makes many things possible in Otis's mind, and convinces him that Caterina's intentions toward him, with or without beans, is only good.

Otis makes a list of subjects to talk to Caterina about on the apple-picking trip:

1. Bad flavors of jelly beans (birthday cake, pomegranate, and, he assumes, jalapeño)
2. Apples
3. Crossword puzzles
4. Bugs: Where does she stand?
5. Robots
6. Math: What subjects does she like? (Otis actually already knows the answer to this, Caterina likes art, and reading and spelling, but he will ask her anyway.)

Otis figures that these subjects will be more than enough to get the ball rolling, and hopefully lead to other conversations. Also, he has used some of the money his dad gave him for a small package of Jelly Bellies to share with Caterina; he has some remarkable good sense in guessing that giving her a present of Jelly Bellies would be too much of a statement (not that he doesn't want to make that statement, but he senses her overall hesitation in who she befriends, and doesn't want to do anything to scare her away), but supposes that sharing his own could take them to the next level, could say, without having to say, *Now that we're sharing beans, would you like to be my lover?* Also in Otis's backpack: pencils, random colored markers, a three-ring binder, a tin robot that's one of his favorites, the lunch his mom has fixed him; in the side pocket, six dollars and change left over from the ten his dad gave him; on the left side, a copy of one of his older crossword puzzles from before he started putting her in them; on the right, some printouts of paper robots he likes to cut out and glue together.

At school, Otis makes a critical mistake in boarding the chartered school bus; he gets on first, before Caterina, but realizes too late that he should have prepared a seating plan. His last-minute plan is to sit close to the front and block anyone but Caterina from sitting next to him, and then to slide over and make room just as Caterina approaches his seat. This isn't exactly how it goes down, but a small miracle happens anyway: she sits across the aisle from him. It's a small miracle because Otis knows Bethany's not far behind on the line and also because there's still potential for someone to try to shove in on his side, too. Mostly, though, the rest of the kids shove down to the end of the bus, and though Bethany does indeed sit next to Caterina, Caterina makes her take the window seat.

And then this: Caterina turns to Otis and speaks. She begins a conversation. This day is already exceeding expectations. What Caterina says almost doesn't even register with Otis, so surprised is he that she has spoken first.

I don't want to sit next to the window in case the bus crashes.

What is this? This fearful confession is opening a door Otis was not expecting. What do you say to this? Otis does not know. He runs through his list of topics and cannot figure out how to tie possible bus crashes in to any of them. He will have to think of something on the spot. Time is moving forward. How long has it been? In reality, about ten seconds, in Otis's mind, the sun is beginning to set. Say something, anything.

Is that better? In a crash? Sitting in the middle?

I think so.

Studying her face closely, Otis sees that Caterina looks extremely worried about the possibility of the bus crashing. She hasn't yet mentioned to Otis that she has just seen the movie *Speed* on TV. Caterina's parents, inattentive in a whole different set of ways to the ones Otis has experienced, have neglected to vet her viewing choices, so over time she has seen numerous films and television programs far more inappropriate than *Speed*, among them *Nip/Tuck*, but for whatever reason *Speed* is the one that has affected her, the one that has reached into her and hit something. Otis knows, now that Caterina has shared her deepest fear with him, that he can share his, too. He knows exactly what to say to begin their marathon, daylong conversation.

Do you ever think that you'll kill yourself?

Caterina does not understand the question. She has, of course, not thought at all about killing herself, though she has, at least indirectly, thought about being killed, as in a bus crash.

I don't think so. Why, do you?

No. But my mother said that's what lovers do.

Again, we can only be thankful that in Caterina's mind the word "lovers" is coming out to mean "people who love" and nothing more. And, in fact, that is more or less how Otis has come to understand it. He loves Caterina, and although he doesn't know if she loves him, his hope that it's possible puts her in the category of people who might possibly kill themselves.

On purpose, you mean?

I guess, Otis says. He has yet to draw any conclusions about the whys or hows of it.

Caterina takes a moment to consider it. *No. If I killed myself it would only be on accident.*

This is the best news Otis has ever heard. The best news ever.

Do you like crossword puzzles?

Caterina has no stance on crossword puzzles. *I don't know.* She shrugs. *I like spelling.*

Of course! Otis thinks. Crossword puzzles are *all about* spelling. He could say something to this effect, but all that comes out is *Oh!* Finally he explains that he makes crossword puzzles and takes out his folder to show her. She nods. Her nod is hard to interpret, but one thing he can see for sure is that the worried face she had a few minutes earlier is gone. Otis has successfully gotten his future lover's attention off of buses crashing, has determined that she is not suicidal.

This alone makes it the best day of Otis's life.

thirty-seven

Gordon has not been getting a lot of work done at the office lately. He feels more energetic since he started taking the memory powder, but that hasn't translated into productivity at work. He's delegated a number of his usual tasks among several people, and so far no one's really noticed. Today he's checking online to see if there's been any response from Trudy. None, *grmph,* and he can see that she's been online because there's a brand-new photo of her at a restaurant with some girlfriends. It's actually kind of sexy: Trudy's wearing a strapless turquoise dress, and the women look slightly drunk. As much as Gordon's mind has been pre-occupied with his—mind—he's a little turned on. He officially does not remember the last time he and Jean made love. This in and of itself is disturbing, as is just about anything he cannot remember now, even things that people commonly forget, things that aren't terribly necessary to keep track of, unless you haven't done it for a while, like the last time you had sex with your wife—unless, of course, it's been a long enough time since you've had sex with your wife that it could be one year or it could be six. He tries to think of what that last time might have been like. It's not as though it had been particularly interesting for a while, but Gordon had never been interested in anything especially unusual. He wasn't a strictly missionary type of guy, but neither would he think to do anything as crazy as—standing up, say. Probably he just got on top of her, maybe rolled her over onto her side or something, he's sure he must have ejaculated, he always did, but he just can't bring up the memory. He remembers the days when he and Jean were newly in love, how much he had wanted her, how he shivered when all she'd really done was run her hands along his side, how much time they'd spent in bed those first years. He was happy just to lie there and look at her unclothed form after they were done, though she'd rarely allowed herself to be seen that way more than briefly. He still wanted her, wished she felt the same.

So anyway this, and the picture of Trudy in her strapless dress, have resulted in the beginning of an erection. No sense wasting that—it has been a while, Gordon supposes—so he reaches in to *make the magic happen* (Jean had come to hate that phrase, which was his go-to, perhaps once been meant to be funny, though it wasn't really, and which hadn't helped the frequency of their lovemaking as time went on) and begins to furiously stroke himself, alternating peeks at Trudy and the one of Jean on his desk. Gordon coming is, well, we don't know if you want to see this, but even with no one watching, he somehow manages to be Gordon while he's spilling his jizz all over the desk. *Aaahngh!* Gordon cries, slamming his free hand down on the desk, almost in victory, forgetting that Doris is in the next room. *Yes! Yes!! YESYESYESYES-YESYES!!!*

Doris has never heard Gordon quite like this. She calls in on the intercom to ask what's going on. Gordon recovers, tries to catch his breath, make his voice sound normal, pushes the intercom on the phone, gets a little jizz on that, too. *Just looking at some numbers, Doris! Fantastic numbers!*

For the good fortune of both of them, Doris takes Gordon's excitement about the numbers at face value, doesn't ask anything more. Meanwhile, Gordon, coming down off his five-minute high, suddenly notices that he's made quite a mess of his desk and begins to clean up. Starting with himself, he grabs a wad of tissues, all he has available at the moment, and now that he's actually looking at himself, notices that his testicles seem somewhat droopier than he remembered. Gordon had always been proud of his balls, firm and high, the size and shape of two perfect eggs of the red-breasted snipe, but now they were just a little bit lower, just a little bit less distinct than he recalled, just a millimeter closer to his father's sagging, amorphous ball sack, he thinks, yet again troubling Gordon on many levels.

thirty-eight

I t's been a while since Taylor's trip to L.A. for the reality show, and she's finally gotten the call letting her know that she's no longer being considered. *Oh, I didn't want it that much anyway*, she reports back to Priscilla. *I just got caught up in the moment*. Priscilla kind of wants to reach through the phone and punch Taylor in the face right now; if she didn't really want it, couldn't she just have dropped out and maybe left room for someone who really did? Priscilla makes up little stories like these that have no basis in how it actually works, the fact being, of course, that if they'd really been interested in Priscilla, Taylor's presence or absence wouldn't factor in. But fuck it, it's over now.

Ever since Priscilla didn't get picked, she has been unable to get that last question out of her head: *What is the accomplishment you are most proud of?* Priscilla is more or less aware that she hasn't accomplished anything to speak of. She's got fifteen credits at community college. Is she proud of that? She thinks she's supposed to feel proud of it, but what she feels is more along the lines of hollow. Is that a feeling? Anyway, it's how she feels. She once drank the high school running back under the table after a homecoming rally, and she was super-proud of it at the time, but that moment has for sure passed. She takes pride in her appearance, but she doesn't see it as an accomplishment so much, mostly wishes others would just do the same.

Priscilla logs on to her social network to look through people's info, see what they've accomplished. Not much, but she comes across a quiz: What were you born to do? OMG, how lucky is that? Priscilla takes the quiz; it's not as super easy as she expected, and the answer just confuses her more. Make trouble? She'd been hoping for something much more specific than this; even something like "be famous" would have been a little more concrete. Even if it had said something like "Marry well," at least she could have rejected it out of hand, since that would have been obvious and total bullshit. But make trouble? Priscilla doesn't have clue one about how to interpret this. Is there any possible way to interpret this as good? She hardly thinks of herself as a rebel, has no interest. Make trouble. What the hell? This is totally bogus. Stupid quizzes.

At the food court again, she polls her girlfriends, but the results are seemingly useless, a series of answers mostly involving boys they dated/are dating. These guys live at home. They're no superstars. Ashley surprises her by saying *Graduating high school*. That's something to be proud of, Priscilla thinks? How hard is that? Was it hard for her? It wasn't easy, but it's nothing she's thought to take pride in. It's just what you do. Priscilla thinks about the fact that school itself is never, ever, a topic of conversation with her friends, except for passing comments about how *bo-ring* it is before the subject shifts to some new social drama. Of course, we already know that P doesn't like school, so in that way it's not surprising; what's surprising right now is that there's this little shift in her perception of Ashley, that something Priscilla's considered relatively insignificant is important to her friend. Priscilla doesn't even know what she was expecting in terms of answers. It doesn't make her feel any less dead about school in general; she just kind of gets that it has significance to someone else, someone who's at least a little bit like her. None of them really has any accomplishments to speak of. They aren't even twenty, remember. How many twenty-year-olds have great accomplishments? If you asked Priscilla a couple of weeks ago, she'd have pointed to a lot of reality stars, but now she's thinking it's not like they were even, you know, doing anything besides showing up and maybe drinking and sleeping with cute rich boys and being pretty. Wasn't that what she wanted, though? Could she be wanting something just a tiny bit more than that?

Taylor reminds Priscilla about that summer she spent babysitting and helped a kid learn how to read. *That was a while ago, though.* Taylor looks a little bummed for a second. Priscilla does, too. She didn't even want to help Otis learn to tie his shoes. She hadn't even wanted to *help* Otis tie his shoes. Priscilla is suddenly feeling like she sucks as a person. That's new.

NOT GETTING SATISFYING ANSWERS from her friends—satisfying here basically meaning learning something about herself to be proud of—Priscilla finally asks her family about their proudest accomplishments.

Her dad says: *I have some new paintings I'm quite pleased with. These may be my finest accomplishment.*

Huh, Priscilla says. *Really? I didn't know you were that into it.*

I've always painted, I just haven't had the time until recently.

What? Is he for real right now?

I studied painting in college.

Huh, Priscilla says. She doesn't know he only means one class. She should, he's mentioned it before, but she doesn't.

Well, no, now hold on. Gordon asks her to come to the garage to look at some of the other paintings, pulls down the tarp he's thrown over them. He hasn't started the rest of the family portraits yet; so far he's just painted himself, Doris, Sheila, and blank-faced Trudy. *This one here is very good, too, very good. Though this one has certain merits as well. Well, I'll say the collection of paintings. That is the accomplishment I am most proud of. Yes.*

Gol, Priscilla thinks, Dad is losing his shit. Plus, that was no help. Plus, those paintings are kind of weird-looking. The people don't look like people really look *at all*.

Is that Mom?

No, that's me!

Priscilla looks closer.

See, there's my watch.

Hunh. I thought your wrist was, like, broken or something.

No, it's my watch!

Priscilla looks at it again. *But except it's flesh-colored? And looks broken?*

Her dad is extremely proud of every detail, even the ones that look nothing like what they're supposed to be. *That's artistic license!* It's fair to say now that Gordon's obsession with his memory has begun to be overshadowed by his newfound passion for painting. What we can't say is whether that's an improvement or not. It may just be a sideways move.

Priscilla takes a moment to look at her dad. He's kind of disheveled, but he seems to have pulled the stick out of his ass. None of this has helped her much in the proudest-accomplishment area, but it helps her just a little bit in the seeing-her-family area, an area she previously hasn't dabbled in.

VIVIAN'S ANSWER: *OH! WELL. My, there are so many. I'm a college graduate, of course; after all, many women didn't go to college in those days. I'm awfully proud of my violets, which have won prizes. I'm quite proud of having kept my shape all these years. And of course your great-grandfather Baron and I were married for sixty marvelous years. Oh, we had a tremendous life. We were very privileged. I suppose that's the accomplishment I'm most proud of.* Priscilla's pretty sure Vivian means the marriage, but isn't totally sure if Vivian means the privileged, and doesn't ask.

THE FIRST THING THAT pops into Theodore's mind is to get his crèche and show it to Priscilla. But that can't be right. He's accomplished other things. *Oh, well, as you know, I've* *always fancied myself a photographer, took quite a few of you when you were younger. You were quite the model back then.*

Priscilla remembers posing in various outfits, how her grandfather always waited patiently while she took her time finding just the right accessories, how he had even let her help pick out which photos to print, which ones to reject. Looking at the photos had actually helped her refine her taste, though she probably hadn't added that up.

Here are some I took the other day. He looks at them before handing them over. *Well. Some are a little blurry. But there are one or two good ones in there.*

Priscilla looks at the photos, thinks some of them are sweet, even the blurry ones. Then she realizes they were taken outside. *Grampa, was someone with you when you took these? Did the caretaker take you out for a walk?*

Theodore nods. *Oh! I'm working on a paper for the optometry convention.* Theodore had always been proud of the papers he'd written and lectured on over the years. Priscilla and everyone else has heard this new paper, of course, the most recent reading of which had left everyone squirming. It just didn't make sense—not to Priscilla, anyway. I mean, not that P knows thing one about optometry, but still. It had seemed like a big random jumble of sentences. *I think this could be my best work yet. Can I read it to you?*

Sure, Grampa. Suddenly, Priscilla wants to cry again.

OTIS WANTS TO ANSWER *I have a girlfriend!*, but he's not sure about trusting his sister with this information, so he says what used to be his proudest accomplishment: *My symmetrical crossword*. Priscilla, who as you know pays as little attention to her baby brother as possible, had been unaware of this, has barely noticed that he was into crosswords at all, and is actually impressed, even though she doesn't know right now that there's not a lot of symmetry in that particular puzzle.

Cool. She musses his hair. This is as affectionate a gesture as she has extended to Otis since he was a baby and she was ten, although the truth is that, when she picked him up that one time, it was as awkward as that blind date she let Taylor fix her up on with her cousin's friend from New York who was supposed to be a model and for sure was not.

Do you want to see it?

Maybe later.

JEAN TAKES A MOMENT to think about the question before she says: *You and Otis are my greatest accomplishment.* Then her mom busts out crying. Priscilla is beginning to wonder if Otis is the only semi-normal one besides herself around here.

What this all adds up to for Priscilla so far: none of these answers help her in terms of figuring out what she's actually proud of. She had been so sure that if she had gotten the TV show, she would have been proud. She still believes she would have been really good at it. But she didn't. Priscilla isn't really excited about anything besides clothes, she realizes. She has no proudest accomplishment.

thirty-nine

Headed out to the garage to paint, Gordon meets his father in the kitchen. Theodore's looking through a pile of photos he's had Otis print out for him.

Come have a look, Otis, Theodore says to his son.

Gordon.

What?

Gordon takes a breath, tries to let it go, sits down with his dad. He's never sure lately if his father is just mixing up names, as he always has, or if he's getting worse. He's also never understood his father's long-standing need to print everything out, to make more piles of paper to lose, when he could just as well look at them on the computer. Gordon has looked at these photos before—or photos like them, hard to say. Theodore's photos, of late, are primarily of the ongoing nature show in the yard. One out of every eight or so is in focus. One out of every sixteen is actually quite lovely: a cardinal in a snowy bush, even the blurry deer grazing. Gordon's hard-pressed to ignore the fact that many of the ones Theodore seems most proud of seem to be of nothing at all: entire frames consisting mostly of grass, leaves, sky. Not so long ago Gordon would have been inclined to fill up the space with a discourse on any one of the featured animals or plant genuses, maybe even likened the way Theodore framed the photo to that of a great artist, pleasing his father to no end. But right now he has no idea what to say, and he's aware that he has nothing to say, which is profoundly different and weird and uncomfortable. In the meantime, Theodore has nodded out again. Finally he opens his eyes, though he still looks drowsy.

Can I help you onto the couch for a nap, Dad?

I probably wouldn't send you to hell for it.

Gordon smiles, gently but firmly guides his father from his walker to the sofa, picks up the photos again.

These are nice, Dad.

Arty, huh?

Gordon can't tell now if this is his father's sense of humor about the state of his ability to take simple photos, or if he's really intended for these photos to be artistic.

One of them is a close-up of only the top half of Theodore's head, from the cheerfully surprised eyes up, and it's sideways.

That one was a mistake, Theodore says. *But it has its merits*, he says, smiling.

Gordon nods. He's avoided being alone with his father for months. He's feeling something here. There's something in his throat like a pill that's gotten stuck.

It does, Dad. Gordon asks his father if he can have a few of the printouts.

Sure! Theodore says. *Take whatever you like!* He closes his eyes as Gordon draws an afghan up over him.

Gordon takes the one of his dad, the cardinal in the bush, and the one of the grass, and heads out to the garage.

forty

What Jean's stuck on today: What could I have done to stop this from happening?

No conclusions are drawn as this new series of questions arise in her. As she starts assembling the makings for tonight's dinner, Jean wonders if she hadn't paid James the same attention that he'd paid to her, if her skills of observation were weaker than she believed, if she might have gotten him to confide in her about his illness if she'd only been more attentive. Could he have thought she'd leave him if she'd known? Jean had never had a plan to end their relationship. She had been happy with things the way they were, had believed that James did as well. Or maybe happy wasn't the right word, but she'd been in that dreamy haze of love for the entire year and a half they'd been together. They hadn't talked much about the future, or at least Jean hadn't. They'd never discussed her ending her marriage. Admittedly, it was something Jean had never been quite prepared to think about. Marriage meant something to her, or it had, or she wanted it to; things like these that she once accepted as just *what people do* were cloudy now, like everything. But certainly her family is important to her, and she sees now that she may have been avoiding this discussion, that James may have hoped for something greater, that perhaps his needs were unmet, that he may have wanted more than just afternoons with Jean, that maybe if she'd looked more closely she'd have realized the pain he was in, and she could have gotten him help.

Plus, she's beginning to have another occasional, odd feeling: that James never existed at all, as though what happened between them was a beautiful dream that ended with a waking nightmare, that that must have been someone else's life, because here's mine, here with this man who talks ceaselessly, with one child who seems to hate me and two seniors in need of constant care, where everything suddenly seems without meaning. Just this morning, as she was making coffee, she thought, Why bother? She'll never drink coffee with James again. Does she even want to have coffee ever again? Coffee brings her no joy now. And now here she is making another meal, chicken with rice and asparagus in butter lemon sauce. Why do we take the time to do this? Jean thinks. What is the meaning of this? It's just food. She could just boil all of it, the chicken and the rice and the asparagus and throw it on a plate, let everyone season it if they want to, although she doesn't know why they should. What is the meaning of flavor, really?

Everything that comes into Jean's view these days is met with this kind of abject indifference. She feels as though she has exhausted her life's allotment of emotion, good and bad. If it's not something that sustains her life, she's ambivalent about it. If it didn't mean going out and shopping for new clothes, she'd wear only gray tees and sweats from here on out. None of the sexier outfits she'd chosen for James had kept him from doing what he did. Why do we continue to dress ourselves as we do, why on earth would Priscilla care so much about what she looks like to anyone, does she not see the purpose-lessness in it all? When Jean turns on the TV, comes across a talk show or a sitcom, hears laughter, she feels empty. That, too, has been taken away from her. That's for other people now. Although, frankly, it's hard for her to understand how anyone can laugh since James died. It seems indulgent. As does sunshine, and sleeping, and breathing. With each breath, Jean thinks, I am breathing, and he is not. He chose not to breathe.

JEAN FEELS LIKE PART of a woman now, like the inside of her has been scooped out like a squash, the best part, and that all she is now is just the skin.

forty-one

Otis's day continues to get better. He has not completely let go of his concern about people killing themselves, in spite of Caterina's assurance that she is not suicidal. It's just that things are going so well that he does stop to think, Well, if he killed himself now, he'd end on a high note. If it's possible to have better days than this one, he has not yet imagined them, and maybe that is the reason why lovers kill themselves. But of course, Otis isn't suicidal, so we don't have to worry about that. Cutting to the chase: well before the end of the apple-picking trip, Caterina agrees to be Otis's girlfriend. Better: it's her idea.

What happens is, everyone is paired up with a buddy as they're walking off the bus and it happens that Otis and Caterina walk off the bus in the luckiest order ever, one extra person in a seat in front of them, or one small misstep could have had him paired with Bethany, a nightmare he doesn't want to imagine. Bethany, needless to say, is super-bummed to be with anyone but Caterina, much less the kid who carries the scrap that's left of his baby blanket in his pocket. (The kids all say it's a known fact, but in truth it's a rumor. No one really knows or has even seen it. It could just as well be a hanky, but even if it's nothing at all, this kid's fate is sealed at least until he switches schools, possibly until he grows up and invents a new Internet.)

Each pair of buddies will pick from one tree, his teacher announces.

This might be the most beautiful sentence Otis has ever heard in his life. He imagines himself in the tree, with Caterina, eating apple pie, candy apples, caramel apples, apples with peanut butter, apples with honey, apples with cheese. They live in the tree and feast on apples and drink apple juice and apple tea and talk about the insects and the birds and the squirrels that live in the tree and they make crosswords together and they hold hands and look up at the constellations and wonder what a harvest moon is and whether there's really a man there or not and they live there forever and ever and no one dies the end.

When you have each gathered a full basket of apples, please sit at the bottom of the tree with your buddy until everyone is finished. Then we will go to the shop and pay and then we will reboard the bus to go back to school.

Reboard the bus. Back to school. There is no time to waste, Otis thinks. Otis and Caterina start picking apples from the tree and continue their conversation from earlier. He has mostly forgotten his original list of questions, except for jelly beans. *Oh!* Otis says, *Jelly beans!* He doesn't mean to say this out loud but it doesn't matter. *I brought jelly beans. Want some?*

Sure. Caterina examines several apples very carefully before deciding on one that looks perfect enough to put in the basket.

Otis digs around in his backpack and pulls out the jelly beans, opens the bag. *So, birthday cake isn't so good, right?*

The truth is that Caterina had mistaken the birthday cake beans for strawberry cheesecake beans, and so thinks that Otis is saying he doesn't like birthday cake. Real birthday cake.

You don't like birthday cake? Not even chocolate?

Otis is confused himself for a moment and the conversation almost goes into extreme who's-on-first territory, fortunately, Otis figures it out quickly enough.

Oh! I love birthday cake! I meant the birthday cake jelly beans.

Oh! Oh. Good. Then you can still come to my birthday party.

Otis spends little time worrying about the horrible implication that "can still come" means he almost couldn't come, and he focuses on the great words that followed: *to my birthday party.*

Oh! Yes!

If you come to my birthday party, though, you'll have to be my boyfriend.

Otis is unprepared for this turn. He had no plan to officially ask Caterina for any such commitment, but he's beyond thrilled to make it. He has no idea why this is a condition of the invitation and could not care less. Now, though, he wonders what this word actually means, to Caterina or to himself. Is it the same as "lover"? Is Caterina, in essence, telling Otis she loves him? Would he agree to pretty much any terms required to hold on to the title? Yes, yes he would. He will do whatever Caterina asks. If Caterina asks him to eat a caterpillar, he will absolutely eat a caterpillar. He cannot think of one thing he wouldn't do for Caterina.

Oh! Okay!

In fact, Caterina doesn't really know what she wants. People in movies get boyfriends at the end and then everything is better. That's pretty much all she's thinking. Better.

After this, the conversation dries up a little bit. As they pick apples, Otis remembers his list of questions but moves through them much more quickly than he anticipated. Caterina is ambivalent about robots. Otis remembers several facts about apples from his dad, but much like his dad, he is rewarded for his efforts with little in the way of conversation. Unlike his father, though, Otis makes note of this reaction for future conversations. He wants them to go both ways. What subjects Caterina likes, as he knows, are reading and art and spelling. Otis is not good on the spot, but he does notice that his basket is almost full and that Caterina only has three in hers.

Don't you like apples? he asks.

Yeah, but I don't like any spots on them. Like from worms and stuff.

Me neither, Otis says, although his basket is full of apples with spots.

In the gift shop, Otis steers Caterina toward Bethany for a minute so he can buy her a red pencil with an apple-shaped eraser for her birthday, to go with the crossword he has in mind to start making as soon as he gets home. He sticks the pencil in his backpack so she doesn't see it and heads back over to retrieve Caterina, empowered by *boyfriend*. He takes her hand and pulls her away; Bethany just keeps talking. They line up for the bus, Otis takes a window seat so Caterina can have the outside. He has not let go of her hand. He will never let go of her hand.

forty-two

Theodore spends an hour reading his paper again. He makes a few pencil marks on it here and there, marks that could possibly be construed as letters, or maybe proofreading symbols, but the truth is, a few minutes after he scribbles them on there, even Theodore is no longer sure what these marks signify. Though he's mentioned many times to the family that he is preparing the paper for a conference, and recently announced his plan to take it to the post office tomorrow (several tomorrows having come and gone since that day), it's been understood by everyone that none of this will actually happen, not the completion of the paper, not the trip to the P.O., and for sure not the conference. Theodore has given several papers since his original diagnosis, but the severity of the recent, rapid decline in his condition is apparent to everyone but him.

His last trip outside with Mott, however, has built his confidence, has proven to Theodore that his family has been entirely too cautious about his moves, and that taking a little walk is no big deal. He shuffles to his desk, opens the drawer with the mailing supplies. Inserting the paper into a manila envelope is a bit tricky—why are envelopes not cooperating as they once were?—but he gets it in on the fourth try and seals it closed. There's no letter attached to the paper at all, a formality he's forgotten about. Theodore takes great care in writing his return address in the upper left-hand corner; he has always been aware that his beloved postal service does make occasional mistakes. He rifles through a pile of papers searching for an address to send it to, a few papers sail to the floor in the process. Events like this, small moments like an article floating to the floor, are the stuff of Theodore's days now; retrieving an item from the floor can take fifteen shifty minutes, getting the paper to stick to his fingers can take five alone, the wily paper scooting away from the tips of his fingers as if on its own, Theodore finally raising himself up only to knock something else off the pile with an uncooperative elbow, a series like this carrying on for any length of time, like a protracted game of Mousetrap. Though he appears at most mildly inconvenienced, our best guess is that Theodore simply experiences time differently now. To the casual observer, it's hard to imagine that this sort of change in physical ability would be anything less than profoundly frustrating, but to Theodore, who may likely be forgetting that he's dropped quite as many papers (if any) as he has, just about as quickly as he drops them again, it's simply the same sequence of events as always. This is what we hope, for his sake, anyway.

Sometime later, he manages to write something on the envelope that in his mind represents a contact and an address.

He opens a drawer on the right side of his desk, where he keeps his postal scale and the postage he's kept on hand for about the last sixty years, a small, modified file folder with glassine envelopes containing stamps of every denomination, some as old as thirty years but mostly fairly current. Though he had adapted easily to email, Theodore had never let go of his fondness for the U.S. Postal System and all its appurtenances. He's had his pocket-sized postal scale since he was a kid, a little brass clip for the envelope with a weight on the end and a curved measuring apparatus with an arrow. He also has a bigger scale for larger items, but for smaller ones this is his trusted go-to. It's really a marvelous thing. Positioning the clip between his shaky fingers so that he can hold it open long enough to place the envelope there takes quite a few tries; suspending the envelope in the air still enough to read the weight is even trickier—dang thing keeps moving, never used to do that. As with the papers, the number of times he tries to pinch the clip before he succeeds could be two or it could be ten. He doesn't perceive it as a huge hurdle. Eventually Theodore gets a good enough idea of the general weight, accounts for an extra half-ounce, and selects a dollar thirty-eight in postage from his folder. He's only partially successful in getting the stamps from the folder to his tongue and then to the envelope; one of the ten-cent stamps sticks to his tongue, then to his fingers, until he finally crumples it off his fingers and into the trash, not to be replaced after he simply forgets he needs to.

He'll have to wait for the right moment to leave the house, this he has learned. Theodore has sometimes been found in places where he's no longer allowed to tread: Jean once caught him with his walker stuck behind a door trying to go upstairs, *just to see if anything was new up there*, and several times Gordon has found him at the door headed outside with his camera hoping to get a better picture of some critter or another. Though the Copelands have the sitter, and there's rarely a time when no one at all is home, Theodore is still trusted, unwisely, to know what he can and can't, should and shouldn't do. The family has assumed that allowing him to continue to move freely between rooms is still okay, but that time has passed.

It's not too hard for Theodore to find a moment to make his escape. The sitter has left for the day, Jean has run to the store, Gordon's not home from work yet, Otis is at a friend's house, Priscilla's upstairs, and his mother has fallen asleep on the sofa. That the post office will be closed by the time Theodore gets there is an overlooked detail. That managing the dog and his envelope simultaneously are two conflicting endeavors is not at the forefront of his mind. Theodore shuffles into the main house; his buddy Mott sidles right up. With a few fumbles, Theodore once again manages to hook the leash onto the dog's collar, takes him through the back door, and walks him outside.

They make it only as far as the front of the house when Theodore becomes winded and decides to take a break. *Hooph*, he says out loud to the dog. *We better stop for a minute.* Theodore steps up to the front porch with the dog and sits on the bench swing. Mott lies down, Theodore makes the bench swing lightly. *This is nice.* Theodore swings for a few minutes; a delightful cluster of sparrows lands on a tree in his sight. The sparrows flitting about will occupy his thoughts until he falls asleep.

forty-three

Priscilla arrives home after work, finds Mott lying by the back door, his leash still on—that's messed up—lets the dog inside, yells into the doorway for her mom and dad, gets no response. What the fuck. She goes into Theodore and Vivian's; Vivian is just waking up from her nap. *Gramma Bibbie, I just found the dog outside. Where is everyone?*

Vivian's still a little out of it, says, *Oh, my!*

Priscilla peeks into her grandfather's room; he's not there, either.

Where's Grampa? Did Mom take him somewhere?

No, she just went to the market. Surely he's in your part of the house.

No, Bibbie.

Oh dear. Oh dear. I hope he hasn't fallen down again.

I'll go look again. I'll be right back.

Priscilla goes into the main house, calls upstairs, *Mom! Dad! Grampa! Otis!* Nobody, nothing. We wish there was a precise phonetic spelling of the exasperated noise Priscilla makes here. Suffice it to say it's loud and multisyllabled and very effectively conveys how tired she is of the increasing incompetence of her family. Goes back outside, doesn't see her grandfather by the pond or in the yard, circles the house, finds him asleep on the bench on the front porch. Thank fucking god. *Grampa. Grampa.* Priscilla sits down next to her grandfather, tries to wake him up, starts to realize he's not budging, not breathing. *Grampa.* Fuck. Priscilla bursts into tears, wipes them away, no time for that right now, *Fuck*, hugs her grandfather, wipes her face again, calls her mom, gets voice mail. *Where the fuck are you?* Calls her dad, gets his secretary, Doris, who tells Priscilla he's on his way home.

Priscilla goes inside to get a blanket for her grampa, realizes that's probably weird, that he's colder than cold, but still feels like she should do something and has no idea what to do next. She sits on the porch with her arm around her grandfather, and her head on his shoulder, until her father gets home.

When Gordon arrives to find no one home before him, he, too, loops around the house, asks Vivian what's going on. She doesn't know but *would very much like to.* He finally goes back outside and finds Priscilla and Theodore on the porch.

Oh, there you are. You guys going out for a walk or something?

Priscilla's blood starts to warm up to a slow boil. Has she ever gone for a walk with her grandfather, since she was, like, eight? Fuck, even her thoughts aren't going the way she wants them to.

You guys fucked up. You fucked up, Dad. You guys fucked up.

Gordon doesn't like it when his daughter talks like this. But it doesn't take him long to see that his father doesn't look so good, starts to put it together that this isn't just Priscilla's typical drama, that something is really wrong with his dad. He tells her to calm down, and as soon as she looks at her father directly in the eye, Gordon realizes what's happened, that his father's gone.

Gordon being Gordon, his first reaction is to try to figure out the hows and whys of his father dying on the porch. He asks Priscilla a bunch of questions, but she doesn't have answers. Priscilla, of course, doesn't know the details, though she has the important gist of it, that her grandfather was left unattended and he wandered out, and is doing everything she can to keep herself from fully exploding right here on the porch. Her father took this on, and he should have been on top of it. *Are you kidding me right now, Dad? Do you realize how disastrous this could have been? Do you? What if he'd gotten hit by a car? What if he'd fallen down in some alley and no one even found him?*

At the moment, Gordon is still more or less simply stunned, though in his mind he can't help thinking that all he'd done was go to work as usual. But Priscilla, at least, doesn't see it that way at all. She's used various forms of the word "disaster" before, rarely about anything worse than a cowlick, has a vague sense that her penchant for exaggeration is hindering her ability to convey the seriousness of the situation to her father, but is thinking that somebody needed to step up, like, five minutes ago. And right now her father is not a great candidate, looking severely blank, like he's checked himself into some little mental isolation tank. The loss of Gordon's mother just a few years earlier—well, we should probably provide some backstory on that, but it probably won't surprise you to know that Gordon's method for processing that loss wasn't your typical Kübler-Ross scenario; if we were to try to represent it as a pie chart, we'd make two separate pies, one with nine-tenths denial (one slim tenth devoted to momentary but unwelcome sadness), and another full pie of Wikipedia. That's not a widely acknowledged stage of grief, the Wikipedia stage, but for folks like Gordon, puzzling it through on the Internet and at the library was all he knew how to do. So Gordon knows a lot about how other people process grief, though it probably goes without saying that his ability to notice that people are processing it is another thing entirely.

Granted, things are a little different now, though Gordon can't necessarily articulate the hows or whys of that, either. He's frozen, and though the moment isn't that long, it's long enough for various images to pass through his head: middle-aged Trudy, brain-photoshopped into his college dorm, an awkward cut-and-paste; his beautiful wife on their wedding day; his sad, faraway wife today; his father in better days, helping him with his homework, showing him how to ink a wood block, center a photo in the frame, his now-perpetually messy chin, his shaky hands, his still-wide eyes. His daughter is right. He hasn't been present. He's been busy trying to solve an unsolvable problem. Still, all these thoughts serve to do right now is to render him all the more immobile. He's frozen.

Dad. Get it together. Seriously. Priscilla doesn't want to yell in front of a dead person, that seems way wrong, but she is mustering the sternest tone of voice available. *Dad.*

You have to call somebody. Like, right now. Does she have to say out loud that they can't leave her grandfather here alone on the porch? She doesn't, does she? Her dad might be out of it, but he's not stupid, god knows he's let them know that often freaking enough. She feels some other things coming in sideways. She'd had a feeling her grandfather had been fibbing when he told her he hadn't been alone when he took those photos he showed her. Why hadn't she told someone? Did she have any part in this? Her dad's just lost his dad. He probably feels bad enough. Right now, though, something needs to happen, no time for that. *Dad!* Priscilla raises her voice slightly, what she hopes is enough, looks at her grampa as though she's worried about waking him up, though she knows better.

Gordon takes a deep breath, *Okay, okay, okay,* he says out loud, and starts making mental plans for what needs to happen next. He calls Jean, leaves her a message to tell her to come home from wherever she is; calls his father's doctor; calls a funeral director; doesn't use the word "died"; tries out *expired* but that's not quite right; settles on *passed*; will stick with that, tells Priscilla he'll wait outside with his father until they come. Priscilla eventually stops muttering how fucked up this is, waits outside with her dad and grandfather. She'd rather be anywhere just about now, but leaving her grampa and her dad doesn't seem like an option given the circumstances. Even if her dad is being a bonehead right now. Gordon tries to fill the silence between calls, but Priscilla is still pissed. *Just don't talk, Dad. Seriously.*

When Jean arrives, Priscilla lets her mom know that she

fucked up, too; Jean knows that her daughter is right. She screws up her mouth, nods, kisses Theodore on the head, whispers to her father-in-law that she's sorry, kisses her husband on the head as well, and starts to cry.

Dad, you should probably go tell Gramma Bibbie, Priscilla says. Jean stays with Theodore and her daughter. *This is so messed up,* Priscilla says.

I know, Jean says. *I know.*

Where is Otis, Mom?

I think he's at Caterina's for dinner.

You think? Priscilla thinks she might start spontaneously bleeding from her ears.

No, he is, he is, Jean says.

Well, what time is he supposed to be back?

They said they'd call when they were on their way.

Well, make sure they come around the back. Just in case.

I will, I will.

Frankly, it's a wonder Vivian hasn't already hustled herself out onto the porch to find out what's going on—it's nearly dinnertime, she does not like it when dinner is late, though that happens more often than not lately—but she's got on a TiVo-ed *Nancy Grace* she can't turn away from. Gordon asks if he can put it on pause; she's not happy about that, but it gives her a minute to notice the time, that dinner is late. *Goodness, what in the devil is going on, Gordon, where is your wife, where is everyone, it's ten minutes past dinnertime. This is happening far too often lately.*

It's Dad, Grandma. It's Dad. Gordon is hoping hard that he doesn't have to say any more than that. He doesn't want to have to tell his grandmother that her son has gone before she has; no one wants to tell any mother that, even if her son was seventy-seven years old. *He's gone, Grandma.*

Well, heavens, where did he go this time? Has he fallen down again? Vivian asks.

No, he's on the porch, Grandma, but, that's not what I meant. I'm trying to say he's gone. He's passed. He's passed. Gordon still doesn't want to say the word "died" out loud, not to his grandmother, not any more than he wants to think about it himself. Vivian looks at Gordon blankly, looks at Nancy Grace's frozen image on the TV, her mouth wide open mid-Nancy-Grace-rant/scream, much the way Vivian might feel right now if she allowed it. All that really is there in her somewhere, but honestly, that level of emotion is unacceptable, it lacks refinement for a woman of her age; she always thought that even Jacqueline Kennedy, a *Democrat*, was a model of poise in this way. Vivian knows that people die, but she has a dignified, proper level of acceptance about that, she's always believed. This time it just happens to be her son. She straightens her sweater. *I see* is all she says, looking down for a minute. She's about to say *Well this was not on the calendar*, but stops herself.

forty-four

The days following Theodore's death proceed largely without incident. Theodore is thankfully retrieved from the porch before Otis returns from Caterina's. Predictably, Otis has a lot of questions about what's happened to his grandfather. His primary understanding of death at this point (aside from the loss of his turtle) is what he's extracted about his mother's lover, James. So when Gordon and Jean sit down with Otis, and Gordon begins to explain death in what he believes to be an age-appropriate fashion, Gordon is not expecting Otis's first question on the subject.

Did Grampa kill himself?

Gordon, naturally, is more than startled by this inquiry. *Goodness no, Otis, where would you get such an idea?*

Well, Mommy said that—

Jean actually has a moment where she realizes that perhaps she had overshared with her young son, and quickly tries to cover. *No, sweetie, Grampa was sick, and he just went to sleep. Forever.*

Gordon looks at his wife, studies her for a moment. She

allows him to catch her eye, in spite of herself. It is this moment that contains the entirety of what will ever be communicated about Jean's transgression. Neither of them wants to discuss it, not Jean, and even less Gordon. He's failed her as much as she's betrayed him. Nothing more needs to be known or said.

Otis is still on *sleep* and *forever*, thinking these through for a moment, his face betraying a series of worried thoughts about the various times he'd been sick and gone to sleep, and had he narrowly escaped death, how had his mother even let him go to bed, this sort of thing. But neither Jean nor Gordon is really looking at his face. Jean has her arm around him and Gordon is looking at the ceiling, hoping it will provide him with the right thing to say. *He was very old, son, and he lived a good life.* Well, that worked out, he thinks, how about that, short and to the point, but it's as much the right thing to say to a young boy as it is exactly what he needs to hear himself. Huh. Never mind that the key words "sleep" and "forever" are already out there, and these are the ones that will stick.

Gordon makes most of the arrangements and calls to family and friends. He's gotten it in his head that he's doing what the patriarch of the family should do, standing up straight, life goes on, what he remembers his father had done when people died. Theodore had made all the necessary arrangements for his own father's service, and still had enough presence of mind when Laura had died to handle all that as well, though he had been visibly heartbroken. So Gordon sits down with Jean to make the funeral arrangements, soberly calls everyone who needs to be called, friends, relatives, tries to make himself sound appropriately grave on the phone, to say things he's picked up from his previous grief research, *Yes, well, he passed peacefully*, as though it were some distant cousin he was talking about, as though he weren't the one who needed the most consolation.

The service is decidedly low-key. Though the family is not religious and has never attended a church service together, Jean suggests that it seems like a nice thing anyway; she has a slight ulterior motive in that she's secretly been interested in checking out a particular nondenominational church she'd heard about. Gordon agrees, contacts the church himself; because there's no official pastor at this church, and because they believe in *speaking as the spirit moves you*, Gordon and Jean decide together that it makes the most sense for Gordon to give the eulogy. Had Theodore died just a few weeks earlier, this might have been an entirely different sort of speech, most likely a much longer one filled with a great deal of material culled from books about what it meant to lose a loved one, but Gordon's head is in a completely different place now. Priscilla still believes it's located as firmly up his ass as always, but Gordon feels he's just setting an example for his family by taking care of the details. He's only dimly aware that his behavior has changed at all since the incident with Trudy. All he knows for sure is that something has changed since he started the Stop Memory Loss program, and now, if intangibly, it's changed again. His father has died. So he does what people do when these things happen, and he writes up some brief thoughts to share, but when he stands up planning to share what he's written, instead, his spirit is moved to some impromptu memories of his father, some from his childhood.

My father was an artist. He made his living as an optometrist, but his humor and his soul belonged to art. He was my inspiration.

When I was a small boy, he taught me to carve wood blocks to make prints. It was as a child that his love of art took root in me. Somewhere along the line that was put aside for practical matters.

He was a beloved husband, son, grandfather, and father to me.

Gordon's peculiar addition of the phrase "to me" here suggests that he was all these things to Gordon, and the mourners are hard-pressed not to take note.

Anecdotes. Gordon hasn't meant to say that word out loud, it was meant to remind him of some of the things he wanted to say, memories of his father in better times. He screws his lips together, trying to recall what else it was he wanted to say. He's never been failed by words this way.

Recently I was implicated in an occurrence in which I became uncertain of my cerebral facilities of which I had previously been very certain.

Here, Gordon thinks he knows exactly what he's just said; unfortunately, it's clear that no one else has.

Imagine, if you can, an encounter whereby everything you think you know is turned on its head in the space of a few minutes.

Gordon waits for the congregation to think of such a thing, then forgets where he was going with the idea, insofar as it had anything to do with his dad.

Oh yes, well, frankly, what it was was that I thought I had lost my mind.

Jean's eyes widen. This is news to her.

Gordon is pausing between sentences now, long enough to make it clear that this speech has not been planned.

Maybe I did, but maybe it's not the disaster I had initially believed it to be. Maybe it's a blessing. Maybe we should all lose our minds and get new ones, now and again.

Gordon nods at his own thought. He likes that one.

I am not one for god, especially, but I think hopefully my father is with my mother, Laura, now, and that his mind rests.

Gordon takes another pause. This doesn't quite seem like an end note. It kind of does to us, but not to him.

Years ago, my father had a quote he liked to say: "The proof of a well-trained mind is that it rejoices in that which is good and grieves at the opposite."

This might be a good time to note that Gordon hasn't shed a tear yet and it doesn't appear he's going to anytime soon. He takes a long pause, looks down. It seems like he might be about to expand on the relevancy of the quote to the occasion of his father's death, but he's given all he's got today. He looks out at the expectant faces, nods, and walks away from the podium.

forty-five

All week long, ever since Theodore's service, Jean has been thinking about going back to church. The folks there were warm and friendly, and there's been an annoying bug in her head since the last support group meeting. More will be revealed. More what? More shit? More of this? More what? More what will be revealed. Was it at all possible that hers was a spiritual crisis, that confession or something could right whatever's been wrong with her since James died? She has no plans to take up religion; she mostly just wants to be healed somehow, maybe get a blessing. She imagines one of those faith healings where you get bopped in the head by a minister with a phony Southern accent, maybe dunked underwater for a good old-fashioned baptism, wash this all away and start over. She wishes she believed that kind of thing had any basis in reality. She could use a good bop in the head right about now.

What Jean discovers about this church is that they consider themselves progressive. The way it works is that the members of the congregation take turns rotating sermons week to week, but they aren't called sermons, they're called leads. The service begins with a brief prayer followed by music. The group is a somewhat scruffy bunch, Jean observes. There's a tambourine player with a long skirt and a colorful woolly hat sliding off the back of her head, a guitar player with torn jeans and bare feet. Jean hadn't expected to hit it on the first try, anyway, thought she'd check out a few churches, although she wasn't expecting the Grateful Dead, which is more along the lines of the music they're playing, albeit with a lot of "angels" and "Lords" thrown in. Still, it's sort of pleasant, and Jean's mind drifts off a bit. The guitar player looks like she imagines James might have about twenty years earlier; the lead singer looks a lot like Gordon when he was younger as well, or what he might have looked like with shaggier hair, very cute, softer—huh, what we know that Jean hasn't noticed is that Gordon is actually in need of a haircut right about now, has let that slide lately along with a lot of other things, and that if she looked at her husband for even as long as she's looking at the guy singing, she, too, would probably soften, that there could be a little window for them, but it hasn't happened yet. The moment serves only to allow a sliver of something Jean hasn't processed yet, in her anger with James, her sadness about him, and now Theodore, her everything else: guilt. It's not that she was ever unaware that she was betraying her husband. It's just that in this moment, seeing this cute young shaggy version of Gordon, she feels a shim of remorse wedge its way into the feed of grief.

The speaker this week is a gentleman named Bob. He looks like a Bob, Jean thinks, has the stature required of a

Bob, tall, with a broad chest, salt-and-pepper hair, kind of a big head. Bob has had an interesting experience with his rescue dog Juliet, and he's talking about how having his dog has been spiritually transformative. Jean has no trouble believing this, much less trouble than believing in some puppet-string-pulling deity that gives you parking spots (but somehow goes AWOL when others are in the mood to hang themselves); it seems almost practical to her in a way. She grew up with dogs, first a Lab named Cotton and then a mutt, some kind of dachshund mix named Doug, and now Mott has been sleeping by her side ever since she brought him home. She hadn't felt her relationship with any of them had been spiritual, not even Mott, but it certainly had been a meaningful bond. She's been sure since she brought him home that Mott feels as sad about James as she does, that he *knows*.

I wanted to talk about Juliet today because I feel that she has saved me, much in the way some believe Jesus Christ saves.

Mmm-hmm, Jean means to say quietly, but it comes out loud. She doesn't especially believe in Christ, but something resonates here.

Bob clicks a PowerPoint slide show with images of Juliet. She's a beautiful brown-and-white pit bull mix with, indeed, soulful yellow-green eyes.

My connection with this dog has been transformative. When she came into my life I was a man who knew how to mess things up but not how to fix them. And I was terribly lonely and sad.

Amen! Jean shouts.

I feel, looking into Juliet's eyes, that we have a true partnership. That there are no errors of communication between us, as with our human partners. That she can see into me, that she sees me the way I was meant to be seen, as god created me. Perfect.

Hallelujah! Jean's head goes down in a deep nod of understanding; her right arm shoots up.

Because of the godly love of my beautiful pit bull Juliet, I feel that I have been freed. Freed to bring myself forward. And that with that liberty I can do anything. Well, almost anything. I can't fly. Bob chuckles; the congregation chuckles with him.

Jean jumps to her feet. *Say it, brother!* she says. The woman sitting next to Jean scooches slightly farther away down the bench, but Jean fails to notice.

Bob continues his lead in this vein and Jean continues her praise. She's entered a zone. There will be no other churches.

So this is my message to you today: Juliet's love is god's merciful love and god's love is for all of us. Bob leaves the pulpit to greet the congregants and the organist begins to play. It's a somber tune, practically a dirge, which is unfortunate. Jean wants to get up and dance down the aisle. She joins the line to introduce herself to Bob. She tells Bob it's her first time, that she was really moved by his sermon, that she hopes to confess, asks Bob if they can sit down to talk. Bob chuckles. *We can talk if you like, but I'm not a priest, or even a pastor. Everyone here is the pastor, you could say. You should give the lead next week. We find it's a wonderful way to connect with new congregants.*

Jean does not have to think about this twice.

Oh! My! Well, yes, yes, of course! Thank you!

Jean nearly runs a red light speeding home, dashes upstairs to begin writing her lead. The truth is, she has no idea what to say, but she's been truly inspired by Bob's honest talk about his dog. She gets it. She sits down with a legal pad, starts scribbling down notes, tearing off sheets, scribbling more notes. None of it is good, but she knows it's coming; she can feel the message bubbling up inside her.

But the week comes and goes, and by Saturday she still has nothing. Sunday morning, two things happen:

1. She steps outside with her morning coffee, lets Mott outside, and remembers a beautiful dream about James.
2. A squirrel, mid–running up a tree with a small nut in its mouth, hears Jean open the door, freezes, swivels its head around to meet her gaze. It's a real moment, an intense two seconds in which the dead stare of this squirrel convinces Jean of the ultimate connection between all living creatures. In spite of the reality— that this squirrel, who, if he has any ability at all to think in the way we understand thinking, is probably thinking something like "This nut is *mine*"— what Jean perceives is what she wants to believe, that the essence of James is in the eyes of this squirrel, and that his message to her is *Yes, Jean, your dreams are true.*

She decides she'll wing it.

forty-six

Heading out to run an errand, Priscilla catches a glimpse of her old dollhouse in the garage. Gordon had moved it a few feet out of his way when he started painting, into a spot that's now in Priscilla's line of sight when she enters the garage. It's been in there collecting dust for several years now, the furniture packed up in a box. Suddenly Priscilla's moved to have another look at it. Holy shit, she thinks. This is insane. Priscilla opens the little closet doors, sees the little shoe shelves inside. He built her a three-way fucking mirror. The dining room and two of the bedrooms have real wallpaper, cream-on-cream paisley in the dining room, tiny florals in the bedrooms. Barbie's bedroom still has the tiny little posters on the walls that he'd photocopied and shrunk down, the casts of *Dawson's Creek* and *Buffy*, her favorites (yes, she'd been too young for these shows; does this surprise anyone?). Theodore had even gone to lengths to set up views outside the windows, building a slot behind them to place a series of photographs he'd taken of the backyard at different times of day. *Or we could put in new ones, a skyline or something, if you want her to be a city girl*, her grandfather had said. The curtains her mother had made still hung in all the windows, in all the colors that were Priscilla's favorites back then: cornflower blues, gunmetal grays. Priscilla opens the box next to it, pulling out items that her mother had made, tiny pillows she'd petit-pointed with single plys of silk thread, embroidered wall hangings done much the same way, blankets and towels, the hooked rug, everything coordinating, everything made with great care, even the little picture frame with a photo of the family, it's about an inch by an inch and a half, one of their old Sears holiday portraits. She wipes away some tears. She can't believe her mom did all this for her. She will not cry.

Priscilla is desperate, so desperate now that when her mother knocks on her door to *See what's going on*, in a singsongy voice she's never heard before, she actually opens it.

What's going on is, I have no proudest accomplishment, Mom. I have nothing to be proud of, except maybe, like, my hair. I could be, like, a hair model. There's an accusatory tone to her voice, which probably isn't anything new, and which does not go unnoticed by Jean, even though she's also scanning the room for clues that her daughter is suicidal. No loose ropes lying around, closet still full of unpaid-for designer clothes, nothing out of the ordinary.

What are you looking at, Mom?

Nothing, sweetheart.

Do you think I'm good at anything?

There's probably no right answer here, as Priscilla has never tried much of anything for anyone to know whether or not she'd be good at it.

Honey, I'm sure you are. Everyone's good at something.

Oh, great. But you, like, have no idea.

No, sweetie, I don't. You're the one who would know. What do you think would be something you'd be proud of doing?

Priscilla explains that she wanted more than anything to be on the reality TV show, that she'd been so sure that it was, like, her *calling. But then it was like god totally punked me, and my one opportunity for happiness was offered up on a plate and then snatched away.*

Priscilla's mother looks her straight in the eye for the first time in years. Jean has no time for anyone's bullshit anymore. She's got god. Or something.

God didn't punk you, daughter. Life is what you make it. Nobody knows this better than me. He doesn't just hand out reality shows. He comes in dreams, in the eyes of squirrels.

Priscilla thinks her mom is speaking metaphorically, hopes so anyway, has never understood why people can't just say things, like, *normally*, but also thinks her mom is losing her shit, that there is a whole lot of shit being lost around here these days. Seriously, it's like a massive breakdown is going on in the family area, and she's suddenly, like, the brains of the operation.

Also? You might try not being such a bitch.

Did her mother just seriously call her a bitch to her face? A rare moment of openmouthed silence from Priscilla.

Jean shrugs. *I'm not saying I don't love you.*

Priscilla is absolutely dumbstruck.

Make your own reality. Jean kisses her daughter on the head and leaves the room.

forty-seven

Otis is working on a heart-shaped crossword for Caterina. There's a week left before Caterina's party; in the past it's taken him anywhere from four days to three weeks to complete a crossword. Symmetrical is out—which is unfortunate, but symmetrical could be the difference between today and eternity. He starts by making a list of things he wants to include, taking a lot of time to consider what Caterina might know or think of (with a few exceptions): jelly beans (pomegranate, birthday cake, jalapeño), apples, spelling, Bethany, *Speed*, buddies, robots, boyfriend, love, pink, pigtails, poop, in your butt, ribbons, bugs, art, reading, math, worms/spots. He uses colors, instead of just black, for the empty squares. He makes a few mistakes in numbering, and when it gets down to the wire he'll have to settle for a few "halfs." This is not preferable, but any more erasing and he'll have holes in the paper. Should he make the clues hard or easy? The truth is, Otis doesn't have the best idea of what might be hard or easy for Caterina. He wants her to be able to fill it in; it's critical that she see the answers. But he doesn't want her to think that he thinks she's dumb. He gets a little help from his father—there are some squares he's filled in with things that look like words but he's not sure. His father explains words like SOU and VEEP, BIAS and SOD, makes him erase ERB (Otis insists he's heard his mom say this, but Gordon explains that the H is silent).

Otis will finish the puzzle the morning of Caterina's party. Asymmetrical though it is, it is his masterpiece.

CLUES:

ACROSS

1. Subject with numbers I like
3. Color you like (I think)
5. Trick ____ Treat
7. Name for a dog (not ours)
9. ~~What is today?~~ The day you were born
12. Fee Fi ____ Fum.
13. Girl who sits behind me in homeroom
15. Number before two
16. Yuck
19. You and me =
20. Talks a lot (girl)
23. Honest ____ Lincoln
24 ½. A long time
25. When you jump into a pool with your hands in front
27. A kind of eggs, or also if you do good on your home-work
28. Not good in your apple
30. Mom
32. You could catch butterflies in this
33. ___dio (listen to songs on it)

34.   My sister does this a lot

35.   Something you sit on made of legs (not a chair)

37.   We picked them together!

40.   My sister calls me this but really it's her

41.   Me!

43.   Some kids do this on the playground

44.   Animals you ride

46.   A short way to say vice president

47.   Not you

48.   Superheroes have this like if they can fly and stuff

50.   It sticks things to things

52.   Bread that has seeds

54.   The playground is there

56.   They sting you

58.   Not off

59.   Means yes with your head

60.   True __ False

61.   I would fight in one for you (with a sword)

63.   A laugh

64.   Some kids take these when they're sleepy (not me)

65.   A bone in your side

67.   (Too hard to explain you can skip this one)

70.   A subject you like with letters

72.   More than one fifth letter

73.   Long cars for famous people to ride in

75.   A boy kid

DOWN

1.   Magazine moms read

2.   Subject with paints and crayons you like

3.   Bad jelly bean

4.   Bop __ (loud toy my sister hates)

6.   (with 9 across) Good at party, bad in jelly bean

7.   That's __ Raven

8.   One part of a fork

9.   Smelly pits

10.   What you say before "butt" to make it funny

11.   Mexican song Ai __ __ __ (repeated)

12.   If you're sick and your forehead is hot you have this

13.   What you say when you find something out

14.   When something's cool

17.   Animal that barks (not a dog)

18.   Dirt under the grass

19.   If you don't lose

21.   Mouse _____ (a game we have, do you?)

22.   If you're excited you might say them

24.   I'm this to you

26.   Likes Reese's Pieces

29.   Mine is named Jean, yours is named Mrs. Belknap

30.   When you stay overnight

31.   You!

35.   I _____ You (+S)

36.   You can make this with apples

38.   Comes out the butt

39.   What you do with food

42.   Scary movie

43.   Sometimes in your pretty hair

45.   Old French coin

49.   Letters my sister says (I don't know what it means)

50 ½. When you have a question you do this

53.   If you say it twice, a toy that rolls up and down

55.   __ You Know the Way to San Jose (that's a song)

57.   Another long time

62.   One part of your mouth

66.   Rings when class is over

67.   A big animal with horns

68. Not out
69. Long ___ and far away
71. Sour yellow fruit
74. Where in the World __ Carmen Sandiego?

forty-eight

Priscilla is at work at Express in the mall. She's always thought Express was pretty lame, but it was between that and Hot Topic, pretty much a no-brainer. She had applied for a job at J.Crew but was told there weren't any jobs. (Not true: right after this, they hired this uppity bitch Olivia she knows from school. What P doesn't know is that they rejected her because when she interviewed she had described her former boss as a kind of a jerk, and also answered a text message from Taylor, right in the middle of the interview. It also hadn't helped that when they asked her about her long-term goals, the pause between the question and her answer was a clear indication of her cluelessness, that by the time she lied and said *Purchasing, I guess*, it was essentially just the first thing that popped into her head that sounded like anything, even though the truth was she hardly knew much more about *purchasing* than that it sounded close to *shopping*.)

More than anything, Priscilla hates folding the clothes. She would prefer to handle this poly-blend crap as little as possible, has gone through way more hand lotion than ever since she started this job. The styles aren't that bad here, but the cuts and the fabrics, the workmanship, eugh. Pull one wrong thread and all the pieces will fall on the floor like when they'd just been cut, she's sure. Sometimes she'd even rather be in the back steaming, where she doesn't have to touch them so much. But Priscilla feels she's best put to use here with the customers.

This is only partly true. She has a knack for styling, to be sure, but her people skills could use some work, depending on who you ask. The employees have been told regularly that they should do what they can to say only that the clothes are flattering. The idea *is* to sell them. No duh. But Priscilla knows she can sell them minus bullshit. Sometimes this is appreciated and sometimes it is not. Today, for example, she's dealt with a size-fourteen woman who's been trying on skinny jeans and a forty-year-old who thinks she's going to pull off a schoolgirl kilt with tights and the plastic Doc Marten–style boots she rode in on. Size Fourteen had appreciated neither Priscilla's look of disdain nor the accompanying comment, *Yeah, that's not gonna work*, but was thankfully too hurt to call a manager to complain, and left red-faced. Which was unfortunate, Priscilla thought, she could have pulled her something that was flattering, modern, *and* age-appropriate—like she did for the Doc Marten lady, who just needed a knee-length skirt and ballet flats, or a tall boot. Plus she'd also sold that lady three pairs of tights and a flattering, drapey cardigan she hadn't planned on. And this was how Priscilla kept her job: she sold clothes.

Ever since her dreams of being a TV star fell all to shit,

though, this job has felt more and more, like, tragic. She hardly wants to move up the ladder at Express. She doesn't really want to be anywhere on the Express ladder, thanks. But today: *Genius!* the Doc Marten lady had said. Priscilla liked the sound of that word. *You're like that TV lady, what does she say, "I die"?*

Rachel Zoe? You think I'm like Rachel Zoe?

Sure! Look at me! Look at you!

The lady looks good, and Priscilla does have a killer outfit on today, and she knows it. Knee-high Anna Sui boots and a knit dress from Agnes B., a handmade scarf around her neck. The only item on her from Express is a cotton cami and tap shorts you can't even see under her dress; this doesn't help her job standing, either.

You're right! A rare, nonsarcastic smile from Priscilla.

P's brain wheel starts whirring. How did she not realize this before? *Make your own reality.* Maybe it wasn't the craziest thing she'd ever heard. She hadn't been able to shake it out of her head since the moment her mother said it. She knew Rachel Zoe had the best job on TV; fuck, she'd do that job *off* TV. She'd almost do it for free if it meant she could style celebrities. She's always dreamed about making over Taylor Momsen. Such a pretty girl, such a freaking goth bullshit mess. Why not do it for a job? How did she not think of this before? How do people get those jobs? Priscilla has no idea.

It's not helping her that she lives in the middle of Fuckall USA. She could move to L.A. Then what? She could move to L.A. and apply to work for Rachel Zoe. She could get hired by Rachel Zoe and go to Cameron Diaz's house and style the shit out of her, put things on her even Rachel Zoe wouldn't think of, and then everyone'd be all *Priscilla Copeland is like a zillion times better even than Rachel Zoe*, and then she'd get her own show and become best friends with Gwen Stefani and Gavin Rossdale and reject guys like Robert Pattinson or even that smokin' hot Asian dude from *Glee* (Priscilla has masturbated more than once thinking about this guy, but has never learned his name) when they tried to ask her out— when they begged. (Priscilla has always loved a good reject-a-hot-guy fantasy, which fits in nicely with her I-should-be-a-superstar-stylist fantasy.) She would have believed all this was seriously possible until recently, before the TV people became severely misguided and picked Taylor over her to fly to Hollywood. Priscilla's confidence was down. But this lady, this Doc Marten lady, lifted her up just a little bit today. Priscilla was genius. She was cooking up some badass ideas. She had clue zero how to put them in motion, but would worry about that later. Make your own fucking reality.

forty-nine

I t has not gone unnoticed by the family that Gordon hasn't shed a tear since his father's death. It's not that this is unusual Gordon behavior, but his endeavors to act strong for the family are typically odd. Gordon, as a rule, is an upbeat kind of guy, but at the moment his cheer is clearly forced, and weirder to observe than ever. Everyone wishes he'd just have a good cry a time or two and get it over with.

Until it actually happens.

This is how it goes down: Gordon finally has a free afternoon after things settle down and goes out to the garage to look at the progress he's making with his paintings. There's still a good bit of work to do to get them where he wants them. He pulls the drop cloth off the one of his dad, mixes some reds and browns, looks at the painting again, dabs at it here and there, and within minutes he is on his knees sobbing as though sobbing has just now been invented—water pouring from his eyes, bizarre, unbidden animal moans coming up from his chest. Gordon allows this to happen largely because he now seems to have no control over it, and in a way he doesn't quite understand, it feels good, letting this wet, colossal sound thing out; it feels like an entity that's been in him for all of his forty-seven years that he had no idea was there. After a few minutes on the cold floor, the sobs mutate into a more manageable weep, enough for Gordon to move himself off the garage floor to the ratty La-Z-Boy that Jean banished here years ago, and he weeps there for he doesn't know how long, until he falls asleep. Jean comes out to call him for dinner, sees him asleep with a wet face, wipes the tears from his cheeks and brings him the afghan from the sofa, lets him sleep through it. Jean hasn't seen Gordon cry since they were married; had thought, at the time, hoped, he had maybe been a little misty saying his vows, but he'd been so under control that she attributed his one tiny *for better or worse* sniffle to allergies (a correct assessment). But this is promising, Jean thinks. This has been a long time coming.

Maybe a little too long. Because when Gordon wakes up and decides to start painting again, feeling strangely refreshed but still weeping, what he doesn't know—what no one knows right now—is that now that the faucet has been turned on, it's not going off anytime soon. Gordon quickly senses that these tears are not going to stop of their own volition, and decides to allow them to come. *It's natural*, he thinks. Why *has* he resisted this feeling for so long? This is a wonderful feeling indeed. He retrieves his paintbrush from the floor, invigorated.

fifty

Following the apple-picking trip, Otis follows Caterina's lead. He does not know what is expected of him in his new status as boyfriend, but is willing to go to great lengths. The truth is that Caterina doesn't really know, either. "Boyfriend" is kind of just a word, something that you have, something that makes things better just by the wordness of it. So, for most of their first official day as boyfriend and girlfriend, Otis kind of just quietly shadows Caterina, doesn't want to make any sudden moves. They sit on the playground together; she shares her jelly beans, even the good flavors. He watches her eat them. Again, it would have seemed unthinkable just a short time ago that the way she eats jelly beans could be even more fascinating, but Caterina-as-girlfriend eating jelly beans in three bites is truly even more miraculous than it was before. He so wants to ask her why she does that, but suddenly worries that it might sound weird, doesn't want to rock the boat. He has seen what has happened with third-grade boyfriends and girlfriends. There aren't a lot of examples, of course, most of the boys do not really like girls yet, or won't admit it, but of the ones he's seen, the longest-lasting was about a month. Supposedly those two had kissed *and everything*, *and everything* being alarmingly nebulous, but he's nowhere near ready for kissing, much less the things his mother has described to him. It's a length Otis is not sure he's willing to go to. For sure he won't be the one making any sudden moves, might, might, might not push Caterina away if she tried to kiss him, but it's not going to happen. It's not the reason she wants a boyfriend. Bethany and this dumb kid Tanner were boyfriend and girlfriend for all of two days before he yelled at her to shut up right in front of everyone in the cafeteria. Otis wants to imagine that this is about Bethany, which of course it pretty much is, but still, he'll pull back on the talking just a little bit at first, just in case.

Otis and Caterina sit down together on the playground, watch the other kids for a while. Thankfully Bethany's tied up with another girl today or she'd be right there with them, yakking. Mostly, they sit there in silence for a while until Caterina finally speaks. They have a playdate set up for this afternoon.

What are we doing after school today?

The amazingest word in this sentence? *We.* Me and Caterina are We.

I could show you my room, and my stuff and things.

I'd prefer to watch TV.

Really, Caterina could have said *I'd prefer to watch the ceiling fan* and it would have been no less perfect.

Sure! We can watch TV!

Priscilla picks up Otis today, Jean is out at some—church thing? Priscilla doesn't really want to know. Otis has his little friend with him; she's awfully cute.

Priscilla, this is my girlfriend, Caterina! Caterina, this is my sister, Priscilla! Priscilla, Caterina is coming over today for a date to watch TV!

Yeah, I know—she stops herself, she's about to call him Baby Freak but thinks better of it with his "girlfriend" there. Huh, that's new. *Mom told me.*

AT HOME, PRISCILLA FIXES the kids a snack, parks them in front of the TV in the living room, figures they'll watch *Dora the Explorer* or maybe a rerun of *The Brady Bunch*, goes to her room.

Mott joins the kids on the couch, puts his big head on Otis's lap. He sniffs Caterina, licks her hand. Uh-oh. This could be bad. He hadn't thought to ask her where she stood on dogs. But Caterina just giggles, pulls her hand away, wipes it on her skirt.

Otis picks up the remote. *I think 'Spongebob' is on.* He's not a huge fan of *Spongebob*, doesn't even watch that much TV.

'Spongebob''s kind of babyish, actually. Can I see the remote?

Otis hands Caterina the remote, she flips channels, can't find anything but dumb kid shows. Checks the TiVo. *Oh! I like this show. Have you seen it?* Caterina hits play. It's *Nip/Tuck*.

I think my sister watches that show. Otis knows he's not allowed to watch this show, and has not ever wished to before this, but Priscilla's upstairs.

The opening sequence alone is enough to make Otis a little queasy, but he toughs it out.

The first scene is a giant close-up of a man's ass, bobbing up and down. At first Otis laughs, butts are funny, but he doesn't know what's going on. Finally it's revealed: he's pushing into a lady on a bed. That doesn't look good. That doesn't look good at all.

Otis can't hold back a gasp. It looks like he's hurting her, and plus also she's naked.

What is he doing to her?

They're making love.

Otis has never heard the term "making love" before, but recalls his mother explaining to him about lying down together. But this does not look special, not at all.

You can probably fill this out yourself, right, where Otis goes with this from here? He flashes back to *goopy soupy delicious*, which in no way describes what he's seeing right now. He hadn't liked the sound of goopy soupy delicious in the first place, but *this*, this is something else entirely. He will never participate in anything like this, not ever in his whole entire life. That is a true fact. He wants to watch something else, anything else. But it's Caterina. She likes this show. He'll just stare into the popcorn bowl for a while, pet Mott until it's over. Unfortunately the next scene is almost worse. It's another close-up, this time of a woman getting her boobs done, although Otis doesn't know what that means, he just sees boobies and blood. It's everything Otis can do not to scream.

See, that's an "augmentation." They're doctors. Caterina is not squeamish at all; she pays close attention to *Nip/Tuck*, thinks maybe she'd like to be a doctor someday. Or a mom.

This is not what Otis has experienced at the doctor's. There are no boobies and there's no blood.

Do you want to play a game? Or I could show you my room?

Shhh, Caterina says without taking her eyes off the TV.

Otis knows that Caterina wants to be a doctor, and the fact that she's not easily grossed out, even though he is, for sure is just another thing that sets Caterina apart—most girls will squeal if a bee buzzes past them—but he doesn't want to be there in the operating room with her. So for now he just closes his eyes until the scene is over. Otis will do what he has to do for the love of Caterina. He's going to stay with her forever no matter what.

For the rest of their time as boyfriend and girlfriend, Otis and Caterina have dates almost every day after school. Most times, after the first day, they end up going to Caterina's house. Otis sits through a couple more episodes of *Nip/Tuck* and one episode of *Jersey Shore*, which seems like a romp to him after *Nip/Tuck*. As the end of the week approaches, Caterina mentions to Otis that it's almost their two-week anniversary. Otis doesn't know what he's supposed to do about that, doesn't know he's supposed to do anything about it. *I would like you to take me to Applebee's*. Otis would like to take Caterina to Applebee's.

Okay, Otis says.

When Jean picks him up from Caterina's house, he mentions the anniversary. *Oh! That's so sweet, Otis.*

She wants to go to Applebee's.

Well, then, we'll go to Applebee's!

Otis is not sure how excited he is about the group We here, doesn't know who's included in this We, likes the Otis and Caterina We much better, but realistically, he's nine, and he doesn't drive and has no money.

fifty-one

Otis's dinner date at Applebee's does not go quite as he imagined it, given that his entire family is in attendance. Otis loves his family but was hoping for more of a *date* date. In his mind it was not unlike his fantasy of the apple tree, but with tables and mozzarella sticks and maybe a violin player like he's seen on TV. He hadn't supposed he'd be so lucky to somehow get dropped off there with Caterina, but had hoped maybe they could sit at a separate table.

There's not a lot here we haven't seen before at a Copeland family dinner, but there's a lot Caterina hasn't seen. It's not as though they're any weirder than her family, they're just differently weird. And you know how it is. Caterina doesn't really even know, won't add it up for a few more years, that her own family is weird. She doesn't know that it's not okay to watch *Nip/Tuck* when you're nine. She doesn't know that it's not normal for your mom to drink wine with breakfast, or that it's unusual to wake up in the middle of the night for a glass of milk and find your dad and his best friend kissing on the couch. Two people kissing is no big deal compared to what they do on *Nip/Tuck*, and it's not like that fazes her. Differently weird is just plain weird. Nevertheless, the weirdness level at Applebee's tonight is definitely dialed up.

We may have misspoken when we said there was nothing we haven't seen before. The Copelands are friendly enough, at least Mr. and Mrs. Copeland are, asking Caterina about her family (although Mr. Copeland kind of asks too many questions, Caterina thinks); Priscilla gets up to take a phone call; Vivian tells the story about her first *special little friend*, when she was just around Otis's age. Otis doesn't quite know what to do. He's thrilled that he's spent time almost every day with Caterina, but he's worried that this dinner could be their undoing.

Gordon, examining the menu, asks the table if they'd like to share an appetizer sampler, waits for responses but mostly gets blank stares and shrugs, though Caterina asks if it comes with potato twisters. Gordon looks at the menu again. *It doesn't seem so, but we'll just order that, too!* Jean, Priscilla, and Vivian have gotten used to Gordon ordering appetizers without asking for their input, which is part one of the weirdness that's taking place right now. It's nothing to get upset about, it's a good thing, right, but still it's a thing they're not used to. Part two is that they're even at Applebee's in the first place. Gordon's let it be known many times in the past that his palate is far too sophisticated to dine at a mid-priced chain restaurant like this.

Part three: after the drinks are ordered, Gordon raises his glass. *I'd like to make a toast*, he says. *First, to Otis and Caterina.*

Priscilla closes her eyes. Is her father seriously toasting the relationship of two nine-year-olds? She tries to shake her head negative subtly enough so her dad will see, but no luck. Has he forgotten what it was like to be nine? *Was* he ever nine? Of course he wasn't. If he was, he was the fortiest nine-year-old ever to live. If he had been, he'd know you don't call attention to these things. Bad enough they've all been forced to tag along here. Her poor little brother.

But Otis and Caterina both like to cheers, so neither is particularly uncomfortable at the outset of the toast.

We are delighted to have you here with us, Caterina, Gordon says. *I wish the two of you a long and lovely friendship.* Priscilla exhales in relief; cheesy, Dad, but good call on "friendship." *I'd also like to toast to my beautiful wife,* he continues. It's here that Gordon begins welling up; these days he's never more than two words away from crying, but no one's used to it yet. They're sure it's a phase, it hasn't been that long since his father died, it's probably normal for anyone else, but never having seen Gordon cry one single time, it's not something anyone else in the family knows how to deal with. Least of all Vivian. This embarrassing display is providing her with some extremely unwanted déjà vu, as she has not forgotten that phase her son went through in his later years, standing up wet-eyed at every meal, it seemed to her, to express his love and gratitude to his wife and family. Time and a place, she thinks; had she not taught him this? And now here her grandson was, doing the very same thing. Honestly. Vivian does not need any more reminders of what's happened.

The loss of my father has brought into my view some things I have not seen with clarity. Jean, I don't think I've been a very good husband to you.

Oh no. Oh no. Oh no, Jean thinks. I mean, it's true, how long has she waited to hear him say such a thing, but now? At Applebee's? And yet no words are coming out of her mouth to stop it.

Though it's true that I provide for the family in the traditional sense, I see now that I have not availed myself to each one of you as I should have. Jean, you have worked tirelessly to care for me and our family, and I have not expressed my gratitude. You are a loving mother, and you have gone over and above your vows in allowing my father and grandmother to remain in their home and caring for them as you have.

Grandmother, I am truly sorry for your devastating loss.

Vivian is not pleased by Gordon's use of the word "devastating" here.

No matter how old, a parent should not have to live to see the death of her child.

Surely her grandson isn't implying *she* should be dead, is he? Because that's what it sounds like to Vivian.

Gordon now has a steady stream of tears down his face, and in between words he's making some noises that we can all agree are slightly nonhuman-sounding. *You raised a wonderful son*, he says, *and father*. Gordon has to take a good long moment before he can speak again. He's entirely unaware that he's pouting like a little boy at this moment, lower lip trembling, but everyone else sees it quite clearly.

Priscilla, I have failed you, and yet I see your emergence happening in spite of my failure. I raise my glass to you as well.

Jean takes a deep breath, Priscilla simply has no idea what her father has just said besides *fail*, though she has a thin sense he's trying to pay her a compliment.

Otis, you are a wonderful boy with your mother's good heart. I don't know what if anything I have given to you, but I believe the world is lucky to have you. Caterina, my son has shared with me his strong feelings for you, and I trust his good judgment; it appears that his choice in mates was as providential as mine due to nothing apparent I have done.

By the time he's finished, Otis is baffled enough to whisper to his sister. *Priscilla, what is Dad talking about, why does he keep crying so much?* Priscilla isn't much more sure than Otis is, but her sisterly qualities seem to be rising in her.

Old people just croak, it totally sucks, you're supposed to be sad.

Why are Mom and Dad acting so weird then?

They always act weird, Otis. Seriously, they were, like, born that way. Don't worry about it.

Otis's main takeaway from this exchange: *My sister called me Otis.*

fifty-two

Make your own reality. It's been running through
Priscilla's head for days now, quite a few more
times even than her mother calling her a bitch.
Priscilla has called her mother worse things behind her
back—no big, really. Make your own reality, though, that's,
like, metaphysical. Seriously, what does that even mean? It's
three words away from make trouble. It's a self-help book.
Right? Gag. But. She wants to be, could for sure be, the next
superstar celebrity stylist. People will forget Rachel Zoe ever
even existed.

Priscilla pops open her laptop, turns on the webcam, and
starts talking. She's done this once or twice before, tried to
keep a video diary, back when she was fifteen, didn't keep it
up. Up until now she hasn't had much to say, and when she's
played the videos back she's kind of wanted to barf. But right
now she's got some wind in her sails. She's supposed to be
on fucking TV. She slams down her laptop again, goes to the
closet, pulls out something better to wear, quickly fixes her
makeup and hair, starts over.

Welcome to 'Make Your Own Fucking Reality,' Bitches. Episode One: My Family Is Batshit Crazy.

Okay, so a few weeks ago I was at the mall eating a Cinnabon with my friends and these dudes came up to us and they were like, "What's up, want to be on a reality show?" and we were like, "Uh, yeah," and so we went and interviewed, and apparently I said all the wrong things and my friend Taylor said all the right things, because she got called back like sixteen times and I did not. In the end, she got rejected, too, otherwise I seriously doubt I could pretend to her face that I wasn't devastated, not to mention I could not understand why she didn't step aside, knowing it meant so much more to me than it ever did to her, but whatever. After this, as you can imagine, I became kind of totally despairing, feeling that I was doing life, like, fully wrong, do you know that feeling? It's a shitty one. Like, after I realized I could almost have been a reality TV star, I really began to think, What am I doing with my life? Why am I still here in this town where seriously nothing happens, where the best job is at Target and even that's in the next town over, where there's not even some great guy to sweep me out of here, a town populated with dickwads like Kyle Woolrich—yes, I just said his name—and oh my god do not even get me started on Kyle Woolrich, but just in case you're interested? His dick? Kinda puny.

So, you know, adding this all up, I'm just thinking, if this is my destiny, then my destiny sucks it. And then my mother walks in and tells me I'm a bitch, which was totes shocking—can you imagine? who does that to their kid?—and even if she's right so the fuck what, you'd be bitchy, too, if you were me.

I haven't even told you about my family yet. Let's see, where should I start, okay, well, my dad is some weird crying Picasso sud-

denly, and Mom's talking to Jesus now or some shit, came home with some random giant drooly dog one day out of the total blue, my sweet grampa bit the dust while no one was looking, my great-gramma gets on my case cause my freaking knees are showing? And wants to take me for a makeover? Priscilla makes a face, almost laughs. *Her hair is freaking purple, people. Plus if I hear one more time about my Ivy League twenty-eighth cousin twice removed I think I'll seriously jump off a bridge. Like, my little brother is seeming like the normal one lately. That's my reality, bitches.* Oh. Em. Effing. Gee. She totally has a catch phrase.

Priscilla has been talking for eight minutes and forty-six seconds by the time she's done. She posts the results on YouTube and links it to her social network page. She means to get around to talking about fashion, but that'll have to be episode two. She had some things to get off her chest today. She doesn't know what will happen next, but she knows it will totally be something.

fifty-three

Caterina and Otis do not end up living happily ever after in the apple tree. They have two and a half somewhat weird, somewhat great weeks together. But they don't even make it through the birthday party before she breaks up with him. He puts the crossword in a manila envelope, wraps the envelope with Ariel birthday wrapping paper, ties the apple pencil into the ribbon, writes on it TO CATERINA FROM OTIS with a red Sharpie, which doesn't show very well over the design.

This is how it goes down: She gets a better present from another boy. That's it. An American Girl doll. It has ribbons like Caterina wears, but her hair is in braids, Caterina never wears braids, and the doll's hair isn't even the same color. This kid doesn't know her at all, Otis thinks. *He's my boyfriend now, sorry*, is what Caterina tells Otis. No, seriously, that's it. Don't you remember being nine? There's no working things out. There's no couples counseling. It doesn't even matter that she and this boy will break up exactly two weeks later, or even that Otis will be witness to this event when it happens on the playground. Getting to see Caterina cry because some boy did to her what she'd done to Otis brings him no comfort or pleasure. The opposite. Nevertheless, Otis will think a lot about all this, for sure—the crossword, the doll. His mother had suggested another present, but Otis had to go and *make* his present, a crossword puzzle all about Caterina. Is Otis's life ruined? You'd think so, right? He's not happy. He goes home and the first thing he does is eat the jalapeño jelly bean. He eats it in one bite; it gets stuck in his back teeth. It's as close as Otis will ever come to saying Fuck you to Caterina, or anyone, ever. And the bean tastes so bad. A caterpillar would have been better, he's sure. It's predictably terrible, the bean, a gummy spicy mess, a flavor that should never have been considered in conjunction with sugar, and he feels a mix of things, including that he deserves to feel this misery in his mouth and he deserves to throw away the precious gift Caterina had given him that day. But the thing is, for two and a half weeks, for a glorious, heaven-sent seventeen days, Caterina was Otis's girlfriend. The power bestowed on him by Caterina that day with the righteous word "boyfriend" is the stuff of legend, it gave him his cape, the power to leap buildings, fight crime. This alone will last him until his next girlfriend, nine years from now.

fifty-four

Make *Your Own Reality* actually gathers some viewers—10,471 last time Priscilla checked, ten minutes
ago. It's not fully viral, but Priscilla has a couple
thousand online friends now, and a lot of them have "liked"
it and shared it, too. Priscilla's done three more webisodes
since the first. She can't seem to avoid talking about her family, her personal life, but the primary focus has shifted to
fashion. It's a strange hybrid of topics if there ever was one,
but it works. It's actually the reason it works.

Priscilla handwrites a sign for her bedroom door in block
letters, in preparation for the fifth episode: TAPING IN PROG-
RESS. There's no one home at the moment though, thankfully. She's got Ashley over in an outfit they put together
intentionally to show how to improve it. Priscilla positions her
laptop to get both her and Ashley in the picture, puts a little
piece of tape on her desk to mark the spot, sits down, turns
the computer back toward herself. She also has a couple of
index cards in front of her with notes for things she wants to
remember to talk about.

What's up, it's me Priscilla, again, back with another episode of 'Make Your Own Reality.' Today I'm gonna stop yapping about my family and show you how to take an iffy outfit and make it better. But first I want to say a few things about my general fashion philosophy, because I've been thinking about this. To me, it seems so super-easy to dress cute, but then, you know, you go out of your house and you see that it's not that easy for everyone else. And there are, like, so many different ways people dress badly. Like those people whose wardrobes are entirely made of T-shirts from places they've been plus cargo shorts and Crocs.

Priscilla shakes her head as though even the word "Crocs" makes her ill.

Or even, to the other extreme, people who try way too hard to be different and so put weird shit together or maybe cover themselves in tattoos but are still kind of weirdly the same. And, um, also, very obviously? Having the money to buy expensive clothes does not necessarily mean you're going to know what to buy or how to wear it when you get it home. I do not have a lot of money, I am for sure on a fashion budget.

We could mention here that, while this seems true to Priscilla, who knows that she can't afford the higher-end designer pieces she'd like, she still spends beyond her means—and though it's true that she wears what she buys, if she were to truly stay within her budget, she would pretty much be limited to shopping at Express or Target.

So but here's what I think. She glances down at the first card. *These are my ABCs of how to dress like a normal person: (a) It's so all about having a few really nice things than it is about having a lot of things.*

Priscilla picks up her laptop and positions it in front of her closet.

Look, I'll show you. Ashley, open the closet door. Ashley opens the closet. Inside are Priscilla's clothes and shoes, neatly hung, and it is by no means jam-packed. She has been buying and returning a certain amount of clothes and accessories for this purpose, but keeps just enough so the stores don't harass her. *See? There's space between the hangers. I'm just saying. Also you'll see I'm not a fan of bright colors, but I'm not saying they're not okay for you. In moderation, please.*

Priscilla sits back down to finish.

Okay, so anyway, (a) a few nice things, (b) it's all about how you put things together, and (c) if you have to spend money on something, spend it on accessories. You can build entire outfits around a great pair of boots or shoes.

She gets up, turns her laptop back around to where the tape mark is. Ashley is wearing black leggings, a pair of flats, and a T-shirt.

Okay, so here's Ashley in what is clearly a weak outfit. I'm not gonna lie, Ashley doesn't really dress this bad, and if she did I wouldn't let her go out this way because that's what friends do—so, side note, if you yourself dress well but you see your friend dressed bad, do everyone in the world a favor please and tell them. Anyway, I work in retail, so trust me I know a lot of you people are out there dressing like this for real, but you shouldn't.

There are two big problem areas here, the top and the bottom, adding up to one giant problem area. Maybe, maybe the T-shirt on its own would be all right, but it's a little on the trendy side with this kind of swirly paisley thing going down the side here, I'm not a big fan of this look—oh, and that reminds me, I want to talk to you another time about how to wear trends without looking like, you know, an idiot. Anyway, the main thing here is that these pants? Are not pants? Are leggings? They go under things? I don't care if you have the tightest butt ever, please, just no. Look, Ashley has a totally cute butt, but no. Ashley smiles and sticks it out for the camera a little bit, they both crack up. *I'm not a fan of leggings really so much anyway, but if you're one of those people, just please try to remember that* they go under things.

Priscilla leans closer into the camera fake-sternly; then a corner of her mouth turns up into a smile. She's cracking herself up.

So I'm going to solve two problems here today, actually. All right, Ashley's going to change now, so I'll talk to you for a minute while she does that.

Okay, last time I was kind of freaking out, obvs, but I've been thinking a lot about my grampa since he died, and how much I miss him. Or, I miss who he used to be anyway. When I was a little kid and I first was into clothes, he used to take pictures of me, and I was already reading the magazines and I'd pick out these outfits and pose like I'd seen the models do, and then I'd save the pictures into a fashion file for myself. She thinks about this for a moment, realizes only now that this isn't what most kids do for fun, that she is in some way different, has been all along. Huh. *Well, anyway, here's one of those pictures.* Priscilla holds the photo up to the camera; she's not just wearing a sophisticated outfit for a child, a gray pleated skirt with a pale pink eyelet blouse with gray tights and a pair of gray Mary Janes (Jean had gone to some lengths to find these for her), but she has a look on her face that, at the time, only her grandfather could have captured. Sweet. Priscilla gets a tear in her eye, isn't quite ready to share that much of herself with the world, sits up straighter, redirects. *I told you what happened, right, that he went out for a walk and died on the porch while nobody was looking after him? Well, but I mean, I wasn't there either, so.* Priscilla looks off, purses her mouth almost the exact same way her mother does, looks over and sees that Ashley is ready and waiting.

Okay, so here's Ashley now, in the new improved outfit. Ashley still has the leggings on, with a long printed top over them. *I got this dress at H&M. Not expensive, like, nineteen ninety-nine or something. Except I need to say something. This dress?* Not a dress! *People! It's a shirt. You can tell by the way it just barely covers her ass. Just because Jessica Simpson or whoever is doing it doesn't mean you should. She shouldn't either. Although FYI her line of shoes is not bad at all if you're on a budget. Anyway. Unless you are five-foot-one or something, this is not a dress. It's a shirt.* Priscilla grabs a double-wrap belt she has handy and puts it around the dress, blousing the top of the dress slightly over the top of the belt. *Right? Super cute. A million times better.* Ashley smiles and poses with her hands on her hips to indicate how much better it is now. *The shoes are fine, but if you want to dress this up just a little you can put it with maybe a wedge sandal with a heel or something.*

Jean knocks on the door but comes right in without waiting for an answer.

Mom-muh, there's a sign! We're taping. Priscilla has yet to figure out how to edit, does everything in one take, for better or worse.

I'm sorry, Priscilla, I didn't see it.

Priscilla tilts her head and leans into the camera again, widens her eyes. *Do you see what I've been talking about?*

I just wanted to know if you're going to be home for dinner.

Yes, Mom.

Okay. Jean starts to leave, Priscilla notices her mother's outfit, a pair of pleated khakis and a blouse tucked in.

Wait, c'mere a minute, Mom. Wanna be on the show?

It's somewhat unprecedented that Jean has just been invited all the way in. Conversations between Priscilla and Jean in this room usually tend to last only as long as Jean's willing to stand in the doorway or until Priscilla hints loudly that she's busy. But Priscilla sees an opportunity.

Oh, I don't know.

C'mon, I can fix that outfit for you.

Jean was unaware that her outfit needed fixing.

C'mon, it'll be fun. Over here. Priscilla gestures for Ashley to move out of the way, positions her mother in camera view. *Okay, so look, there's nothing super tragic here, just some little mistakes, although, well, these pants need to go. Ashley, would you grab me those J.Crew khakis I showed you before? There are two basic things wrong here: pleated pants from, like, 1984, and the top is tucked in.* Priscilla untucks the top, the outfit is quickly improved. *Put these pants on.* Priscilla turns the camera away so her mother can change, looks into the camera again. *Yes, they're showing pleated pants again, but listen, you know who looks good in them? Supermodels with teeny waists and giraffe legs. Are you a supermodel? Or a giraffe? Then you can't wear them. And what else is . . . never tuck anything in. If you're a man who wears a suit to work you can tuck in. Otherwise no. I need to write down a list of rules, they're so simple.*

Jean finishes dressing; Priscilla turns the camera her way. Jean looks at the outfit in Priscilla's mirror. She's never been clothes-conscious at all, but she can see the difference. *See,* Priscilla says, pleased. *Better already, right?* Ashley has been instructed in advance to nod vigorously at statements like these. Jean has not. *It does,* Jean says, studying her daughter for a moment. She sees that Priscilla's entire demeanor is different in this arena. She's kind of sparkly, even more so on camera. It's the reason she got called back for the reality show as many times as she did, though she doesn't know this.

The shoes are heinous though, Mom. Jean looks down at her scuffed slides.

Priscilla sits down in front of the camera again. *Here's a really good tip—if you look at yourself in the mirror, and you think, what would this outfit look like in ten years if I looked at a photo, really think about it, and the answer is Oh, wow, this crop top or whatever, is maybe not such a timeless look after all, you know, there's still time for you to change.* She holds up the picture of her again as a kid. *Like, this holds up.*

Next week, how to be yourself, but not too much, and busting fashion myths. For a preview I'll just say that that thing you read in every magazine about how a must-have item is a trenchcoat? Whatever. A trenchcoat? We're not spies in old movies. You don't need a trenchcoat.

Thanks Ashley and Mom for helping me out with the show today. Later everyone! Priscilla mugs for the camera, closes the laptop.

THE VIEWERS KIND OF root for her in spite of themselves. They're not loving to hate her. It's a kind of love. And she loves them back. There's a thread of 368 comments, mostly from preteen girls with usernames like JoDiDaBomb and LuvScilla: *Keepz it realz! Totally like me! Luv Ur Style! That's like, my house! Where did u get that rad ruffle vest? Go bitch!* (Also a few comments from horny dudes. *Hotttt. Rubbin my dick 2 U.*) It moves slightly outside of the circle of sixteen-to-twenty-one-year-old girls and catches the attention of some more well-known style bloggers. Some of them say she's a natural, others aren't buying it. A conversation begins. The word "hoax" comes up. A few contend that this is just a typical vacuous American girl telling the truth as she sees it and she's maybe not super insightful, not right now, anyway, but there are tiny moments, tiny moments when Priscilla tilts her head a micrometer one way or the other, or casts her eyes away from the camera in tiny moments of actual contemplation, that are definitely real, for better or worse. Priscilla isn't dumb like we've said, but she's not smart enough to concoct a hoax. But this is the discussion. There have been precedents set in online fakery. P is more than happy to address this directly, insisting she's just her, she's *real*, come up to her and ask her to her face if she's real. *Easy to type some shit in and hit send, Anonymous*, she says, with a face that says I dare you. But she doesn't really care about the haters. She's got their eyes and ears. Let them hate. QVC just called her up. So did TVLand. They fucking looked her up and called her up on the phone. She's flying to L.A. next week to meet them and some agents, too. QVC is starting a new, younger-focused channel, needs hosts. TVLand asked for a pitch. It should be stated that out of these calls, at least one is interested in the idea of a reality show that includes Priscilla's entire family. Our guess is that this would not be her first pick, if she even has a pick, but having lost what she thought was her original chance, she is now willing to consider all options.

Priscilla has no idea how this will all shake out, but she's not worried; it's obvious destiny really is on her side after all. She has a proudest accomplishment.

fifty-five

It's an eventful day for Vivian.

It starts when she goes out front to look for the news-paper. Usually someone brings it in by this time; for a long time that someone was Theodore. Briefly Vivian wonders why her son hasn't brought it in today, before she remembers, then pushes away any further thoughts about that. Bending down to pick up the paper, Vivian discovers, under the porch swing, the letter Theodore had intended to mail the day he died. At first she doesn't recognize the handwriting, it looks like a child's, maybe Otis's. But the return address clearly reads "Theodore Copeland." Vivian finds herself feeling a little light-headed, seeing this, sits down on the porch swing for a moment. She examines the envelope again. The handwriting is familiar now. It's al-most identical to what Theodore's penmanship looked like when he first learned cursive: careful and overly rounded, the unsteady but slow hand of a child learning to write. Vivian looks up and away, clasps the letter in both hands like a prayer. A few tears come up into her eyes before she dabs at them with a handkerchief, takes a deep breath, puts the letter in her pocket, and goes back inside.

This afternoon, Vivian has a luncheon with her friends at their favorite restaurant, The Iris. They have a key lime pie that's always worth commenting on. *Real key limes!* one of them always says, though no one really knows this for sure. She has a pleasant time as always, but feels a little more restless today than usual, undoubtedly made worse by finding the letter and by the fact that her friends have all expressed their condolences once again. This might have been all right had their sympathies been brief. Vivian had always felt she and her friends shared a sense of decorum on subjects like these, believed there was an unspoken amount of time that should be devoted to conversations about such things—which, in Vivian's mind, ought to be limited to a single comment or two per person. Today, though, her friends share their own experiences with losses, of which they've all had many. This puts Vivian into something of a pickle; though there are known limits, you also don't want to be the one to interrupt someone talking about how much they miss their spouse, although you can be sure Vivian is considering it and hoping to the heavens that someone else will. This conversation goes on for an interminable eight or nine minutes before Florence mentions something about her great-grandchild, which Vivian sticks to like a wad of gum in a second-grader's hair. Never before has Vivian seemed so interested in a person, place, or thing other than herself.

Vivian walks home from lunch as usual. The Iris is just a few blocks away from home and it's a gorgeous day. A block down from the restaurant, Vivian spies a convertible in the drugstore parking lot. Oh, it's a shiny thing; she has no idea what model, that's hardly anything she's interested in. What catches her eye is the beautiful aqua color, the sunlight glinting off the silver trim, the white leather upholstery. Oh my! She's never seen such a thing. For those of you who care, it's a 1956 Thunderbird. There's a vintage car show in town. Vintage models from all eras have been spotted on the streets this week. But Vivian can hardly tell it's a vintage car. She's never been one to pay attention to new cars when they come out, can hardly tell a wagon from a minivan, but she can sure recognize a convertible when she sees one, and to her this one looks brand spanking new.

Well, it certainly can't do any harm to just touch those seats. Vivian runs a gloved hand across the leather, takes her glove off to touch it again. Oh my. Isn't that something? Oh, that is quite nice. Well, it couldn't do any harm just to sit behind the wheel for a moment. Who's going to get upset with a ninety-eight-year-old lady in a smart suit? Vivian slides in, runs her hand along the seats again, looks at the dash, the silvery chrome of the dials, puts her hands on the bright white steering wheel, the keys in the ignition! Oh, who would notice if she just turned that little key . . .

Oh, the purr of that engine! How has she never felt such a thing before, never felt this marvelous rumble in her chest! Maybe just a spin around the block; who would know? Did she dare?

Vivian looks around. There's no one in sight. She puts the car in reverse, like she's seen her husband do a thousand times, pulls the bar down until it clicks the R into place, slowly backs the car out of the spot, shifts into drive, and *goes*. Down Main Street, over to the wealthy section of town. Oh, wouldn't it be just marvelous if her friends could see her, if anyone she knows would see her right now? She knows she must look like she was just born to drive this car, up the hilly, winding road past mansions and into the woods. The wind is blowing back her curls—she'll probably look a fright when she gets back, but she'll deal with that later. Vivian keeps going, past the last estate, through the woods, past farms, cities, skylines, past mountains and oceans until the car lifts up off the ground, over the trees, and right into the stars.

fifty-six

The morning of the sermon, Jean comes back inside to get dressed, looks in her closet, and finds herself suddenly appalled at the swath of khaki pants and black cardigans in her eyesight. Did these seem different to her when she bought them? She knows this church isn't a fancy place where women put on elaborate hats, wonders if anyone really gets dressed up for church anymore; still, she's speaking today, and she wants to look nice. Maybe Priscilla has something. She creeps into her daughter's room—she's still sleeping—pokes around in the closet. Lots of things with tags; where is Priscilla getting the money for this stuff?

Nothing looks quite right. She pushes some things around, pulls out a pair of gray wool trousers, a long lavender cardigan, a pair of suede pumps still in the box. Jean takes the clothes back to her room to get dressed, goes downstairs to make breakfast. When Priscilla comes down and pours herself coffee, it takes a minute for it to register.

Are those my clothes?

Mmm, no. Mine is all Jean says.

No they're not, those are mine. Were you in my room?

Guess so.

Priscilla is hardly awake enough or she'd have a full-on invasion-of-privacy shit fit. Plus, her mom is so far on the weird side this morning, there's no telling how that would go.

Where are you going, anyway?

I'm going to church.

Priscilla so does not want to know anything else about that. Things are bad enough with Dad sobbing all the time now. She thought maybe things would get a little more normal around here after her grandfather died—well, maybe that's harsh, it's not like she wanted him to die, but he was less and less his old self and more and more hard to care for and that just is what it is. But her dad is being weirder than ever, much as that would have once seemed impossible, and she's not fully over her mom calling her a bitch, even though in the end that method seemed to have worked, though she'll for sure never admit that. The last thing this family needs now is Jesus or some shit. But her mom is wearing her nicest clothes and she still looks like a hot mess. *Okay, well, at least . . . you've got the sweater on wrong.* Priscilla starts to adjust it a bit; it's hard for her not to do her thing, but as she does, she sees something in her mom's eye, sees the corners of her mom's lips turn up just the slightest bit and recognizes this as a moment coming on between them, backs away. *Okay, that's fine, I guess.* She shakes her head, takes her coffee mug back to her room.

Jean hasn't even put the shoes on yet. She won't put them on until she gets to the church—she knows she can't drive in them—so she drives barefoot, puts the heels on when she arrives at the church, takes a few awkward steps, can't remember the last time she had on heels, at her wedding maybe? But then quickly finds a stride, walks up the church steps and down to the front pew of church. She's ready.

Jean walks up to the podium after the music ends. Her daughter's clothes feel foreign; that may have been a rash choice, but the shoes make up the difference. In the shoes, her posture is different, straighter; her person feels like it's matching up with her body. This is how tall I should have been, she thinks. *If I'd been this tall, things could have gone differently for me from the beginning.* Wait, did she say that out loud? She did, people are laughing. That's good, right? She starts by talking a little about how she'd come to the church, has a hard time looking out at the congregation at first, but talks a bit about how welcomed she had felt when her father-in-law died; segues quickly into her certainty that heaven is a high school dance filled with movie stars, with astrophysicists and dinosaurs, with long-gone pets, literary greats and your loved ones, anyone you imagine; looks up long enough to see a few nods in the front row, enough for now, though there are as many more who aren't sure where she's going with this, more than a few are thinking high school dances were their idea of hell, but on the other hand, they've heard weirder things around here. Jean latches onto Bob's serene face, doesn't look down again.

And in heaven, when you dance with your dead lover, you will no longer have the need to ask him Why the fuck, *you will no longer have that horrible, indelible image in your mind of his lifeless, sad body hanging in the place where you once made beautiful love, you will no longer ask yourself a million questions that can't be answered, like what if you hadn't had an extra cup of coffee that day, or how did you miss goddamned everything, what kind of blackout shades had you pulled down over your life to miss goddamned everything, how could you be so stupid to not see one single clue that your lover was so depressed that he would hang himself, what story were you telling yourself about what was going on between you, about who he was? You will no longer ask yourself if he had set you up from the beginning, knowing he was living his last days, not wanting to hurt his family, so instead putting it on you. You will stop asking if your entire relationship was made out of nothing but air, created solely for the purpose of having some random person find you hanging rather than having one of your family members find you hanging, because let me tell you I spent a good long time on that one. For a while it made as much sense as anything to me. It's hard to come up with any good reason why someone would do that to a person he supposedly loved—unless what he felt wasn't love at all, was something more like complete dispassion, or hate. But these are the questions. There's an additional line of questions relating to Who the goddamn are you, lady, that you could do such a thing in the first place, tell this epic lie to your family and friends, sneak around and tell yourself the great love you think you have rights out any wrongs. That's a movie-star lie.*

I have heard it said that if you commit suicide, you go straight to hell. I know now that this is nothing but a myth. I'm just saying there is no hell. Whatever god is, if there even is one, he/she/it loves and forgives everyone. Everyone. That's what I'm going with. Probably even a psychopath, that's the kind of love I'm talking about—that god can love a psychopath, love him so much that forgiveness isn't even part of it, it's just pure love. Don't misunderstand, I think it's clear enough that god can't stop a psychopath, can't even stop you from doing whatever shit you have in mind to do. And he can't give you parking spaces, not even if there's a puppy stuck up a flaming tree that needs your help. And yet I see now, really, it's all got to be about god. It's all happening in god's world, right? Psychopaths and parking spaces, rainbows and lollipops. There is a great loving and forgiving something out there even if it's not pushing things around the way we might like. I believe it.

I'm not saying it's okay to commit suicide. Don't do it, please. Seriously, please don't commit suicide. Please, if you have terrible thoughts like that, you should tell someone—anyone. No one thinks it's better if you do that. I mean, if you're a child molester or something, for a second, yes, I might be glad you killed yourself—I can't lie about that, I am a mother—but still, someone loves you. Someone always loves you. Just turn yourself in and let your sister or your nephew visit you in jail. Don't fucking kill yourself. We enter the world pure and clean. We are heavenly in body, mind, and spirit. I have witnessed a miracle in this dream, and to witness a miracle is to know yourself, vital, brilliant, heavenly in spirit.

We hesitate to disrupt Jean's groove here, but it may need to be pointed out that she's just quoted the label from the face cream she had only recently been so disturbed by.

Yesterday I looked into the eyes of a squirrel and I saw my dead lover, James, who said, Yes, it's true about heaven.

I am sure, now, that my lover, James, must have known about this heaven, because I have tried and tried to understand what made him take his life away from me and have, until this dream, failed. Failed to understand. I know now that this dream was James contacting me from heaven, to tell me, Look, my beloved, I am here dancing with Rita Hayworth, everything is beautiful.

fifty-seven

Gordon holds a "gallery opening" in the garage for his family. He has completed the family series. He's covered a workbench with a paper tablecloth, put out some club soda, a cheese plate, and a box of wine (itself indicating to Jean and Priscilla that Gordon is not his usual self, considering how many lessons on fine wine they've gotten over the years). Gordon is positively beaming, still weepy but beaming, and for once in his life he says little. He wants the work to speak for itself. Whether or not it has actual artistic merit, we may not be the ones to say, nor do we know if it will ever be seen outside of this garage. Gordon hasn't thought that far ahead.

The family looks at the paintings. For the most part, their initial responses are a bit blank. Everyone is silent. The portrait of Priscilla shows her inside of a TV set; the edge of the canvas is the edge of the TV (proportions here being entirely skewed, considering this is a vertical rectangle). Her arms are crossed against her chest, but there's a new elegance to her, a slight difference in her stance, a hint of an intelligence in her eyes, a focus. The painting of Otis shows him with a pencil in his mouth, holding a hand that presumably belongs to Caterina, but she is not in the picture. His expression is at once beatific and furrowed. Vivian is standing in her rose garden. She's wearing a crown. Gordon added that in at the last minute. He'd captured her regal posture so well he thought she needed a crown. But there's an underlying note, if you look closely, an uncertainty in her eyes. Behind the roses in the background is a dirt road, at the end of which appears to be a tiny aqua blur that disappears up into the clouds. Given what we know of Gordon's skills as a painter, we cannot interpret his meaning here, or know whether that aqua blur is merely a mistake he tried to cover up with some clouds. We will only say that Vivian is not present and we'll say no more about it.

Theodore's painting is based on one of his accidental photographs, the one of the top half of his head; in this garage, anyway, it seems near as big as a Chuck Close, Gordon's father's bright eyes the size of softballs, the top of his head taking up the rest of the canvas. He's oriented the painting vertically, unlike the photo it was based on. The background is grass, and there's a bright red cardinal perched on top of Theodore's head.

The self-portrait Gordon had shown Priscilla earlier is also included, though the watch is now a slightly darker brown to better contrast against his skin. Also, the expression in his eyes has been altered slightly. Gordon's intention was to create the illusion that he was looking out from the canvas, directly at the viewer. Whether he's actually accomplished this is hard for us to say.

Even Mott has a painting. He's curled up in his spot at the head of the bed, the backs of Jean and Gordon on either side of him, the rest of them off the sides of the painting, but his head is up, facing the viewer. Jean's portrait is a nude. She has a penetrating stare, and she's standing with her legs slightly apart, arms by her hips at the ready, like a nude gunslinger. This one is his favorite.

Everyone has thoughts about the paintings: thoughts about their individual paintings, and thoughts about the other paintings, and thoughts about the paintings together. Are they stunned? Maybe? Do they see themselves in these paintings, any little part of themselves, as Gordon has, finally, or do they think Gordon's gotten it right about everyone but themselves, or is it a mixed bag? Is there a chance they'll somehow connect now, where they see themselves as their father sees them, or do they not get it? For once, we have no idea. We only know so much. What do you think?

acknowledgments

Endless gratitude for all my awesome and great friends who read various and/or multiple drafts: Nina Solomon, Kirk Walsh, Jami Attenberg, Jamie Quatro, Anne Hutchison Hensley, Ike Turner—you people know what's up.

Cal Morgan, jeez, it's impossible to overstate the hand you've had in making this what it is. You rock it.

The fine people of JVNLA, most especially Alice Tasman, but also the whole team, Tara, Jessica, Jean, Jennifer, who have all worked hard on my behalf—for a long time!

The Corporation of Yaddo, and the inspiring place of Yaddo, where this thing got off the ground. I went there with no plan to write a novel, and you gave me that lovely little cabin, and Sylvia Plath's thermos, I'm certain, and this happened.

My UCR colleagues who I admire so, and who continue to inspire and amuse me.

My Chicago writers group: Gina Frangello, Megan Stielstra, Emily Gray Tedrowe, Patrick Somerville, Thea Goodman, Billy Lombardo, cheerleaders always that I am honored to have sat among and absorbed their mad wisdoms.

Also, a special shout-out to those of you who read the draft of the thing that got put on more or less permanent hold for this: Nina, Ben, Alice, Kirk, Gina, Peter Birkenhead, Deanne Stillman, and Donny Ward. Your time, wisdom, and encouragement are invaluable.

And for Ben, 'cause you know.

About the author

2 A Letter from Elizabeth Crane

About the book

5 From Short Story to Novel: The Making of *We Only Know So Much*

Read On

13 Author's Picks

Insights,
Interviews
& More . . .

A Letter from Elizabeth Crane

DEAR PERSON Holding This Book,

Usually, when I tell the story of how I became a writer, I talk about how Harriet the Spy changed my life when I was eight, and that is true enough. Weird little misfit girl in NYC taking notes on everything around her? *I'm in*. I started writing right then and I never stopped.

How I became a *good* writer (if I can make any claim to that adjective) is another story entirely, and it happened somewhat by accident.

Back when I was a kid, one of our primary means of communication was actual mail. Telephones existed (I'm not *that* old), but long-distance calls were expensive, and my father lived a thousand miles away in a magical land called Iowa (where stepmoms took you to the grocery store and let you put *frosted Pop-Tarts and grape soda and anything else you wanted* in the cart). So we wrote letters. For several years, my stepbrothers and I built an organization dedicated to spying on my dad (called the S.F.W.A.—the Secret Fred Watchers Association—that revolved entirely around anonymous, typed letters issuing extremely silly demands for things we wanted, at the cost of some absurd peril if our needs weren't met). During the summers, I'd write letters to my best friend, Nina (another future author). And somewhere along the way I started writing rough drafts. *Of my letters.*

I was hardly fabricating stories at this point, but there's no question, looking at it now, that I was honing my voice. At the time, I was just aiming to entertain, ideally to make my intended reader laugh via my ongoing missteps and romantic kerfuffles. (Okay, well, who am I kidding? This is still my MO.) Anyway, people claimed to love my letters, and I loved writing them, and these people always told me I should be a writer, and I would say I *was* a writer, even though I was making a living as a waiter, a preschool teacher, and about sixteen other things over the years.

Mind you, the stories I was writing over those years bore no resemblance to my letters whatsoever. I spent a lot of years trying to be all fancy-like, describing stuff I had no business describing, and trying to make my storylines neat and tidy. Did I know from neat and tidy? I did not. There had always been a few writers I loved, but it was years before I read anything that rocked my world—enough to show me that the way I wrote letters was the way I *actually wrote.* (I've named these people ninety hundred times before, but David Foster Wallace was the first; then I finally discovered people like Rick Moody, Lorrie Moore, George Saunders, and Lydia Davis, and my universe more or less exploded.) So after, what was it— let's say twenty-five—years of writing, after these writers fell into my hands my writing started to improve, and started to really sound like *me.* It turned out ▶

A Letter from Elizabeth Crane *(continued)*

my writerly instincts had been pretty good all along; I'd just been ignoring them.

No one ever said I was a quick learner. (See also: my love life. But that worked out nicely too in the end.)

Your friend,

E. Crane ∾

From Short Story to Novel: The Making of *We Only Know So Much*

WELL, THIS WAS AN INTERESTING THING.

I really didn't plan to write a novel. After three collections of stories, I was pretty sure they were my thing, and that was fine. I love short stories; I love to read them and I love to write them. The novel thing eluded me, and a few false starts from time to time confirmed to me that I just had no idea how to do it.

Then, in the summer of 2010, I had the good fortune to spend a month at the Yaddo writers' colony, in a sweet little cabin in the woods,[1] and set about writing a short story. I had some characters in mind who would eventually become the four younger members of the Copeland family, but that was about it. In fact, I had initially thought these characters would each be the center of their own individual stories, unrelated to one another. There were some things I was wondering about: What would it be like if your daughter was a bitch? What would it be like if someone came up to you and told you that you'd dated him for a year—and ▸

[1] A similar one makes a guest appearance in this book.

you had zero memory of that person?[2]
What would it be like to lose someone to
suicide?

So I started some character sketches
of these folks, but they quickly became
a family. In a short time I had thirty
pages, but I was nowhere near finishing
this "story." Sixty pages in—and having
a lot of fun, I might add, but still
nowhere near done telling this family's
story—I began to think, Well, now I'm
totally screwed! Because it still felt like a
short story to me, and I liked that about
it, but there aren't a lot of places that
publish sixty-page short stories. It
wasn't until I hit ninety pages that
I started to realize—or maybe *accept*
is a better word—that I was probably
maybe possibly writing a novel.

The first (semicomplete) draft of
the book was very short, in the ballpark
of 150 pages, or forty-six thousand
words. My agent read it and loved
what I had, and more or less said
Keep writing, at which point I had
a sudden inspiration: that if Gordon
was caring for a father who had
Parkinson's—who was dealing with
real cognitive decline (vs. Gordon's

---

[2] The opposite actually happened to me. I ran
into an ex who couldn't remember me at all.
In real life, this guy was essentially unfazed
(and in turn, knowing him, I was unfazed
by his unfazedness), entirely unlike the way
Gordon responds. But the incident sparked my
imagination to think about how a relatively sane
person would react in the same situation.

mostly imaginary one)—it would serve to exacerbate Gordon's fear that he's losing his own mind, and might add depth to the story. This idea was sudden, but not totally random. My dad had Parkinson's, and though he was lucid to a great extent, in recent years he had been suffering from not just physical but various cognitive issues. So I threw a version of him into the mix, and added his mother, my grandmother, for good measure.

My father had actually cared for his parents in their old age, and my grandmother was a pretty rich character as well. But I would be grafting both of these real-life people onto an entirely fictional family, and I had no idea if that would be believable in the end. Still, I proceeded to develop these two new characters, and moved them into the Copelands' house. I gave each of them their own issues and then interspersed these chapters where they seemed to make sense—though one of my concerns had always been the order of the chapters, as they weren't entirely written in order. And since I'd never written a novel before, that was just one of my concerns about structure.

I had originally been opposed to traditional chapter breaks. I really, really wanted the novel to maintain the feel of a short story, to keep the Crane-ish tone and voice of my shorter work, and I had the idea that if this novel didn't have breaks it would have the movement ▶

of a story, and you'd just keep reading. I knew there were novels that were written this way—particularly shorter ones, as mine was. But in many cases I wasn't sure where those breaks should go, so this was something I held on to until almost the last minute. Finally, I sat down and forced myself to choose the appropriate breaks, and not long before we submitted the book to publishers—I think it was actually the night before—I actually broke down and numbered the chapters. (Which I now like just fine.)

I also really didn't *necessarily* want the characters to change too much, which may seem problematic (and possibly even hilarious) to those who know how novels are supposed to work. But, again, I wanted it to feel like a short story, like *my* work, and I wanted any changes the characters went through to be subtle.

Somewhere in here, my agent[3] had also brought up another reasonable but troublesome idea: she thought the characters should interact more. At first I was still attached to the idea that the story was all about what was going on in each of their individual heads, that it would all be very internal (or interior, as my colleague David Ulin likes to say); that they would interact with people *outside* of the family, but what little interaction they would actually have

---

[3] Yes, she does have a name, Alice, and it's a nice one I think, so henceforth I will use it.

with each other would be riddled with something like miscommunication, inappropriateness, or latent hostility of some kind. (Which is still more or less the case.) But apparently this is not terribly "novelistic," whatever that means, so Alice encouraged me to write more dialogue between family members, confident that I could do this in a way that wouldn't compromise my (*brilliant artistic*) vision, in which, no matter what their interactions were like, they were still very much in their own little mental worlds, and not connecting very well even when they were in the same room.

Okay. So I worked on it a little more, we sent it out, the awesome and great Cal Morgan at Harper Perennial made an offer I couldn't refuse. Before we'd finalized the deal, he called me up, told me at length how much he loved the book, and made a few casual suggestions for me to think about. One of them was something Alice had talked about— which was to have more scenes in which the family members interact with one another—but the other was that he thought the family needed what he called a "game changer." Specifically, he thought—and he was certainly not at all adamant about this—that if the grandfather died, the family would have an opportunity to connect (or not), that it could serve to tie their storylines together and give any or all of them an opportunity to change.

Sigh. So. Initially, I was very, very, ▶

From Short Story to Novel: The Making of
We Only Know So Much (continued)

very resistant to this. I'm not
superstitious in any way, and yet I felt
extremely uncomfortable about the
idea of killing off a character based on
someone I was close to. (Cal, it should
be said, had *no* idea about my dad's
condition when he made this
suggestion.) I have no issue creating
characters based on real people once
they're gone, and/or even real people
when they're alive. But this is something
I'd given some previous thought to, and
I just didn't want to do it. I understood
very clearly why this might make a lot of
sense for this book, and I wanted it to be
the best book it could possibly be, so
I sat with the idea for a good while, and
I mentioned it to my stepmom as well.

My dad knew I was writing my fourth
book, and I think he even knew he was
a character in it, but we both knew that
no matter how I went ahead with the
storyline, his reading days were behind
him. He believed he'd read it, and was
excited about it, as always, but we knew
he wouldn't actually read it, as he'd
given up reading at least a year or two
before this. My stepmom said that she
completely understood, and that she had
no problem with it, and that if that was
the choice I made it would be totally fine.
Now, this may be an extremely specific
editorial issue, and if you're a writer,
you probably won't be asked to kill off
your living family members. You may,
however, be asked to make changes
that are similarly difficult for you to

consider, though they may not be quite as personal. But I tried to remember that it is fiction, and that fiction writers should remain open to any solution that makes the best story and the best work.

Cal also suggested that at some point Gordon should discover Jean's infidelity, which I was also very, very resistant to. It wasn't what the story was about to me; I wanted her processing this entirely on her own, and not particularly well, and I didn't want them to have a conversation about it, a) because Gordon is supposed to be historically, vastly inattentive to his wife, more now than ever because of his obsession with his memory, and b) because I feared that having this come out into the open would make the book a story about infidelity. This may seem weird, but to me the infidelity is a subject that belongs to Jean alone, whereas the overall story is about this family's inability to communicate.

Eventually, though, with Cal's insanely detailed guidance—he provided me with *twenty-two single-spaced pages of notes*—I was able to accomplish both of these critical changes, without compromising what I had in mind creatively, and ultimately I think they made it a vastly better book. (And side note: in the case of this particular book, the editorial work involved *developing* material. Very little of what I had originally sent was cut—maybe sentences or short bits here and ▶

there—and by the end we had added about fifty pages.)

While I was in the process of editing, as it happened, my dad died. That sucked, but he was eighty-four, and it was very obviously going to happen a little sooner for him than it had for his parents, who lived past one hundred. (Yes, I actually made Vivian younger than my real grandmother!) But my father was my biggest fan, and I was pretty sure he wouldn't mind being immortalized in this way. My grandmother, well, that's another story. :) She might have had a thing or two to say about it, but she only lived to be a hundred and four, so she's not here to argue. But I hope I've finally done something better with my life than the time all those years ago when I lay perfectly still on a baby blanket. ❧

Author's Picks

AS A RULE, I don't tend to seek out any particular reading material when I'm starting a new writing project. That said, on some unconscious level, some things do seep in. Generally, my taste in reading is a bit all over the map— I tend to gravitate to things that are weird, or offbeat, or surreal, or untraditional in some way, whether it's a matter of structure or a voice that to my ear sounds like a real person is talking to me.

These were some of the writers who inspired me during the time I spent working on this book.

Deb Olin Unferth: *Minor Robberies*. Worth it for the story "Deb Olin Unferth" alone, but every last story is a little gem.

Lydia Davis: Do yourself a favor and just get *The Collected Stories*. If you read one, you'll want to read more. A huge inspiration.

Steven Millhauser: *Dangerous Laughter*. Third-person plural, weird worlds, amazing images and language— what's not to love?

Donald Antrim: *The Hundred Brothers*. Holy crap, this book blew my mind. This is the kind of book that makes you think you can write a book like this, but you can't. (You, here = me.) ▶

Author's Picks *(continued)*

Colum McCann: *Let the Great World Spin*. Another one that rocked my world. Gorgeously written, seamlessly interwoven storylines in my hometown and my era: messed-up, grungy, crime-ridden 1970s NYC! Yeah!

Patrick Somerville: *The Universe in Miniature in Miniature*. Dude can write some freaking sentences. ∾

Don't miss the next book by your favorite author. Sign up now for AuthorTracker by visiting www.AuthorTracker.com.